Love in Transit

The Last Stop Was You

Honeymoon Aljabri

Honeymoon Publishing House

Published by [Honeymoon Publishing House] Texas. / Global Distribution

ISBN: 979-8-9934488-7-9

First Edition: 2026

Printed in the United States of America / United Kingdom / Australia (via IngramSpark) (Amazon KDP)

Dedication:

To my beloved family, who are forever entwined with my being, and whose love, however reluctantly expressed at times, is my constant anchor thank you for being my unbreakable foundation.

To my extraordinary friends, those rare souls who chose to love me, knowing full well the complex, sometimes challenging, heart of a Capricorn. Thank you for seeing me, for embracing me, and for always choosing to walk this path beside me.

To my mother, my guiding light, my first love , I love you, *Da zuu*.

To all my ex-boyfriends, without whose impeccable timing and well-executed departures, I might never have discovered the boundless landscapes of my imagination. Thank you for dumping me, for fueling the fantasy train ride of a hopeless romantic, and for inspiring the very worlds I now create.

To every soul I have ever met, who offered a listening ear or shared a story, giving me the opportunity to listen in return your presence has enriched my journey immeasurably.

A special, heartfelt thank you to my incredible Editor, Joi, whose tireless dedication, keen eye, and unwavering belief worked magic to shape this book into what it is today. Your brilliance is a gift.

To my dear **Auntie Babe Jeuri**: Whatever ink I drop, whatever words I weave in the quiet solitude of midnight, you are always, always with me. I love you, and I will forever carry you in my heart. Rest in eternal peace, my beautiful one.

To **Miss Maggie Richie**, the woman I met when she was ninety, yet who remained a teenager in her heart: You became my best friend and my mentor. You were the editor who taught me that the heartbeat of a story matters more than the mechanics of the pen. You told me:

"When you write a novel, do not care about grammar I can fix that. But do not give me a novel without a soul. Honeymoon, you have to breathe life into it. Give it emotion. Your words have to belong somewhere; they must be attached to the heart, not just hanging in the air. Perfect grammar doesn't make a novel emotions do."

Miss Maggie, you helped me develop this story. You helped me breathe value and humanity into these characters. As I write these final words, my tears are falling because you aren't here to see the seed we planted together finally bloom. I love you, and I will always love you, my "Old Lady." I miss you.

Rest in Peace.

A Love Letter to My Continent: The Heart of Africa

Thank you

"I am an African. I owe my being to the hills and the valleys, the mountains and the glades, the rivers, the deserts, the trees, the flowers, the seas and the ever-changing seasons that define the face of our native land." - Thabo Mbeki

Indeed, I am an African. I owe my very soul to this ancient, pulsing land that cradled my ancestors and birthed my spirit. It is this profound belonging, this fierce love, that I yearn to gift to you, my cherished reader, especially those who have never set foot upon our soil, those who carry only distant echoes or veiled perceptions of our magnificent continent. I want to welcome you, to honor my people, my land, and my pride: Africa.

As an author, my journey has been a tapestry woven with threads of love, discovery, and a deep reverence for culture. "Love in Transit" is my fourth novel, a culmination of stories that began with the vibrant spirit of "Leila," followed by the poignant memories of "Remembering Us," and the heartfelt passion of "Heartstrings." Each narrative, like a brushstroke on a vast canvas, has sought to open a window into worlds often unseen or misunderstood.

This particular story, "Love in Transit," was born from a simple spark a mesmerizing YouTube tour of the Rovos Rail Luxury train. As I watched those elegant carriages glide through sun-drenched landscapes, a deeper truth began to stir within me. For too long, when many think of Africa, they see only the scars, the dark shadows of a history defined by external forces, the fractured tapestry left behind by the infamous scramble of 1884 in Berlin. They see a "Dark Continent," a land of burden, often overlooking the iridescent beauty, the vibrant tapestry of cultures, and the resilient spirit that thrives here. They do not see the unique, breathtaking grandeur, the soil that holds not just ancient dust, but the very essence of countless souls, of profound love, and of an enduring, unshakeable hope.

Through the pages of Luca and Amelia's journey, I wanted to part that veil. I am giving you my land, my pride, my beating heart. And if, after reading this story, you find yourself touched, intrigued, and yearning, then I welcome you. Choose any part of our magnificent 54 countries and step onto the motherland. Let her embrace you, let her whispered histories wash over you, and allow her vibrant spirit to awaken something primal within your own soul. Come, experience the true, unvarnished glory that is Africa.

My love for storytelling extends beyond novels. While crafting "Heartstrings," I found myself falling completely in love with the culinary magic of Italy, which inspired my cooking book, "Not So Italian" a playful exploration of flavors and traditions. And for our youngest explorers, I have poured my heart into children's books, creating the "Amani" series, where a curious young girl journeys across all African countries, experiencing their rich history, diverse heritages, and captivating cultures.

With each ink drop, with each carefully chosen word, with every beautiful brushstroke of a character's heart, I want you to open your own heart. Open it to my people, to our stories, to the vibrant, undeniable truth of our land.

We write what we know... and I know the land that made me. Africa, I dream to beautify you, to offer you flowers that shine like the bright stars of the Kalahari and the sunrise of the Sahara. I seek to write with a depth like the Blue and White Nile in Khartoum, reaching for the heights of Kilimanjaro and the Giza Pyramids. With every drop of ink, I honor you, my land.

Thank you, dear reader, for embarking on this journey with me, for allowing "Love in Transit" to carry you across oceans and into the very soul of Africa. May your own heart find its true destination.

With all my love and gratitude,

Honeymoon Aljabri

Shukran. (Thank You.)

The Author

Honeymoon Aljabri is more than an author; she is a filmmaker and journalist whose work serves as a magnificent testament to her vow: to place Africa at the center of the universe.

While her roots are African, her growth was nurtured under the wide, open skies of **Houston, Texas**. A proud graduate of **Texas Southern University**, she honors the city that molded her from a girl into a woman the "713" area code that she chose as her home. Her storytelling is a unique tapestry woven from global perspective and indomitable spirit.

A Legacy of Storytelling from the sweeping romance of *Love in Transit* to the soulful verses of *Love Letter to Africa*, Honeymoon's literary landscape is vast:

Novels of Heart: *Leila*, *Remembering Us*, *Heartstrings*, and *Love in Transit.*

Poetry: *Love Letter to Africa*, a rhythmic tribute to the motherland.

Culinary Arts: *Not So Italian*, a bridge between her deep affection for Italian culture and her African roots.

For the Youth: The *Amani* series, inviting the next generation to journey across the diverse landscapes of the continent.

Through meticulously drawn characters and vivid settings, Honeymoon Aljabri invites the world to see the resilience and profound love that pulses through the African continent. She remains a firm believer in the power of story to dismantle misconceptions and build bridges that lead straight back to the heart of the motherland.

The Rovos Rail

The air in Pretoria was electric, alive with an anticipation that felt almost heavy. It was a sensory feast: the faint scent of freshly polished mahogany mingled with the lingering, honeyed sweetness of the blooming jacaranda trees. Before her sat the Rovos Rail, a vision of vintage opulence gleaming under the relentless gold of the South African sun. Its deep green carriages, trimmed in polished brass, didn't just look like a train; they looked like a promise of a bygone era.

This wasn't merely a departure; it was a celebration. The platform was a stage of high-society bustle, filled with porters in crisp, stiff uniforms and guests balancing crystal champagne flutes alongside high-end cameras. Today felt particularly grand because this journey was the crown jewel of "The Pride of Africa." Since 1986, Rohan Vos had poured his soul into this "land cruise," vowing to reveal the continent's heart in a way no one else dared. To be here was to step into a living history book.

Amelia clutched her ticket, her fingers trembling slightly. She had dreamed of this journey for years, ever since she'd first traced the glossy photos in *People of Africa* magazine. It was supposed to be a shared dream. She was meant to be standing here with

Houston, his hand on the small of her back. But the echoes of their harsh breakup still rang louder than the festive chatter on the platform. After the tears had dried, she'd had to painstakingly rearrange everything the dates, the cabin, the very trajectory of her life.

Now, standing alone amidst the crowd, she looked toward the podium. There stood a man who exuded the same quiet pride as the vintage engine behind him, preparing to invite the passengers into a world she had only ever seen in her dreams.

Amelia Blake adjusted the strap of her leather tote bag as she stepped further onto the platform. At five-foot-seven, she possessed a natural elegance that commanded the space around her without a single word. Her long braids cascaded over her shoulders like a dark waterfall, punctuated by copper cuffs that caught the South African sun and sent glints of light dancing across the station.

She had chosen her outfit with the care of a woman starting over: a tailored white linen jumpsuit that hugged her curves in all the right places, exuding a blend of sophisticated grace and subtle daring. Her deep brown skin glowed with a radiant luster against the crisp fabric, and her large, expressive eyes scanned the crowd with a mixture of curiosity and a lingering, quiet ache. Even in this sea of world travelers and champagne, Amelia stood out a woman who looked like she belonged in the very magazine pages that had inspired her to come here.

As her gaze wandered, it landed on him.

He stood tall, effortlessly commanding the space around him. Dressed in a well-fitted navy blazer and a white shirt open at the collar, he radiated the quiet confidence of a man accustomed to admiration. His jet-black hair was swept back with precision, framing a face that could have been sculpted from marble sharp cheekbones, a strong jawline, and a slight shadow of stubble that added a rugged edge to his sophistication. His wire-rimmed glasses lent him a scholarly charm, but it was his smile, dazzling and boyish, that stole the air from her lungs.

Their eyes met, and for a heartbeat, the chaos of the station the steam, the shouting, the clinking of glasses simply ceased to exist. His gaze was piercing, as if he weren't just looking at her, but seeing her. Amelia felt a heat crawl up her neck that had nothing to do with the sun. Her lips curved into a tentative smile, and he responded in kind, his expression softening with a look of pure, unexpected recognition.

Before the moment could deepen, a woman's sharp, melodic voice broke the spell.

"Luca! Don't forget my bag!"

Amelia's heart thudded back to a dull, heavy rhythm as a slender brunette approached him, looping an arm around his shoulder with a familiarity that made Amelia's stomach twist. The woman was dressed in an elegant floral dress, her sunhat **tilted at a playful angle** as she spoke in rapid, melodic Italian.

Luca's lips quirked into a grin as he reached down to pick up her luggage, his attention completely diverted. Amelia exhaled slowly, a flush of embarrassment warming her cheeks. She turned away quickly, focusing her attention on the grand announcement being made at the platform's edge to distract herself from the pair.

A man in a sharp, tailored suit Rohan Vos himself stood on a mahogany podium. Behind him, the engine loomed like a massive, gleaming promise of adventure. "Ladies and gentlemen, welcome to the Pride of Africa," he declared, his voice rich and carrying across the hushed crowd. “This train is more than a mode of transport; it is a journey through time, a window into the soul of this great continent.”

Amelia moved closer, drawn to his words. To calm her nerves, she reached into the leather gift bag she’d been handed at check-in. Inside, she found a heavy, cream-colored brochure and a detailed map of the route. As she unfolded the glossy pages, she began to visualize the world waiting behind those green-and-gold walls. She could almost smell the faint scent of leather and cedar. Based on the photos, she pictured the plush velvet seats and the polished mahogany tables set with crystal glasses a vintage sanctuary that felt miles away from the heartbreak she’d left behind in DC.

As she enter inside the train, Amelia ran her fingers over the smooth wood-paneled walls of her compartment, the subtle fragrance of lilies mingling with the faint metallic hum of the train. She sighed and shook her head, trying to shake off the image of him. She knew nothing about the man except that he had a woman, who was probably counting her blessings to have him at her side.

"How lucky she must be," Amelia muttered to herself, a bittersweet smile playing on her lips. "And here I am, on the solo adventure of a lifetime, thinking about a stranger."

The gentle lurch of the train brought her back to reality. She turned to the window, watching as Pretoria’s bustling platform faded into a blur of golden hues, dotted with trees and small towns. South Africa was calling, and with it came the promise of discovery, of stepping out of her routine and into something new.

The room was smaller than she expected, a cozy single she had booked by mistake instead of the double she initially wanted. She laughed, thinking, Well, at least I won't have to share the mirror.

She threw herself onto the plush bed, spreading her arms out wide. "I could be naked if I wanted," she mused with a grin. The thought made her giggle, a sound that echoed softly in the quiet room.

A soft rhythm began to rise in the distance drums, steady and enchanting. Amelia glanced at her watch. 6:30. Dinner was being announced in the most dramatic, Rovos Railway. The ceremonial drumming resonated through the train like an ancient call to gather.

Amelia stretched lazily before hopping up to prepare. In the compact but luxurious bathroom, she let the warm water of the shower wash away her fatigue. After toweling off, she reached for her yellow dress, its satin fabric shimmering like sunlight. Paired with sleek black heels and her favorite gold earrings, she felt every bit the radiant queen she wanted to be tonight.

Her braids, freshly moisturized and styled, cascaded over her shoulders. She leaned into the mirror, carefully applying her makeup just enough to highlight her striking eyes and full lips. A spritz of her signature perfume added the finishing touch.

Amelia stepped back from the mirror, smiling at her reflection. She mimicked the voice of the Rovos Rail owner from earlier, waving her hand regally. "No cellphones, official dinner attire." She winked at herself. "Guess we're here to create memories, not take pictures."

Satisfied, she grabbed her small clutch and stepped out of her room. The hallways were alive with faint murmurs of fellow passengers and the sound of soft piano notes floating from the dining car. Amelia felt her heart quicken not just at the idea of the lavish meal awaiting her, but the possibility of crossing paths with him again.

As she entered the dining car, the opulence was intoxicating. Crystal chandeliers hung from the ceiling, casting a warm glow over tables set with fine china and polished silver. Guests were already seated, their laughter and chatter blending harmoniously with the clink of glasses.

And there he was. Luca.

Seated at a table near the window, his dark eyes flicked upward, catching hers. For a moment, the world narrowed to just the two of them. His lips curved into that devastating smile once more, and Amelia felt the heat rise in her che eks.Taking a steadying breath, she smiled back and walked toward her assigned table. Tonight was just beginning, and so, perhaps, was something else entirely.

After the exquisite three-course meal, paired with wines that tasted like bottled African sunsets, the Pride of Africa train kept its rhythm rolling steadily through the night as Amelia's heart and Luca's soul danced to the melody of perfect strangers.

The dining car buzzed with soft conversations and the occasional burst of laughter. Luca's sister Sofia, animated and exuberant, spoke to him in rapid Italian, her hands moving as though she were painting the air with her words. Luca nodded along, his attention seemingly devoted to her, but every so often, his gaze would wander, searching, until it found Amelia.

Seated across the room, Amelia pretended not to notice. But her last sip of wine felt heavier than the others, weighted by the heat of his glances. As she placed her empty glass down, she stood with deliberate calmness, excused herself politely, and walked back to her room, her steps slow but purposeful.

Inside her compartment, she exhaled deeply and smiled to herself. She reached for her diary, the leather soft and familiar in her hands, and began writing. Her pen moved tenderly across the page as she described him the man she'd just met, the man who seemed to have rooted himself somewhere between her mind and her heart. She read over the words, chuckling softly before pressing her fingers to the page as if to seal her feelings within.

After brushing her teeth, she slipped into her soft cotton pajamas and lay down, letting the gentle swaying of the train lull her into sleep beneath Africa's starlit sky.

By dawn, a cool breeze whispered through the small gap in her window, carrying the scent of damp earth and wild grass. Amelia stirred, glancing at her watch: 6:00 a.m.

As she pulled on her silk robe, she thought of the frantic life she'd left behind in D.C. As a busy teaching, her days were usually a blur of deadlines. This trip from Pretoria to Cape Town was supposed to be her sanctuary, a "land cruise" where she could finally breathe after the messy end of her relationship with Houston. She'd chosen to continue with her plans without Houston, selecting the *Rovos Rail* for its reputation, its slow, rhythmic pace, and those traditional touchstones like the beating of the cowhide drums that would soon echo through the halls to announce breakfast It was the perfect place to get lost.

The lounge car was faintly illuminated by the early morning light, the polished wood glowing softly. As she entered, she froze.

There he was. The man from the platform. He was standing by the silver coffee service, holding two steaming cups, looking far too awake and handsome for the hour.

His face lit up when he saw her. Before she could even manage a "Good morning," he blurted out, "Which car are you in?"

Amelia laughed softly, her voice still husky from sleep. "Good morning to you, too, stranger."

He chuckled, shaking his head at his own eagerness. "Good morning, perfect stranger. Forgive me I just realized this train is nearly half a kilometer long. If I didn't ask now, I feared I might never run into you again."

They shared a quiet, breathless laugh that felt oddly intimate in the stillness of the dawn.

"I'm in the Pullman suite, Car C," he said, choosing to be a bit more specific so he wouldn't have to search a hundred cabins. "Suite 12. And you?"

"Car D, right behind you," she replied, his eyes sparkling behind his glasses.

They stood there for a long moment, the silence stretching. For thirty seconds, neither moved, just smiling as the train swayed gently beneath their feet.

"You better go before that coffee gets cold," Amelia teased, nodding toward the two cups. A tiny, unbidden spark of jealousy flickered in her chest was the second cup for the woman with the floral dress?

Luca glanced down at the cups. "Right. Yes. My... well, she's waiting for her caffeine fix. I'll see you around ."

He turned to leave, his steps light. Amelia stood there for a moment, biting her lip and watching him disappear. She didn't even know his name, yet her heart was racing faster than the locomotive.

Her morning had just started, and already, the day held a spark of something extraordinary Amelia wasn't in the mood for the dining car that morning. Instead, she opted for a granola bar from her bag and the coffee she'd managed to snag earlier. Sitting by the window, her laptop balanced on her knees, she opened her inbox to find an email from her boss in Washington, D.C. Work was a constant companion, even on this luxury escape. She sighed, replying quickly while the train hummed along the tracks.

Time slipped by unnoticed. By the time she glanced at the clock, it was nearing lunch. She jumped up, taking a quick shower before slipping into a red jumpsuit that clung to her curves in all the right places. A pair of chic flat shoes completed the look, and with her signature red lipstick and oversized black sunglasses, she could've been mistaken for a model straight off the pages of a glamour magazine.

As she stepped into the train's aisle, Amelia walked with effortless grace, each step echoing like a catwalk strut. She felt the presence of someone behind her, the soft rhythm of footsteps matching hers, but she didn't turn around.

Behind her was Luca, utterly captivated. Each sway of her hips, each confident stride, felt like an unspoken invitation to a private dance that only he could see. She was mesmerizing, and Luca couldn't look away, his thoughts a blur of admiration and longing.

Amelia entered the dining car and took a seat at one of the elegantly set tables. Moments later, Luca appeared, pulling out the chair next to hers with a charming smile.

"Is this seat taken?" he asked, his voice warm and teasing.

Amelia looked up, her lips curling into a smirk. She gestured toward the chair with a graceful hand, her smile all the invitation Luca needed.

"Perfect stranger," he began, leaning slightly toward her, "what's your name?"

Amelia laughed softly, shaking his outstretched hand. "I think I'll keep the 'perfect stranger' title. It suits us, don't you think?"

Luca nodded, his grin widening. "Alright, Perfect Stranger. Nice to officially meet you."

The waitress appeared, and they ordered their meals. The conversation flowed as if they'd known each other for years. They talked about everything and nothing travel dreams, embarrassing stories, favorite meals. But neither asked the obvious questions: phone numbers, relationship status, or even last names. It felt unnecessary, as though naming their connection might break the spell.

Time passed too quickly, and before they knew it, the train began to slow for the first ground tour a safari.

As Amelia stood to leave, she caught sight of Sofia approaching from the opposite direction. Not wanting to create an awkward situation, she smiled politely and excused herself.

"It was wonderful talking to you, Perfect Stranger," she said, grabbing her bag. "I need to go change for the safari tour." Luca stood as well, his gaze following her every move. "See you then," he said, his voice filled with anticipation.

As Amelia walked away, Luca watched her disappear down the corridor, already counting the moments until their paths crossed again. The air between them was charged, the promise of something undeniable hanging just out of reach. Sofia walked up to him, placing two fingers under his chin to close his slightly ajar mouth. "Dude, you're literally dropping your face. She's gone." Her tone was sharp, but her smirk betrayed her amusement.

"Please, not again. You promised me this trip was supposed to be just us. I hate when you start doing this," Sofia added, pointing at him with an exaggerated, dramatic flourish that drew looks from the other passengers. "We've never had a proper brother-sister getaway without you falling in love with a stranger."

Luca chuckled, a bit of color rising to his cheeks as he ran a hand through his hair. "Oh, come on, Sof. That's not true!"

Sofia arched a perfectly manicured eyebrow, completely unimpressed. "How about Spain? Ring any bells, *Lupe*?" a smirk playing on her lips.

Luca sighed dramatically, leaning back against the plush velvet of the seat. "Spain doesn't count. That was... different."

"It *so* counts," she shot back, collapsing into her seat and eyeing the extra glass of wine he had yet to finish. "You didn't even remember her name two weeks after that whirlwind romance. You get swept up in the scenery, Luca. You're a romantic, and it's dangerous."

They both laughed, the easy, lived-in laughter of people who had grown up side-by-side. Just then, the train began to hiss and slow to a rhythmic stop, signaling their arrival for the ground safari tour. Sofia stood up and, with a mischievous glint in her eyes, handed him her heavy designer handbag.

"Carry this for me," she said, smiling with fake sweetness.

Luca frowned, looking at the bag as if it were a trap. "Do I have to? What is it with you and these heavy handbags? What do you have in here, bricks?"

She grinned, leaning in close as if sharing a grand conspiracy. "Because when other women see you dutifully holding my bag, they'll assume I'm your girlfriend or your wife. Consider it a repellent for your habit of falling for strangers. It's for your own good, big brother. I'm saving you from yourself."

Luca groaned, but he dutifully slung the bag over his shoulder, the feminine strap looking ridiculous against his broad chest. He muttered under his breath, "If you weren't my sister..."

Sofia just laughed, walking toward the exit with the confidence of someone who had successfully marked her territory, unaware that her "protection" was about to cause the very heartbreak she claimed to be preventing.

As they disembarked, tourists bustled around, eagerly finding their assigned vehicles for the game drive. Luca glanced around but didn't see Amelia. He mumbled an excuse and ducked into the restroom.

The air was fresh, carrying the faint mineral scent of Warmbaths, Bela Bela a town famous for its hot springs. Luca's sister, impatient as ever, climbed into their car and saved him a seat. She glanced up, realizing he was nowhere in sight.

When she finally spotted him emerging from the restroom, he was too far away to stop the inevitable. Another passenger was about to take his saved seat. Luca spotted Amelia heading toward a different car and quickly waved to his sister, gesturing he'd ride elsewhere.

Sofia rolled her eyes. "Unbelievable," she muttered as the driver started the engine.

Meanwhile, Luca slipped into the car with Amelia. Coincidentally or perhaps by fate the couple assigned to join them had canceled last minute, leaving them alone.

Amelia noticed his sister's bag still slung over his shoulder and burst into laughter. I love your handbag!

Luca laughed, shaking his head. "Women. Always making things complicated."

She tilted her head. "What's really complicated is why you're carrying it in the first place."

"Forget the bag," he said, brushing it aside. "What made you take this trip solo?"

Amelia chuckled. "If that's your way of asking if I'm single, the answer is yes."

Luca's eyes lit up mischievously. "Are you sure?"

Before he could finish his thought, Amelia leaned in and kissed him. It was quick but confident, leaving Luca utterly breathless. His heart pounded like the drumbeats signaling a Maasai celebration.

Amelia pulled back, a teasing grin playing on her lips. "Oops. Did I just pull a 'me too' moment on you?"

Luca shook his head, leaning closer this time, and kissed her. This time, the kiss lingered, their connection deepening with each passing second.

The driver's abrupt swerve into a pothole jolted them apart, their gazes darting to the rearview mirror where the driver's poorly hidden smirk confirmed he'd seen everything.

They both sat back, flustered but grinning. As they neared the other vehicles, Amelia caught sight of Sofia. Guilt flickered across her face, and she turned to look out the window.

Luca leaned in close, his breath tickling her ear. "This isn't over."

Amelia laughed softly, shaking her head. "We'll see, Perfect Stranger."

For now, they let the moment pass, enjoying the wild beauty of the African landscape and the promise of what was yet to come.

After the safari tour, the train continued its journey, winding through the darkened African landscape. After the safari tour, most passengers retreated to their compartments, exhausted from the day's adventures. The rhythmic hum of the rails lulled them into a quiet reprieve.

Amelia, however, was filled with a renewed energy. Dinner was calling, and she was determined to make an unforgettable impression. She chose her best dress for the occasion a long, flowing gown in a stunning periwinkle hue that clung to her curves in all the right places. The neckline offered a teasing glimpse of her décolletage, a subtle yet provocative invitation. She pinned her braids into an elegant updo, her face glowing with the soft shimmer of expertly applied makeup. Her black Christian Louboutin heels, with their signature red soles, were her finishing touch a statement of power and allure.

When she entered the dining car, the effect was immediate. Conversations paused, heads turned, and all eyes were drawn to her. But for Luca, time stopped entirely. He watched her from the moment she stepped in, unable to tear his gaze away. She was radiant, her presence commanding every flicker of the candlelight.

Sofia, seated beside him, was chatting animatedly, but her words were lost to him. His mind was elsewhere, spinning fantasies of how he might seize a moment with Amelia, away from the eyes of others.

Dinner was a luxurious affair, with courses paired expertly with fine South African wines. The dim lighting, the clinking of glasses, and the soft murmur of conversation created a perfect backdrop for longing glances and stolen smiles.

As people began to return to their rooms, the candlelight dimming with each departing guest, Amelia rose gracefully from her seat. Her movements were deliberate, her hips swaying ever so slightly as she walked past Luca, heading toward her compartment. He watched her leave, his heart racing, the primal pull toward her growing stronger with every second.

After ensuring his sister was comfortably tucked into bed, lulled to sleep by wine and the gentle sway of the train, Luca slipped out of the room. His pulse quickened as he made his way through the train cars, knocking softly on doors under the pretense of searching for someone's lost watch.

When he finally reached her door and knocked, it opened almost instantly. Amelia stood there; her lips slightly parted as if she had been waiting for him. Without a word, she grabbed his hand, pulled him inside, and shut the door.

Their eyes locked, and the tension between them snapped. Amelia leaned in, her lips capturing his in a kiss that was both tender and fiery. Luca responded eagerly, his hands finding her waist and pulling her closer.

The train rocked gently as they moved together, the motion mirroring their rhythm. Amelia's fingers worked at the buttons of Luca's shirt, her touch sending shivers down his spine. He slid the straps of her dress from her shoulders, the fabric pooling at her feet, revealing her luminous skin beneath.

The air was thick with desire, their breaths mingling as they explored each other. Every kiss, every touch, every whispered word was electric. The sounds of the train the hum of the engine, the occasional whistle faded into the background. The only reality was each other.

Luca's lips traced a path down her neck, his hands roaming her curves with reverence. Amelia's fingers tangled in his hair, her head falling back as she surrendered to the moment. The world outside the window was a blur, the African sky scattered with stars bearing silent witness to their passion.

Hours passed as they lost themselves in one another, their connection as deep and endless as the landscapes rushing by. When they finally lay entwined, their breathing steadying in unison, the train's rhythm sang them into a peaceful slumber.

Above them, the sky glittered, the Southern Cross shining brightly a celestial nod to a love that was as fleeting as it was unforgettable.

Amelia lay wrapped in the soft sheets of her cabin, her breathing steady, her body relaxed from the intensity of the night. The rhythmic hum of the train blended with her serene slumber. Luca sat at the edge of the bed, gazing at her peaceful face. The night had been nothing short of magical passion intertwining with tenderness, their bodies moving in perfect harmony under the vast African sky.

He reached out and brushed a strand of hair from her face. She murmured softly in her sleep, and Luca smiled, his heart swelling with an emotion he wasn't sure he could name. He wanted to freeze time, to stay in this moment forever.

But forever wasn't theirs to claim.

Quietly, he dressed, the reality of their separate paths creeping back into his mind. Before leaving, he found a piece of paper on the desk. With the train swaying gently beneath him, he wrote:

Dear Perfect Stranger,

This night, time folded in on itself, and within those fleeting hours, we lived a thousand lifetimes. The world outside disappeared, and in its place, you only you became my universe. You've left an indelible mark on my soul, one I never sought but now cannot imagine living without. I came on this journey expecting landscapes and solitude, but instead, I found you a force I can neither name nor resist. As I write, the memory of you lingers like the final notes of a beautiful song, bittersweet and endless. My heart feels both impossibly full and achingly hollow. How cruel that something so profound can slip through the fingers of time. But if fate should ever bring you to Florence, know that I am waiting. Find me at Via della Vita, No. 8 a street that translates to "The Way of Life," fitting, as you've become mine...

folded the note and carefully slipped it into her handbag. As he lingered by the door, he whispered, "Goodbye, Perfect Stranger," and left.

Back in his room, Luca found his sister still fast asleep. He lay on his bed, staring at the ceiling, replaying every moment with Amelia the touch of her hand, the way her laughter lit up the room, the way she looked at him as if she'd known him for a lifetime.

But as the train continued its journey, another memory crept in: his father's laughter, his deep voice, the way he'd always known the right thing to say.

The tears came before Luca could stop them. He pressed a hand over his mouth to stifle the sobs, his body shaking. This trip had always been about his father, about honoring a man who had given him and his sister everything. And now, here he was, caught between the past and the future, between duty and desire.

Unspoken sorrow

Before the hum of the train pulled her back to reality, Sofia was somewhere else.

In her dream, the air was thick with the scent of Ugandan rain and rich, red earth. She was a little girl again, standing in the shade of a massive acacia tree. Her father was there, his skin bronzed by the African sun he had loved more than the Tuscan hills of his birth. He was an Italian man with a nomad's heart, a man who had moved his life to Uganda not for his job, but for the rhythm of the land.

In the dream, he knelt before her and Luca, his hands roughened by years of work but his touch as gentle as a breeze. *"When the time comes,"* he whispered in his melodic, gravelly Italian, *"do not leave me in a cold stone vault. Take me back to the smoke that thunders. Take me to Victoria Falls. It is the most magical place I have ever been the place where the earth meets the sky. I want to rest where the water never stops singing."*

He had laughed then, a deep, resonant sound that felt like home, and reached out to pull them both into an embrace that promised he would never leave.

But the laughter began to fade, turning into the rhythmic, metallic clatter of wheels on tracks. The warmth of his arms dissolved into the cool silk of her bedsheets.

Sofia's eyes fluttered open to the muted hum of the train gliding along its tracks, the world outside bathed in a soft golden light. The first rays of morning spilled through the window, painting Luca in a glow that softened the weariness etched on his face. He sat quietly, his gaze fixed on the endless plains of the savannah, his eyes rimmed with the red of sleepless nights and unspoken sorrow.

Without a word, she slid beside him, her presence a silent comfort. Resting her head on his shoulder, she whispered, "I miss him."

Luca turned to her, his voice low and rough, as if the words themselves carried weight. "Me too."

Their eyes met, a mirror of pain and love shared between siblings who had lost the man who had shaped their lives. Without hesitation, Sofia wrapped her arms around him, her tears spilling freely. Luca held her close, his own silent grief flowing between them like a river.

"This journey," she began, her voice trembling, "it's to lay him to rest, but it feels so much heavier than that."

"It's because it's not just about saying goodbye," Luca replied. "It's about holding onto everything he was and everything he taught us to be."

Sofia shook her head. "I don't think I can go to breakfast. Or lunch. I just... I can't face the world today."

Luca nodded, his agreement unspoken but clear. He reached for his laptop, opening a folder that had been untouched for months. The screen flickered to life, revealing a home video. The two of them as children, running barefoot across their father's garden, laughter ringing out like music. Their father's deep, warm voice called to them, his arms outstretched in a gesture of love so profound it transcended the screen.

They sat together, the rhythmic sway of the train a gentle backdrop to their mourning. They laughed softly at the silly moments their father had captured, the joy of those days momentarily replacing the ache in their hearts. Then they cried again, their tears falling in sync with the rain that had begun to tap gently against the window, as though the world wept with them.

The train moved steadily onward, carrying them closer to Victoria Falls and the place where they would say their final goodbye. But in that morning wrapped in memories, in each other's presence, and in the love their father had left behind they found something unexpected.

Not closure, but peace. A quiet understanding that though their father's journey on earth had ended, his legacy was alive in their laughter, their tears, and the bond that would never break.

And as the train cut through the golden landscape, the two of them sat in that cabin, letting the past heal their wounds and the present prepare them for what lay ahead.

Victoria Falls

The train came to a smooth halt at Victoria Falls, its final destination. Outside the grand windows, mist rose like a ghostly veil from the thundering cascade. Passengers eagerly stepped down, cameras and curiosity in hand, drawn by the magnetic pull of the majestic wonder ahead.

For Luca and Sofia, however, this was no ordinary journey. They stood together at the edge of the falls, the roaring waters echoing the storm of emotions within them. The spray kissed their faces, mingling with tears neither had the strength to hide.

Sofia held the urn close to her chest, her fingers trembling. She turned to Luca, her voice barely audible over the relentless rush of the falls. "Do you think he'd be proud of us?"

Luca's jaw tightened as he swallowed the lump in his throat. "He'd be proud of you," he said, his voice breaking. "You've kept us together, Sof. Through everything."

Together, they unscrewed the urn's lid, their hands steadying each other as they prepared for the final goodbye. The ashes danced on the wind before merging with the mist, becoming one with the falls that seemed to roar louder as if to welcome their father home.

Sofia collapsed into Luca's arms, her grief spilling out in sobs that racked her body. He held her tightly, whispering words of comfort, though his own tears fell freely, carving silent paths down his face. In that moment, their bond as siblings was unshakable a lifeline in a sea of loss.

From a distance, Amelia arrived, her heart caught in a tangle of emotions. She had told herself she wanted to see the falls, but the pull to find Luca had been stronger.

Her steps faltered as she saw them. Luca and Sofia, locked in an embrace, tears flowing unchecked. A wave of guilt swept over her, a sharp, suffocating pang that settled heavily in her chest.

"I slept with a married man," she thought, shame washing over her like the mist from the falls. Her gaze darted to Sofia. The way Luca held her, the intimacy of their shared grief it could only mean one thing. "That's his wife," she whispered to herself, her throat tightening.

She turned away, unable to bear the sight, her mind a whirlwind of emotions. She felt shame, yes, but also something deeper, something raw. The connection she had felt with Luca the night before wasn't just physical. It had reached into her very soul, pulling something alive and vulnerable to the surface.

Amelia quickened her steps, her resolve hardening with each one. She found the first boat heading back toward the train station, her body trembling as though trying to shake off the memory of his touch, his voice, his presence.

Her mind screamed at her to flee, to put distance between herself and a love that could only bring ruin. Yet her heart clung stubbornly to the moments they had shared, moments that had felt more real than anything she had known in years.

As the boat pulled away, she looked back one last time, the falls fading into the horizon. Her chest ached with the weight of her decision, and her soul whispered a quiet goodbye to the man who had unknowingly awakened it.

The taxi bounced gently over the cobblestone streets, carrying Amelia away from the station, the faint roar of Victoria Falls still echoing in her ears. She leaned her forehead against the cool glass window, watching the vibrant landscape blur past. Her heart was heavy, each beat an ache she couldn't shake.

She had made up her mind. She couldn't face Luca again, not after what she'd seen. The memory of his arms wrapped protectively around another woman his tears falling freely played on a loop in her mind. She had felt something profound with him, something she didn't know was possible. But now, that connection felt like an illusion, tainted by misunderstanding and guilt.

"Where to, miss?" the taxi driver asked, glancing at her through the rearview mirror.

"The airport," she said softly, her voice fragile, as if even speaking might crack her resolve.

Back at the station, Luca looking around, his body and mind still raw from the emotions of the morning. He glanced around the platform, expecting to find her waiting, her warm smile lighting up the chaos around them. But she wasn't there.

A small knot of worry tightened in his chest. He walked briskly through the crowd, scanning every face, looking for her. As the minutes passed and the platform began to empty, unease turned to panic.

He approached a porter, his voice tight. "Have you seen the woman has black braids hair, wearing a light blue scarf?"

The porter frowned in thought before shaking his head. "Not sure, but maybe the tour guide can help."

Luca turned quickly, finding the guide who had been with their group. "A woman I was with yesterday did you see where she went?"

The guide nodded sympathetically. "She took a taxi not long ago. Seemed in a rush, asked to be taken to the airport."

"The airport?" Luca's heart sank. "Did she say anything? Leave a message?"

"No, she didn't say much," the guide replied. "She looked...sad."

Luca stood there, stunned, the world spinning around him. He felt an unbearable weight settle in his chest, a sense of loss he couldn't put into words. She was leaving, slipping through his fingers, and there was nothing he could do to stop her.

His mind raced. Who was she really? He knew the curve of her smile, the way her laughter warmed the air around them, the softness of her touch but he didn't know her name. He didn't know her story, where she was going, or why she had left without a word.

He sank onto a nearby bench, staring out at the horizon where the taxi had disappeared. The vibrant hum of the station dulled, and the lively chatter of passengers faded into an unbearable silence.

In the distance, the faint sound of Victoria Falls echoed, a reminder of the journey that had brought them together and now, the one tearing them apart.

Luca closed his eyes, his head in his hands. The chances of finding her again in a world so vast seemed impossible. Yet, deep within, a flicker of hope refused to be extinguished. He wouldn't let her memory slip away, even if she was already gone.

In the Sky

Amelia sat by the window, the hum of the plane a dull roar in her ears. Below, the vast expanse of the Atlantic shimmered like liquid silver, endless and indifferent. She rested her forehead against the cool glass, trying to silence the storm in her heart.

As she reached into her bag, searching for her journal, her fingers brushed against something unfamiliar paper, folded neatly, as if placed there with care. Her breath hitched. She pulled it out, her hands trembling as she assume this would be Perfect stranger's handwriting.

For a moment, she stared at the note, afraid to open it, as if the words inside could undo her fragile composure. Finally, she unfolded it, the creases soft beneath her fingertips.

His words spilled onto the page like poetry, raw and unguarded she slowly she opens he lips and finish reading.

> "What we shared wasn't just a moment it was eternity wrapped in a fleeting hour. You've imprinted yourself on my soul, and no matter the distance, I will carry you with me. Until then, carry me with you as I will carry you. Always.

Eternally yours perfect stranger,

Always,

Tears blurred her vision, each word carving its way into her heart. She pressed the note to her lips, as if by doing so, she could close the distance between them. The plane's cabin felt smaller, the air heavier, as if the weight of her emotions defied gravity itself. Her chest tightened, a longing so profound it left her breathless. She whispered to herself, a name that now felt like a prayer. "Perfect stranger..."

Across the continent,

The luxury train sped toward Tanzania, cutting through the golden savannah under a burning orange sky. Luca sat by the window; his reflection ghostlike against the glass.

The ache of her absence was unbearable, like a wound he couldn't heal. His thoughts were a tangled mess of regret, hope, and the memory of her the way her laughter had lit up even the darkest corners of his heart, the warmth of her touch, the way she had whispered his name as if it were sacred.

He closed his eyes, the rhythmic clatter of the train amplifying the silence within him. She was out there somewhere, carrying a piece of him he could never reclaim.

Two souls, bound by a fleeting but eternal connection, traveled in opposite directions one across the sky, the other across the earth. Yet, the threads of fate rarely unravel so easily.

Amelia clutched the note tighter, her heart torn between the life waiting for her and the man she'd left behind. Questions swirled in her mind: What if? What now? What could have been? how about the girl?

Luca stared out at the fading horizon, his heart heavy but alive with a quiet resolve. He didn't know her name, her destination, or her story but he knew one thing: he would find her.

Somewhere, in the vastness of the world, their paths had crossed. Somewhere, they would cross again...

Amelia stared at the letter in her lap, the words trembling in her hands. Her breath caught somewhere between her chest and her throat. She hadn't expected honesty. She hadn't expected... this.

As the plane hummed beneath her and clouds blurred outside the window, she reached for her phone maybe just to ground herself. A notification blinked across the screen

1 New Message Houston

"Baby, you won. I can't live without you. Let's talk. I still love you."

She blinked, heart cracking in two directions. One name lit her phone. The other still echoed from the letter.

The scent of cherry blossoms

Amelia stepped off the plane into the soft embrace of Washington, DC's spring air. The scent of cherry blossoms floated lightly, like a whispered promise, wrapping around her senses and stirring something gentle inside her. The city glowed in the afternoon sun, petals shimmering pink and white, a delicate celebration of new beginnings.

She moved with a lightness in her step, her fingers grazing the worn leather strap of her bag as she reached the carousel. A slow, deep breath filled her lungs. It was sweet. Fresh. Alive. She was finally home. Her lips curved into a smile, soft and tentative, as if she was greeting an old friend she hadn't seen in years.

Inside the restroom, the cool tile kissed her feet as she washed away the remnants of travel. Water dripped down her face, cool and awakening, mingling with the warmth rising in her cheeks. She carefully applied her favorite rose-colored lipstick, the color blooming like a secret thrill. A touch of blush warmed her skin, and with a shy glance in the mirror, she whispered, "Home sweet home."

But then just for a heartbeat Luca's image flickered behind her eyes. His lips, soft and inviting, pressed against hers, sending a shiver that raced through her like a sudden electric current. Her pulse quickened, and she tucked her eyeliner into her bag with a steadying breath.

The humid air of Washington D.C. felt heavy and stagnant compared to the crisp, wild breezes of the African plains. As Amelia walked through the sliding glass doors of the airport, her phone buzzed with the text he'd sent while she was at baggage claim: *I'm at the front ...in the Jeep. Can't wait to see you.*

She spotted him immediately. Houston was leaning against the black hood of his Wrangler, "southern boy" charm that had first captured her heart. He looked good too good. His sleeves were rolled up, revealing tanned forearms, and his smile was wide and genuine.

As she approached, a jagged flashback sliced through her mind, sharp as a razor.

Two weeks before their scheduled flight to Pretoria. She had walked into his office to surprise him with lunch, only to find him pressed against his mahogany desk, his hands tangled in his co-worker's hair. The air in that room had tasted like betrayal. The "harsh breakup" hadn't just been an argument; it had been an explosion.

Now, standing here, she felt the familiar pull of his gravity. She was exhausted, lonely, and terrified of being single at thirty. She wanted to believe his "safe harbor" was real.

"Hey, beautiful," Houston called out, his arms opening wide.

Amelia stepped into his embrace, letting him pull her into a hug so full of warmth it almost made her forget the ache buried deep inside. *Almost.*

As he pressed a kiss to her temple, her mind betrayed her. She wasn't in D.C.; she was back in the dimly lit carriage of the Rovos Rail. She could still feel the phantom sensation of Luca's hands on her skin, a touch that had left her breathless in the shadow of Victoria Falls a place where love had roared like thunder.

She pulled back, forcing a smile that didn't reach her eyes. She was an expert at hiding what her heart whispered in silence. She laughed at his jokes as he loaded her bags, playing the part of the happy girlfriend returned home. But as she climbed into the passenger seat, she knew the truth: she had brought a ghost back with her, and Houston had no idea he was already being replaced.

The ride through DC was effortless, the streets nearly empty on this gentle Sunday afternoon. The sunlight filtered through budding trees, casting playful shadows on the pavement. They rolled into Yuma Street, turning onto Connecticut Avenue, the familiar corners anchoring her to this moment in time.

Before heading inside their apartment, Houston suggested brunch nearby, a quaint spot just steps from the Van Ness station. Though exhaustion weighed heavily on her, Amelia nodded, grateful for the extra minutes to linger outside, to delay the closeness she wasn't ready to face.

Over buttery toast and steaming cups of coffee, they shared quiet conversation. The world was calm, but Amelia's heart was a storm of longing and memory, caught somewhere between two continents, two loves.

Back at the garage, the jeep's engine hummed softly as they packed up. Amelia's thoughts drifted like the last petals falling from the cherry trees.

Stepping into the shower, the warm water spilled over her skin, soothing the ache in her muscles and soul. Then Houston was there, bare and bold, his presence a tender invitation.

His eyes darkened with desire. "Mind if I join?"

For a moment, she hesitated, then gave in to the pull. His body pressed close, the heat radiating through the spray, his hands tracing promises on her wet skin.

As the water cascaded down her back, it carried her away to the misty roar of Victoria Falls, to the phantom touch of Luca's hands. Her breath hitched, a delicious ache blooming deep inside her.

Their lips met, hungry and soft, a kiss that spoke of the distance between them and the fire she longed to feel again.

Afterward, Houston pulled back with a grin, breath ragged. "Africa gave you something I want to keep. Next trip's on me you're bringing that magic back."

They laughed softly, the sound mingling with the night's quiet, and Amelia let herself drift into sleep, jet lag and longing wrapped tight around her heart.

The months that followed her return were a beautiful, curated lie. Spring turned into a humid D.C. summer, with long afternoons spent at outdoor cafes and weekend drives in Houston's Jeep. By the time the leaves began to turn gold across the **Howard University** campus, where Amelia spent her days lecturing on literature she and Houston seemed like the perfect couple again.

On the surface, they were thriving. They hosted dinners, celebrated holidays with family, and Houston was the attentive, "Southern boy" lover he had always promised to be. He was watering the garden of their relationship, desperate to make it grow over the cracks of his past mistakes.

But Amelia's heart was a locked room.

One rainy October night, after they had made love, the silence of the bedroom felt deafening. Houston lay beside her, his breathing heavy and rhythmic in the deep sleep of a man who believed he was forgiven. Amelia sat up slowly, the ghost of a sensation lingering on her skin. In the heat of their intimacy moments ago, she had almost whispered it the words *"perfect stranger"* had hovered on the tip of her tongue, a private tribute to the man on the train.

She reached into her nightstand and pulled out her leather-bound diary. Her pen flew across the page, the ink bleeding with her truth:

Houston is here, but I am still in Car C. Every time he touches me, I am comparing the pressure of his hands to the memory of perfect stranger's. It wasn't just sex; it was a soul-shift. How can a stranger from a three-day journey rewrite the map of my entire body? I look at the man I'm supposed to love, and all I see is the person who isn't him.

She wrote about the way the light hit perfect stranger's glasses, the way his voice sounded over the roar of the falls, and how that "perfect stranger" had ruined her for any other man.

Closing the diary with a soft *thud*, she looked at Houston's sleeping form. A pang of guilt struck her, but it wasn't enough to erase the memory. She stood up, walked to her closet, and tucked the diary deep into the hidden pocket of her handbag.

She was an assistant Professor Amelia Lockhart at one of the most prestigious universities in the country, a woman of logic and intellect. Yet, as she stared out at the D.C. skyline, she realized she was failing the simplest test of all: she was physically in Washington, but her heart had never gotten off that train.

Return to Sender

A year had slipped by since Amelia returned from her solo journey through Southern Africa the luxury train that wound from South Africa to Zimbabwe, carrying her through landscapes both wild and breathtaking. That trip hadn't just changed her; it had transformed her, like the gentle erosion of stone by a river, shaping a woman who had finally learned to love herself fiercely, without apology. She had discovered a deep, unyielding courage the kind that fights for what it believes in, and loves not just others but the very essence of one's own soul.

She had tried to reach Luca in letters, fragile paper bridges thrown across oceans and borders, only to have them come back, stamped "Return to Sender" in cold black ink. Yet, she kept one letter from him their last tether safe and sacred inside the worn lining of her handbag. It was a talisman on the darkest days, a whispered echo of a love that once promised eternity. Whenever the world pressed heavy on her chest, she would slip her fingers inside her bag, pull out the letter, and lose herself in his words, carried away to a time and place where hearts beat in sync and promises were alive.

Houston had noticed. Quietly, carefully. He had watched her clutch that letter, eyes shining with tears or distant memories, and though it stirred a wild ache inside him, he said nothing. Because he loved her. Because he had betrayed her once, and in the fragile aftermath, he had learned the sharpest lesson silence sometimes shelters love from the wounds of truth.

The evening began with a sweetness that felt earned. Houston walked through the front door, the screen door clicking shut behind him, carrying a vibrant bouquet of sunflowers Amelia's favorite. He found her in the kitchen, her silhouette framed by the amber glow of the setting D.C. sun.

"For the smartest professor at Howard," he murmured, stepping up behind her. He pressed a warm kiss to the nape of her neck, his hands lingering on her waist.

Amelia leaned back into him for a second, a small smile playing on her lips as she stirred the pan. "They're beautiful, Houston. Thank you."

The kitchen was filled with the domestic comfort of a couple in rhythm the aroma of shrimp sizzling in butter and garlic, the soft hum of the refrigerator, the sound of their easy conversation about her lectures that day. For a moment, it felt like they had finally made it back to solid ground.

Then, the shrill ring of her phone broke the quiet. It was vibrating on the dining table across the room.

"Can you bring me my bag, babe?" Amelia asked softly, her attention on the stove. "The phone is right next to it."

Houston nodded, dropping the flowers on the counter. He walked over and lifted the worn leather tote from the chair. As he reached for the phone, the bag tilted, and the zipper left slightly ajar gave way. A single piece of cream-colored stationery slipped out, fluttering to the floor like a wounded bird.

His heart thundered in his chest a wild, chaotic rhythm like drums beating through an African jungle. He recognized the paper. It wasn't a bill or a flyer. His hands trembled. He wanted to look away, to set the bag down and walk back to the woman he loves, but the pull of curiosity and long-buried suspicion was too strong.

He bent to retrieve the letter, his fingertips grazing the fragile paper. Unfolding it carefully, he began to read. Words meant for another time, another place, filled with a raw longing that he had never felt from her. He could almost see Amelia in his mind's eye her hands tangled in the hair of another man, their bodies pressed close in a shadowed train cabin. The ache of it clawed through him, shredding the peace of the last year.

Driven by a turmoil he barely understood, he searched further. He unzipped the smaller pocket and pulled out the soft leather diary. With shaking fingers, he opened it. His eyes scanned pages dense with secrets tears dried into the ink, confessions carved in the silence of the nights they had spent together. His breath hitched, sweat prickling his brow as if he were standing under the unforgiving midday sun of a desert.

He walked back to the kitchen doorway, holding the letter and diary like fragile, damning relics. Amelia turned, a question on her lips, but she froze when she saw his face. Their eyes locked two souls suspended on the edge of a breaking wave, weighted with inevitability.

Houston stepped forward, the pain finally shattering his carefully guarded walls. Tears brimmed in his eyes. "I should ask...

but I already know," he said, his voice cracking and desperate. "I read everything. The letter from perfect stranger, the ones you sent back, the diary... the nights you cried for him while you were lying next to me. So, tell me... was he better than me? Did you ever really love me?"

Amelia's breath caught, silence swallowing the room.

"Was he better than me?" he demanded, his voice rising in anguish.

Tears spilled freely down Amelia's cheeks as she met his gaze. "I don't know how to answer," she whispered. "He was... different. Special. He touched something inside me my soul, my heart. I don't know how to explain it."

Turning away, she faced the stove where the shrimp began to burn. The scent was sharp and bitter now, curling into the smoky air. She didn't want to lie, but the truth was a blade that cut both ways. Her sobs fractured the stillness.

Houston pressed his hands to the counter, struggling to steady himself. "Answer me," he demanded softly.

Her voice trembled, barely audible over the hiss of the pan. "Yes... but in a different way. We had something I can't forget. He reached parts of me no one else has."

Without another word, Houston grabbed a lighter from the counter. He held the flickering flame to the letter. The paper curled, blackened, and turned to ash the last physical thread to the man in Africa.

He turned away, his footsteps heavy and silent.

Alone, Amelia sank to the floor, her tears falling onto the scattered ashes like rain on dry earth. She whispered through broken sobs, "I can't lie to my soul."

Driven by a desperate need to reach him, she ran to the garage. The sound of an engine starting made her freeze. Houston's Jeep was pulling out. She stepped into his path, forcing the vehicle to stop.

"We need to talk," she said, her voice trembling but steady.

He climbed out and gathered her into one last, fierce embrace. "Amelia," he said, his voice low and steady as the fading light. "I'm a Texan, with a pride as wide as the eagle that soars over my land. I'm a southern boy who loves you maybe I will always love you but I have to walk away with that pride intact. This is goodbye. Don't call. Don't try to reach me. Let's make it easier for both of us."

Amelia pressed her lips to his one last time, a soft and trembling ghost of a kiss, then stepped back to watch him drive away. This was no ordinary departure; this was Houston leaving her life forever.

She stood rooted in the cold night, the scent of burnt shrimp and grit lingering like a bitter memory. Slowly, she turned back to the kitchen, her hands trembling as she began to clean the charred remains each motion a painful rhythm in the silence of a love finally unraveling.

Via della Vita

The late afternoon sun draped Milan's streets in a warm, honeyed light as Sofia's apartment at Via della Vita, No. 8 came alive with the sounds of family. After moving from their childhood home in Florence, Sofia had settled here, filling the space with laughter and the intoxicating aromas of home cooking. But Florence was still home for Luca, where the siblings had grown up side by side, the cobblestones and narrow alleys holding memories of their youth.

Tonight, their villa in Milan was the heart of the storm a bustling sanctuary where family spilled in through the doors like a rushing river. This wasn't just a typical Sunday; it was **Adrian's second birthday**, and in an Italian household, that was a summons no one dared ignore.

The kitchen was a fragrant symphony, a masterpiece of domestic chaos. The air was thick with garlic sizzling in golden olive oil and the scent of fresh basil being crushed between hurried fingers. On the stove, a deep pot of ripe tomatoes simmered into a rich, dark sauce, the steam mingling with the warm, yeasty aroma of freshly baked focaccia. In every corner, the sharp sweetness of red wine poured from bottles labeled from their own family vineyards in Tuscany breathed in half-full glasses.

Baby Adrian was the undisputed star of the evening. Barely two years old, his chubby hands reached eagerly for handfuls of warm bread as aunts and cousins swooped in to shower him with wrapped gifts and loud, wet kisses. His wide eyes the same deep, liquid brown as his mother Sofia's sparkled, reflecting the vibrant chaos around him: the laughter, the playful shouts, and the constant, rhythmic clatter of heirloom plates.

The room pulsed with a thousand voices, all speaking at once in a rapid-fire melody of Italian warmth. Children darted between the legs of uncles, and elders raised their voices to be heard over the animated stories of past summers.

In the midst of it all, Sofia moved with practiced grace, her fiery hair catching the light as she wove between groups. She raised her glass of Chianti, catching Luca's eye across the room. His smile was easy, tinged with the familiar comfort only siblings share.

""Cousin!" Sofia called out playfully, coming to his side and nudging him with her shoulder. "I have to brag there was one time I cockblocked Luca. Only once, but it counts."

Laughter erupted around them, voices raising in approval and delight. In this house, Luca was the golden boy, but Sofia was the one who kept his feet on the ground.

"Tell us!" Maria's eyes sparkled with anticipation, leaning over her wine glass.

Sofia lowered her voice, the hint of a mischievous secret curling her lips. "Picture this: a luxury train gliding through the wilds from Pretoria to Victoria Falls, the African sun beating down, the landscape a blur of ochre and sky. You remember that trip when we scattered Dad's ashes into the roaring falls? Our beautiful Italian father, who left the hills of Tuscany to become a legend in Uganda... we were taking him to his final rest."

Niko shook his head with a grin. "That doesn't count you weren't on vacation! It was family business."

Sofia shrugged with a sly smile. "Maybe, but I swear he was trying. There was this American girl Black, stunning, a vision in white linen and I swear, I saw his eyes linger on her. I stopped him. I made sure I was the only woman on his arm. I'm proud."

Cheers and laughter rose up again, filling the space like fireworks. They saw it as a sister's protection, unaware of the heart she had accidentally broken.

Maria jumped in, a smirk tugging at her lips. "You know Maria? My best friend? He dumped her. My friend never talks to me because of Luca. And that was not enough Luca showed up in Rome again!" she said with a laughing voice. "And Lily, my co-worker, aka my Boss, thought she found a soulmate. Nope. He dumped her. I almost lost my job. Cheers to that!"

Luca took a slow drink and smiled, his wire-rimmed glasses catching the candlelight. "Cousin, Lily gave me her number at your place. She said she was sick and needed a doctor. And when she showed up in the hospital, she wanted a *doctor*... not medication. And there I was what is my fault, cousin?" He laughed, the deep, rich sound of a man who spent his days saving lives as a **Cardiologist** and his nights trying to outrun his own heart.

Glasses clinked, the sound sparkling bright and clear. Sofia raised her glass toward the memory of the mystery woman with playful reverence. "To the woman who has the power to cockblock Mr. Luca cheers!"

The laughter rolled on, a joyful tide that filled every corner of the Milanese apartment. Eventually, Maria asked about photos from the Victoria Falls trip. "Do you have pictures?"

"Yeah, wait I'll grab them," Sofia said, disappearing into the other room.

Luca chuckled, shaking his head. He leaned in toward Niko. "No way she actually did it. I tapped her, the last night of the train ride..."

Sofia spun around, returning with a stack of prints and her phone, a glint in her eye. "What? Yes, I did. Most crazy thing I don't even know how to find her now."

As Sofia scrolled through the pictures, Luca's eyes caught on one face Amelia's. She was standing just behind the group in the station at Pretoria, looking like a queen among commoners. A slow smile spread over his lips. While the cousins were distracted, he slipped the physical photo quietly into his hip pocket, careful not to draw attention.

"Omg, that's her!" Sofia gasped, pointing at the screen. "We were listening to Rohan Vos, the train owner, before boarding in South Africa."

The cousins leaned in, murmuring their approval. Luca's mixed heritage the sharp Italian features of his mother and the deep, soulful gaze of his father who had lived so long in Africa seemed to glow in the light of the room.

"Dude, why do all these women keep chasing you?" someone teased.

Luca shrugged with a grin. "Cousin, I'm magical."

Hours passed with stories, teasing, and songs. The apartment hummed with life the clinking of glasses, the soft scrape of a guitar in the background, the whisper of old family tales shared in quiet moments. Eventually, the crowd thinned. Guests hugged and kissed their goodbyes, leaving behind the warm glow of shared memories. Luca lingered with Sofia and **Baby Adrian**, the air thick with unspoken understanding.

"Sis," Luca said softly, "I've got the first train in the morning back to the clinic. I should get some sleep."

Sofia gathered her things, her husband holding her hand tenderly as they moved toward the quiet of their room. The door clicked shut behind them, leaving the apartment bathed in soft candlelight and the lingering scent of family, food, and love.

Luca stepped quietly into the guest room, the soft click of the door closing behind him muffled by the fading laughter. His fingers brushed the smooth fabric of his jacket as he reached into his pocket and pulled out the photograph the one that held Amelia's smile, tucked just beneath the surface of his heart.

He moved to the window. The vast Milan skyline stretched before him in the fading dusk rooftops layered like terracotta waves, spires piercing the pink-tinged sky, and lights flickering on, one by one, like distant stars awakening.

His lips curved into a gentle smile. Holding the photo close, he pressed a soft kiss to the corner, as if trying to seal a secret promise within its edges. The memory of the train came rushing back the rhythm of wheels against tracks, the wild African sun casting a golden haze over the plains, the taste of dust and hope mingling on his tongue. He could almost feel the warmth of her hand in his.

"I left her my address," he murmured to the quiet room, his voice low, almost afraid to shatter the moment. "I guess she never felt the same..."

He shed his jacket and shirt, the cool air touching his skin, and moved to the mirror. Brushing his teeth with practiced ease, he caught his own reflection a face carved by time and experience, dark eyes heavy with dreams, full lips softened by a hint of a smile. Even in the simplicity of underwear and casual motion, Luca carried the effortless grace of a model strutting down a Milan runway.

He rinsed and set the toothbrush down, bare feet sliding onto the floor as he made his way to the bed. The crisp linens whispered under him as he settled in, lying back and staring up at the ceiling. Fingers trembling slightly, he pulled the photo close, eyes tracing Amelia's face in the dim light.

"I don't know what it is," he whispered, his voice thick with wonder and longing. "But girl... you touched my soul."

He smiled softly, clutching a pillow to his chest as if it could hold her warmth. His eyes fluttered closed, and in the quiet of the night, her presence wrapped around him like a gentle breeze.

"Good night," he breathed. "Sweet dreams."

And with that, Luca slipped into sleep, carrying her with him into the dark. Tomorrow, the train would carry him away again to Florence, to his patients, to his duties as a doctor. But tonight, he was home in the silence, in the memories, in the bittersweet promise of a love still waiting to be written

Possibility ...and longing

A few weeks had passed since Luca arrived back from Milan, yet his mind remained tangled in the thought of Amelia how to reach her, how to bridge the invisible miles that stretched between them. Each day, he wrestled with the quiet storm of hope and hesitation that churned within his chest, a slow fire that refused to die.

One evening, as the city lights flickered softly below, Luca stood by the open window of his living room. The cool night breeze slipped in like a whispered secret, carrying with it the distant hum of life flowing through ancient cobblestone streets. Above him, the moon hung low and luminous, its silver fingers gently brushing the weathered stone buildings that had cradled his childhood dreams, his laughter, his heartbreaks.

The scent of jasmine from a nearby terrace drifted through the air, mingling with the faint trace of roasting chestnuts from a street vendor far below. Luca closed his eyes for a moment, breathing it all in the texture of the night, thick with possibility and longing.

Turning away from the window, he moved toward his computer desk. From the drawer, he carefully pulled out the photograph the one that held the echo of her. Though the picture had never been meant to capture Amelia's face, to Luca it was all he saw: her shy smile, the light that danced in her eyes, a spark of something mysterious and unspoken. His fingertips traced the edges as memories spilled forth, vivid and tender.

He breathed deeply, the sharp, earthy scent of olive trees from the Tuscan hills flooding his mind, blending with the warmth of

Florence's golden sun on his skin. He remembered the laughter echoing through narrow alleys where he and Sofia had grown up, those endless summer afternoons filled with light and life. Beneath it all, distant but never forgotten, was the roar of Victoria Falls, the raw, earthy scent of the African wilderness, the vast wild plains where he had walked beside her two worlds woven together in the tangled threads of his heart.

Luca closed his eyes again, the night air filling his lungs as the ache of what might have been and what still could be settled deep inside him, a fragile ache like the flicker of a candle flame, delicate and shimmering in the dark.

A small, hopeful smile tugged at his lips. "If I don't try," he whispered to the empty room, "I will regret it forever."

With renewed resolve, he pulled out his chair and sat before his computer. His fingers danced across the keyboard as he began to search each query a tiny step toward a bridge that might reach her. Hundreds of faces appeared on the screen, a sea of strangers, until just as he was about to give up, one photo flickered into view: Amelia's face.

His heart clenched and then swelled with tears he did not try to stop. She was there real, vivid, alive on the screen. He clicked through to her social media, his eyes drinking in the scant traces of her life. A LinkedIn post caught his attention a congratulatory message for a new position. She was about to begin teaching literature at Howard University in Washington, D.C.

He stood up, the room spinning slightly as a laugh escaped him, raw and joyful. "Yes," he said aloud, "Yes, I found you."

With trembling hands, he sent her a friend request.

And now, the waiting began.

LinkedIn was a labyrinth a digital jungle thick with guarded doors and silent watchers. Luca sat alone in the dim glow of his apartment, the city's soft murmurs barely reaching his ears. His fingers hovered over the keyboard, trembling with a mix of desperation and hope. How could he reach Amelia without overstepping? Without breaking the fragile barrier between them?

He stared at her profile her name like a secret carved into his mind. But the coldness of the screen, the impersonal click of keys, felt like miles of distance stretching between them. He wanted to write her, to tell her everything, to bare his soul in words she might never see. Yet respect whispered to him, caution kept his fingers frozen.

He tried posting a picture beneath her latest post an elegant shot of the luxury train they'd ridden, bathed in the golden African sun. But it went unnoticed, swallowed in the silence of her inactivity. Amelia was elusive here like a ghost drifting through a world that barely knew her.

A bitter laugh escaped him, raw and low. "Stupid is as stupid does," he whispered, voice thick with a mix of frustration and fondness. "Maybe I'm about to be the biggest fool of all."

The truth burned hot in his chest. If he didn't leap, he would never know.

He rose, pacing the room like a caged lion. "Washington, D.C .," he murmured, tasting the name on his tongue like forbidden wine. "If I don't find her there, at least I'll have the city to lose myself in."

The decision crystallized like a promise, sharp and unyielding.

Hopelessly stupid

The afternoon in Verona was a slow-motion dream. They sat in the heart of **Piazza Bra**, where the ancient pink marble of the **Arena** stood like a silent sentinel against a sky so blue it looked painted. The square was a tapestry of life: elegant Italians in linen suits, the distant chime of bells from the San Zeno basilica, and the sweet, heavy scent of blooming oleander drifting on the breeze.

At their table, the world slowed down. Sofia laughed as she tore into a loaf of crusty bread, dipping it into olive oil that glowed like liquid gold. They feasted on *Pastissada de caval* and thick *Bigoli* pasta, the rich aromas mingling with the cool, crisp notes of a chilled *Soave* wine. To any observer, they were just two beautiful siblings enjoying the "City of Love," lost in the easy rhythm of a spring lunch.

They talked of everything and nothing the family in Milan, Adrian's birthday, the latest gossip from the hospital. Luca was a master of the mask; he smiled and nodded, his wire-rimmed glasses reflecting the shimmering heat of the square.

"You know," Sofia said, leaning back with a satisfied sigh, "there's a reason people say Shakespeare picked this city for a reason. You can feel it in the air, can't you? That feeling that something legendary is about to happen."

Luca took a slow sip of his wine, his gaze fixed on the ancient Roman arches of the coliseum. "I found her, Sofia."

The casual lightness of the table shifted instantly. Sofia paused with her glass halfway to her lips. "What? You found the American? How?"

"A LinkedIn post for a faculty position," Luca replied, his voice low but vibrating with an intensity that cut through the sounds of the piazza. "She's in Washington, D.C. She's a Professor of Literature at Howard University."

Sofia blinked, a playful smirk returning to her face. "Well, congratulations, Luca. You're a world-class stalker. So, what now? You going to send her a digital 'poke' and hope she remembers the man from the train?" She laughed, shaking her head. "Honestly, if you were a real romantic, you wouldn't be sitting here eating pasta. You'd be boarding a plane. You'd go to America and show up at her door like a hero in one of her books."

She took a long sip of wine, waiting for him to join in the joke.

"I leave on Tuesday," Luca said.

The silence that followed was deafening. Sofia nearly choked, her glass hitting the table with a sharp *clack*. "Excuse me?"

"My flight is Tuesday morning. Direct to Dulles," Luca said, his expression completely serious. The surprise hit Sofia like a physical blow. "I've already cleared my surgical schedule for the next two weeks. I've booked a room at The The Willard InterContinental."

"Luca, you're insane!" Sofia hissed, her eyes wide as she looked around the crowded square. "You're going to fly across the Atlantic for a woman who hasn't even accepted your friend request? This isn't a poem, it's a psychiatric episode!"

Luca reached across the table, his hand steady as he covered hers. The playful, scholarly doctor was gone; in his place was the man who had chased the horizon across the African plains.

"You're the one who told me to be wonderfully, hopelessly stupid, Sofia," he reminded her with a soft, dangerous smile. "I'm just taking your advice."

He stood up smiles and walked away toward the shadows of the Arena, Sofia remained frozen in the sunlight, the remnants of her lunch forgotten. The surprise was total not just for her, but for the universe itself. Luca wasn't just dreaming of Juliet anymore; he was going to find her.

Cherry blossoms drifting

The flight across the Atlantic felt like a suspension of time itself. Outside the cabin window, the sky was an endless canvas of indigo, with clouds drifting like ghost ships across a boundless, dark sea. As the plane soared, its wings slicing through the thin, cold air, it carried more than just passengers; it carried Luca's heartbeat and a year's worth of suppressed hope into the night.

When the wheels finally kissed the tarmac at Dulles International, the screech of rubber against the ground sent a jolt of adrenaline through him. This was no longer a digital search or a daydream over a bottle of *Valpolicella*. It was a pulse, beating in real time.

He moved through the terminal, the energy of the airport electric and chaotic. Voices hummed in a dozen different accents around him, and the sound of suitcases rolling over the polished floors echoed like the ticking of a clock counting down to his destiny.

At immigration, he stood in the "Visitors" line, his tall frame and tailored Italian wool coat making him stand out amongst the weary travelers. The officer behind the glass booth looked up, his smile brief but genuine.

"Can I have your passport, please?"

Luca handed over the document, his gaze steady, his expression a mixture of quiet confidence and a raw, hidden yearning. The officer scanned the pages, his eyes flickering to Luca's face.

"Purpose of your visit, Mr. Luca?"

"I am.... Tourist," Luca replied, the truth tasting like iron on his tongue.

The officer offered a knowing, tired smirk and stamped the page with a heavy *thud*. "Mr. Luca, welcome to America."

"America indeed," Luca whispered, his voice thick with an emotion he couldn't quite name. "Thank you."

As he walked out of the terminal and into the crisp Virginia air, the vast unknown shimmered before him. He was here, standing on the edge of a fire that might burn bright enough to light his path, or simply burn him whole. But as he climbed into the back of a black car, watching the green highway signs for *Washington* flash by, he knew he would never turn back.

The city welcomed him with open arms and a sharp, autumnal chill. The air was tinged with the scent of dried leaves and rain-slicked pavement the soft, persistent buzz of D.C. life threading through every street and alley. Every breath he took felt heavier, charged with a strange electricity, as if the very atmosphere of the capital pulsed with her presence. Somewhere out there, among the marble monuments and the red-brick halls of Howard University, Amelia was breathing the same air.

He checked into **The Willard InterContinental**, the hotel's grand Beaux-Arts lobby reflecting the sophisticated world he had left behind in Italy. Once inside his room, Luca stood by the floor-to-ceiling window. Below him, the city lights flickered like a constellation of hopes and buried memories. His mind raced, his heart thundering against his ribs. The ache of longing pressed deep into his skin tender, sharp, and impossible to ignore.

His hand trembled slightly as he pulled out his phone. He needed to hear a voice that knew the man he used to be before he became this version of himself the one chasing a ghost. He dialed Sofia.

The line crackled for a second before her familiar voice broke through the silence. "You're there? You actually did it?"

"I'm here," Luca confessed, his voice rough. "And Sofia... I don't know what this is. Is it love? Is it an obsession? Is it a psychiatric break? I barely know her, yet she has turned my entire world upside down from across an ocean."

Sofia's laughter was rich and warm, a bridge of sound reaching across the miles to soothe his restless soul. "Luca, my dear brother, you've been touched deeply. It doesn't happen often to men like you. So go. Take the leap. Do the stupid thing and either regret it for a lifetime or find joy in being wonderfully, hopelessly stupid."

Their laughter mingled across the Atlantic, light and freeing, breaking the tension that had held him since Verona.

"Then it's settled," Luca said, his eyes catching his own reflection in the window blazing with a fierce, new fire. "Washington, D.C., here I come."

The Willard,

Washington D.C. welcomed Luca with spring's gentle breath. Cherry blossoms drifted lazily in the breeze like pink snowflakes, landing here and there with quiet grace. He had taken a day to rest at **The Willard**, a necessary pause before the rhythm of the university returned before Amelia's world would open to him again.

He wandered through the city streets that afternoon, feeling the pulse of the place beneath his feet. The rich, earthy smell of fresh rain mingled with the sharp tang of blooming flowers and the faint aroma of roasted coffee beans from bustling cafes near the White House. He let the sounds wash over him: the hum of conversation in a nearby park, the clatter of footsteps on cobblestone, and the soft jazz drifting from a street corner saxophone. Everything was alive, vibrant, wrapped in the warmth of possibility.

At a small, high-end diner, Luca tasted America for the first time a thick burger, juicy and smoky, with crispy fries kissed by salt. The flavors were bold and new, grounding him in this foreign land that was already feeling like it held the chapters of his future. As night fell, he wandered beneath the glowing street lamps of Pennsylvania Avenue, the city's nightlife humming softly around him laughter spilling from open doors, the clink of glasses, the murmur of strangers sharing stories. The stars twinkled overhead, a silent audience to his restless heart.

Then, it was Monday. He had prepared for the day to step fully into the story he had been living quietly in his mind.

That morning, Luca stood before the ornate mirror in his suite at **The Willard**, the soft morning light filtering through sheer silk curtains. His reflection met his gaze a strong jawline, dark eyes full of hope, a quiet confidence wrapped in vulnerability. He adjusted the collar of his bespoke navy blazer and reached for his cologne, a fragrance that reminded him of the cedarwood forests back in Italy, with a hint of fresh citrus to brighten the edges.

He spritzed it lightly, the scent settling into his skin like a warm promise.

"Mirror, you better tell me the truth," he murmured, his voice soft with a mix of nerves and humor. "Am I a catch? Or just a fool chasing shadows?"

He offered himself a slow, steady smile that stilled the fluttering in his chest. With a deep breath, he stepped away, ready to face whatever the day held.

Down in the grand lobby, beneath the crystal chandeliers, he asked the receptionist for directions to Howard University. The woman's smile was kind, her eyes bright with warmth as she took in his polished appearance.

"You're not far at all, sir. Honestly, the traffic in the District is a nightmare this time of morning. You don't even need a car. Take one of the electric scooters it's just a straight shot up 11th Street. You'll be there in minutes."

Luca's eyes sparkled with a sudden rush of excitement. "Perfect. I'd rather feel the wind than sit in a taxi."

Outside, the lime-green scooter gleamed under the morning sun, sleek and inviting against the historic backdrop of the hotel. Luca swung his leg over, looking every bit the sophisticated Italian explorer, and felt a thrill ripple through him. The chase was real now not just a dream or a hope, but a journey unfolding beneath his fingertips.

As he hummed toward the campus, the university's historic walls rose ahead old stones alive with the whispers of the thousands who had walked these paths before: students, dreamers, lovers. Luca's heart beat faster, a wild rhythm echoing through his veins.

He paused near the Yard when a group of young women passed, their faces bright with the fresh light of new beginnings. He approached them, holding up the worn photograph of Amelia, his voice steady but hopeful.

"Do you know her? Where she teaches? Or where I might find her?"

Their faces lit up immediately, warm smiles blooming like spring flowers. "We just came out of her class! I think she went for lunch. There's a picnic area behind that building lots of students eat there. She might be there."

"Grazie," Luca breathed, the word soft and full of gratitude.

His steps quickened, his heart pounding like a drumbeat beneath his ribs. And then, there she was.

Amelia.

She was seated alone on a weathered wooden bench, bathed in the golden light of midday, her hair catching the sun like strands of silk. She nibbled on a sandwich, lost in thought, the soft rise and fall of her breath a gentle rhythm that steadied his soul.

Luca's breath hitched, his body humming with a sudden, fierce tenderness. He moved closer, the world narrowing until it was only her only the scent of her shampoo, the subtle warmth of her skin through the fabric of her blouse, and the curve of her neck catching the light.

"Hi, perfect stranger," he said, his voice barely more than a breath.

She turned, eyes wide with surprise, then recognition flaring bright and undeniable. Their gazes locked, and in that instant, the air between them shimmered like firelight. She stood, and without hesitation, wrapped her arms around him, pulling him close. Their lips met soft, slow, electric a kiss that spoke of longing and promises, of memories and futures yet to be written.

As he held her, Luca's hands found the gentle, unexpected swell of her belly. A tender question rose in his chest, his heart stuttering. The moment stilled, a sacred pause filled with unspoken truths. Respect, wonder, and a quiet fear mingled in the space between them.

He pulled back gently and settled beside her on the bench, their fingers intertwining like fragile threads of hope. They talked then words dripping with vulnerability and an ache that both understood. Amelia spoke of the letters she had sent that were returned unopened, of the year she spent waiting and hoping. Luca shared his own silent vigil, the empty mailbox in Milan that had held his heart hostage.

Hours slipped by, filled with laughter, tears, and the quiet music of two souls reconnecting. At last, Amelia glanced at her watch, a soft sigh escaping her lips.

"I have a class to teach," she said, her voice barely above a whisper. "But... maybe we could meet again later? After I'm done?"

Amelia's pulse quickened. "Where will you be?"

He smiled, a mischievous sparkle lighting his eyes, though his mind was already racing with the discovery he had just made. "I'm at the Willard, but I noticed a Restaurant just across from the campus earlier. I'll be there waiting for you, so you don't have to travel far."

Before he could say another word, she leaned close, her breath warm against his ear, her voice a playful promise. "I'll come by. After I finish teaching."

She whispered then, recalling their last words in Africa. "You know this isn't over."

They laughed softly, the sound wrapping around them like a shared secret. But as Luca walked back toward the city, his mind spun with questions. Who was the father? Why hadn't she mentioned her situation in the letters he never received? The subtle changes in her frame the fullness of her belly, the softness in her eyes spoke of a story he wasn't sure he was ready to hear.

His fingers trembled as he dialed Sofia's number, the weight of the secret pressing heavy on his heart.

"Sofia," he said as soon as she answered, his voice breathless. "She's pregnant."

Sofia's laugh was sharp across the line a sudden, startled sound before it softened with immediate sisterly care.

"It's late here, Luca," she murmured, her voice thick with the quiet of the Milan night. "But I'm listening. Tell me everything."

Standing by the floor-to-ceiling window of his suite at **The Willard**, Luca watched the distant glow of the Capitol dome. He told her everything the electric shock of the kiss, the sun hitting the cherry blossoms, and finally, the tender, terrifying mystery he had felt beneath his palms when he held Amelia.

"I'm sorry, brother," Sofia said, her voice heavy with empathy. "At least you tried. At least you know she still wants you. Now, enjoy the city. But please... be careful."

Luca's worry spilled through the line, his voice dropping to a jagged whisper. "She didn't say anything about the father. She didn't mention being with anyone else. And yet, she wants to come to my hotel tonight... and she kissed me as if no time had passed. What do I do, Sof?"

Sofia's voice was steady, a beacon of reason in his dark room.

"Let her lead, Luca. But be cautious. Before you become a father before you let your heart believe this child is yours ask the questions you need to ask. Don't lose yourself in the romance. And remember," she added, a flash of her usual wit returning, "this is America. They have guns there, Luca! Don't let some jealous husband shoot you before I see you again."

They laughed then, a fragile, necessary sound that bridged the ocean between them. They spoke long into the evening, the city alive beneath his window, its lights flickering like the fragile hope in his heart.

Before she hung up, Sofia's voice turned soft and incredibly tender, the playfulness gone. "Brother, be careful. You are the only one I've got. It's okay to love harder, to fall deeper... do not live with regrets. Whatever the truth is, I love you."

"I love you too, Sof," Luca breathed.

He heard the soft click as she hung up, leaving him in the silence of the suite. Luca breathed deeply, the scent of his own cedarwood cologne still clinging to the air. He felt the slow, sweet fire of love burning in his soul, but beneath it was a new, sharp resolve. He was ready to face whatever came next.

Tonight, the "perfect stranger" was coming to his door, and this time, there would be no secrets left in the shadows.

Table for two

The lobby of **The Willard** didn't just glow; it breathed. It had that heavy, velvet-silent warmth that Luca usually only found in the grand hotels of Rome or Milan amber light spilling across white marble floors, shadows pooling in the corners like whispered secrets of the presidents and poets who had walked here before him.

Luca sat in a high-backed leather chair, perfectly still, his hands resting on the cool mahogany arms. He felt as though any sudden movement might cause the fragile memory of the morning to dissolve into the D.C. humidity.

Amelia.

He closed his eyes, and suddenly he wasn't in Washington. He was back on the **Rovos Rail**, in a world of polished teak and brass. He could still smell it: the scent of fine vintage wine, the heavy dust of the South African plains, and something far more intoxicating the scent of her skin. They had made love under the rhythmic, mechanical lullaby of the train, a night of unhurried hands and soft gasps, as if the tracks themselves had granted them a temporary sanctuary from the rest of the world.

And then, the journey had ended. The tracks had pulled them apart, and the sanctuary had vanished.

Until now.

He glanced at his watch. **7:58 p.m.** Dinner was a secondary thought. Hunger was an abstraction. What he craved was the specific curve of her lips when she half-smiled, the way her voice wrapped around his "perfect stranger" like a silk ribbon, and the way her eyes had looked at him on the campus bench as if she could see right through the expensive navy blazer and the cardiologist's degree to the shivering soul beneath.

But the fear, cold and sharp, began to prick at his confidence. *What if she had only been kind?* What if there was a man a husband, a partner already waiting for her in a house he would never see? What if the night on the train, the night that had rearranged the stars for him, had been just a beautiful stopover for her?

8:24 p.m. Time was slipping through his fingers like dry sand.

He rose, the silence of the lobby suddenly feeling like a weight. He began to walk toward the dining room, but a sudden realization stopped him halfway. He turned on his heel and crossed back to the marble reception desk.

"I'm waiting for a guest," he told the receptionist. His voice was low, steady, but there was a tremor of Italian urgency beneath it. "She's about five-foot-seven... skin like warm bronze, dark curls that fall just past her shoulders. Her eyes..."

He paused, catching himself before he gave away too much of his heart to a stranger. "If she comes, tell her I'm in the dining room."

As he walked away, a bitter, self-deprecating laugh escaped him. *I never even told her my name on the Rovos train. Or at the Howard.* The realization hit him like a physical blow. *How would she even ask for me?* He was a ghost chasing a ghost.

The dining room was a cathedral of candlelight. The quiet murmur of D.C.'s elite rose and fell like soft waves against the shore. He chose a table by the window, where the city stretched out in a grid of shadow and gold. A glass of chilled white wine sat before him, the condensation sweating delicately down the crystal. Beside it, a basket of bread sat untouched. It was American bread bland, soft, and lacking the rustic crust of his home.

He looked at it and whispered to the empty chair across from him, "When in Rome..."

He took a sip of the wine, his eyes fixed on the door, waiting for the woman who held his future in her hands

Then, **8:46.**

A hand on his shoulder. Warm. Familiar. A spark of electricity, almost imperceptible, yet it coursed through Luca's entire being, awakening every nerve. He turned, slowly, as if unwrapping a precious gift.

Amelia stood there, bathed in the soft, amber light of **The Willard's** magnificent dining room. The light seemed to cling to her, swirling around her like an aura, as if the room itself knew who she was and bowed in reverence. The years had only deepened her beauty not the fleeting perfection of youth, but a profound, resonant kind that drew you in by the sheer truth in her eyes, the quiet strength in her posture. Her skin, the color of warm bronze, glowed against the elegant ivory of her dress, a simple garment that somehow highlighted the gentle curve of her form. Her dark curls framed her face like a halo in shadow, a cascade he remembered vividly.

He rose, his chair scraping softly against the polished floor, a minor disruption in the cathedral-like silence that had fallen between them. Their eyes locked, and in that instant, the air between them vibrated, thrummed, with everything unsaid, everything yearned for. A year of waiting, of unanswered letters, of silent longing, collapsed into this single, potent moment.

And then he kissed her. It started slow, a tender exploration, a question asked on soft lips. Then, as the memory flooded back the exact taste of her, the way she softened against him, the scent that was uniquely hers it deepened. It became a kiss of recognition, of promises remembered from that night on the train. She rose slightly on her toes, meeting his intensity, but he met her halfway, one hand brushing the gentle curve of her waist, not possessive, but grounding her against him, as if he were afraid she might vanish again. Her fingers, cool and soft, curled around the lapels of his blazer, clinging to him as if he were her last tether to solid ground.

A polite, almost apologetic cough broke them apart, though not completely. The world, it seemed, still insisted on its mundane realities.

"Sir, your food is here," the waiter murmured, his gaze respectfully averted.

They laughed, a soft, shared sound that held the tremor of nerves and the dizzying joy of reunion. They settled into their chairs, still impossibly close, like two people expertly pretending this wasn't the most important, most surreal night of their lives.

"Thank you," Luca managed, his voice slightly rough with emotion, his gaze still fixed on Amelia. He gestured to her. "You can take her order too."

She stole a spoonful from his plate a rich, savory pasta her lips curling in a familiar, mischievous smile he had longed to see. "Don't worry. We'll share." Then, turning to the waiter, her voice steady despite the blush that dusted her cheeks, "A virgin mimosa... and more bread, please." She caught Luca's eye, a silent apology for the drink order, a quiet acknowledgement of the secret that lay between them.

When the waiter finally left, Luca reached for her phone, his fingers brushing hers, sending another jolt through him. "My name is Luca," he said, his voice a low confession as he tapped in his number. "And my email. What else should I add? Blood type? Passport number?"

She laughed a sound he had missed without knowing he'd been missing it, a melody that filled the elegant dining room and made the chandeliers seem to sparkle brighter. She took his phone and mirrored the act, her touch lingering as she slid it back across the table.

They shook hands then, with playful ceremony, their palms meeting in a firm, lingering press that felt more like a promise. "Nice to meet you, perfect stranger."

They talked about everything and nothing. They spoke of the sprawling vineyards of Tuscany and the historic halls of Howard University. They discussed books, art, music, places they had seen, and dreams they still held. They carefully navigated the shimmering surface of their lives, always circling, but never quite touching, the years between them. Never about why he had traveled thousands of miles to Washington, or why she had left the train without a goodbye. Not yet.

When the plates were finally cleared, the last sips of wine gone, Amelia leaned forward, her voice dropping to a low, intimate murmur that was barely audible above the soft hum of conversation around them. "I'd like to freshen up... in your room."

He stood without a word, his chair a gentle whisper against the floor. He simply took her hand, his fingers intertwining with hers, a silent, powerful affirmation. The elevator doors closed, trapping them in the quiet hum of the machinery, and the far more intense hum of their own heartbeats. She leaned into him, her head resting on his shoulder, her scent jasmine and something darker, more elemental pulling him back, completely, to that night when the train swayed and the stars kept their secrets.

This time, he promised himself, his grip tightening on her hand, she wouldn't disappear.

The Room With the City Below

The door clicked shut behind them, sealing them into a world that was suddenly smaller, quieter, and infinite all at once.

Amelia walked ahead, her heels making the faintest whispers on the thick carpet, the muted thud of each step syncing with the racing pulse in her chest. Without a word, she disappeared into the bathroom, the golden spill of light softening the edges of the doorway.

Luca stayed by the window, tall and still, a silhouette carved against Washington D.C.'s night skyline. The city wasn't a show-off no jagged peaks of glass clawing at the clouds but it held itself with a kind of understated grace, lights scattered like a thousand private invitations across the horizon. He watched them the way one might watch a harbor from a ship, waiting for something precious to come into view.

In the mirror, Amelia regarded the reflection of a woman who had been through storms and come out softer, not harder. She reached into her handbag and drew out the lingerie she'd chosen without really knowing why black and yellow satin, like sunflowers turning toward light they couldn't resist. The silk slipped over her skin like a whisper, framing her curves, embracing the gentle, undeniable swell of life she carried.

She freshened her lipstick, exhaled, and murmured to her reflection: *Game time.*

When she stepped back into the room, the world shifted.

Luca turned and stopped. His breath caught in his throat, his eyes taking her in with something between awe and disbelief. Half-clothed, her belly round and radiant, her skin carrying that impossible glow of creation she was the kind of beauty that didn't just live in the body; it lived in the soul.

He crossed the room in two strides, gathering her into his arms and kissing her like a man anchoring himself to the one shore he'd been searching for. Lifting her with effortless care, he set her on the dresser, their faces so close he could feel the brush of her breath.

"I don't know what to say," he murmured, his Italian vowels curling like silk around each word. "You are stealing my heart at a skyrocket speed. Who are you, Amelia? I want to know *everything*."

He lowered himself, pressing a reverent kiss to her belly not tentative, not cautious, but as though he was kissing a secret he had waited years to be told.

"Who is the lucky man?" His voice carried no jealousy, no judgment only the ache of wanting to understand. "Whatever the truth is, I want to know. I can't control what is outside my heart... and you are holding it in your hands."

Her fingers tangled in his hair, and she held him as though afraid the moment would vanish.

"There is no one," she said softly. "I chose her."

Luca's brows drew together. "Darling... be blunt. What do you mean you chose her? Who is the father? Is he in the picture? I am in I just want to know what I'm stepping into."

She took his hand in both of hers, as though it were something rare and breakable. "After South Africa, ...My EX and I... fixed our problems.. as I though.. then, mmm... The breakup I had was messy, loud... the kind of ending that takes pieces of you with it. I was alone for a long time. But I never... I never started over. My heart stayed with a stranger I met on a train to Victoria Falls."

He froze. "You carried your heart to Africa... and left it with me."

She nodded, her eyes glistening. "And I carried it back to Italy... without you."

Something in his chest gave way. He pulled her close, the scent of her hair filling him with every memory he'd fought to bury. "I'm sorry," he whispered. Amelia looked him straight into his eyes "I wish we had spoken. I thought you someone's husband..."She hesitated.

"You thought Sofia was my wife?" he asked with a wry smile.

"When I saw you hugging her, crying," she said, "I thought she'd found out about us... and you were apologizing."

"No," he said, shaking his head. "She was crying because we were sending our father home. That trip... that was for him. He loved Victoria Falls, and after he passed, he asked to be returned there."

Their laughter rose gently between them, tangled with grief, dissolving the heavy shadow of misunderstanding.

His gaze drifted again to her belly. "So... who is the father?"

She smiled faintly, a touch of mischief in her eyes. "I've never met him. He's an Italian sperm donor."

Luca's eyes widened then he laughed, head tipping back. "Amelia... why?"

"I wanted an Italian man. The one I lost. So... I found a way to keep an Italian in my life."

Something shifted in the air warmer, heavier, certain. He sank to his knees, both hands cradling her belly as though she might slip away if he let go. "Hey there," he murmured, "I don't know if you're a boy or a girl"

"She," Amelia said, her voice soft but sure.

His eyes lit up. "Then... I will call you Livia."

The baby kicked, sharp enough for them both to feel.

"She likes it," Amelia laughed, startled.

"It means olive tree," Luca said, his eyes never leaving hers. "Peace. Harmony. Fruitfulness. And it was my grandmother's name."

Another kick. They both laughed, astonished.

Luca moved beside her, his voice lower now, as though the next words might carry the weight of his whole life. "I lost you once. I've thought of you on more nights than I could count. Livia has already agreed to be my daughter... so I ask you, Amelia will you let me be her father?"

Her throat tightened. She couldn't speak; the tears came too fast. So she kissed him, her answer in the way she pressed her lips to his, the way she let the tears fall freely between them.

They made love slowly, not to possess but to remember. Every touch was a rediscovery, every kiss a thread binding the years apart into nothingness. He moved over her with the reverence of a man memorizing a prayer, his hands gentle, his breath unhurried.

When he paused, she teased, "I'm not fragile, Luca. Just pregnant."

"I know," he smiled against her collarbone. "But I don't want to push my daughter around."

Their laughter melted into sighs, into the low music of whispered Italian and her name spoken like a vow. It was the same language they had spoken once before, in a swaying train carriage under the African moon only now, it was richer, heavier with the knowing that they had found each other *again*.

Later, when Amelia lay back with water in hand, her belly shifted, another kick. Luca looked at it as though witnessing a miracle for the first time.

"Does she always do that?"

"Talk to her," Amelia said, taking his hand. "She's never done this before."

Luca bent close. "Livia... your papa is here now. Go to sleep, bella

. I loved you before I even met you."

The kicking stopped, as if in perfect understanding.

And for the first time in years, the night felt whole.

The night had folded itself around them like a whispered secret, and now the first soft light of dawn spilled in from the east, delicate and golden.

Through sheer white silk curtains that fluttered gently in the morning breeze, the city of Washington, D.C., lay quietly beneath a pale sky. The glow of morning wrapped the room in a peaceful hush, as if time itself had slowed to watch them breathe.

Amelia stirred first. Her face caught the light every curve, every shadow softened into a portrait of serenity. She rose slowly, the yellow silk of her lingerie catching the dawn like sunlight trapped in fabric, black lace tracing delicate paths along her skin.

She moved to the window, standing tall and radiant against the shimmering white curtains, the breeze teasing the fabric and her hair. Outside, the city stretched like a masterpiece painted by Da Vinci calm, intricate, and full of silent promises.

Luca woke to the faintest movement beside him, his fingers brushing the cool sheets before his eyes fluttered open. His heart raced the moment he saw her silhouette bathed in morning light a living, breathing promise framed by the window.

For a moment, fear stirred in his chest the thought that she might leave without a word, like a dream fading at dawn. But then he saw her standing there, looking out, and all the fears dissolved into something warmer hope, and love reborn.

He rose quietly, walked behind her, and wrapped his arms around her waist, pulling her close. His lips found hers in a kiss that spoke of every longing and every sleepless night they had spent apart.

"My heart," he whispered in his rich Italian accent, voice thick with feeling, "I know it may be too soon to say this... but after two years of planting the seed, I have the right to say it now."

He kissed her again, tender and fierce.

"I love you... mia cara, mio cuore."

He lifted her face to his, searching her eyes.

"And how is my daughter doing? Talk to her, Amelia."

He spoke softly to the curve of her belly in Italian, the words flowing like a lullaby.

"Mia bambina, non vedo l'ora di vederti. Voglio insegnarti l'italiano, voglio amarti come nessun altro."

Amelia laughed, the sound bright and clear.

"I don't understand a word, but I like the way it sounds."

He hugged her tightly.

"Well, you better get used to it. When she arrives, her first language will be Italian."

They laughed together, their joy spilling over in gentle kisses.

Luca took her hand and carried her toward the bathroom, the warmth of the morning filling the space between them.

Under the cascade of water like the roaring Victoria Falls they had once seen together they found each other again.

Amelia clung to him, breath mingling with water, her voice soft and searching.

The shower came alive with a soft murmur, warm water pouring like molten silk from the curved spout above, spilling over their bodies in shimmering ribbons. Each drop was a gentle caress a delicate touch tracing invisible paths across skin and soul alike, dissolving the months, the years, the distance that had stretched between them.

Steam rose in lazy curls, a misty curtain wrapping them in a private world where only breath and heartbeat existed. The room smelled of jasmine and fresh rain, subtle and intoxicating, as if the earth itself had lent its fragrance to bless their reunion.

Amelia leaned into him, the heat from the water mingling with the warmth of Luca's skin pressed against hers. The satin of her yellow and black lingerie clung like a secret, wet and soft, every curve more vivid beneath the glistening sheen of water. Luca's fingers moved like a whispered prayer, reverent and slow, exploring the swell of her belly, the tender curve that held their daughter, the delicate arch of her back, the softness of her arms where his hands rested like a promise.

Her breath caught when his lips brushed the hollow of her neck, cool water mingling with the heat of his kiss, the faint taste of soap and jasmine on his tongue. Her skin tingled under his touch, alive with a hunger that had waited years to be fed.

She closed her eyes, surrendering to the gentle rhythm the water's pulse, his hands' slow dance, their shared warmth every nerve awake and alive, every heartbeat a note in the symphony of their love.

Luca's fingers found the lace of her soaked lingerie, tracing the delicate threads before slipping beneath the fabric to caress the skin beneath. He kissed her again, deeper now, the taste of rain and desire mingling as their mouths moved in a tender duet.

"Amelia," he whispered, voice husky with longing, "I want to memorize every inch of you. Every line, every curve, every breath."

She smiled against his lips, water cascading over her cheek like a lover's gentle hand. "I'm yours," she breathed. "All of me."

The water flowed over them, a warm embrace that seemed to wash away all hesitation and fear. Water trickled between their fingers, dripped slowly in shimmering beads from tangled hair and entwined arms. The world outside faded until nothing remained but the pulse of their bodies moving in perfect, reverent harmony.

When their bodies came together fully, it was with a tenderness that spoke of reverence and rediscovery, slow and deliberate a sacred dance that bound their hearts more tightly than words ever could.

Luca was careful, mindful of the life growing inside her, cherishing the miracle they had made the love that bridged continents, years, and silence.

The water poured down, mingling with their sweat, their tears, their whispered promises. Their breaths rose and fell in unison, a quiet song sung by two souls who had found their way back home.

And as they moved beneath the cascade beneath the veil of steam and light it was clear: this was no ordinary love. This was a love forged by time and distance, tested by silence and hope, now blooming in a fierce, tender flame that would burn for a lifetime.

Luca stepped out of the shower, steam swirling around him like a soft mist of promises. He wrapped a warm robe around his shoulders, the fabric heavy with warmth and comfort. Moving toward Amelia, he gently draped the robe over her damp skin, his fingers lingering at the curve of her shoulders with reverence.

With eyes full of tenderness, he lifted her effortlessly into his arms, carrying her toward the bedroom like a man cradling the most precious thing in the world. Amelia's lips curled into a soft chuckle, tears of joy tracing silent rivers down her cheeks, shimmering in the morning light.

"What next, Luca?" she whispered, voice trembling with love and hope.

He held her close, his lips trailing gentle kisses along her wet skin, their hearts beating together like a secret rhythm only they could hear.

"No one is promised tomorrow,...Nessuno ha la certezza del domani." he said, his voice low and unwavering. "But as long as I wake up, I will make sure I am beside you and our daughter."

His arms tightened around her, his whisper a vow.

"I don't know if it will be in Italy or America... but this I know I will be with you."

The world beyond the window stretched wide and bright, but inside, time folded softly around them. The memory of water cascading, of hands and lips and whispered promises, lingered in the air an eternal melody that had finally found its home.

In this quiet, glowing dawn, two souls torn by distance, mended by love became one.

And in that perfect, fragile moment, love was not just enough.

It was everything.

He kissed her gently, his lips lingering with all the gratitude and longing he carried. In a voice soft and full of emotion, he whispered,

"Grazie per aver salvato la mia anima... I love you

Atlantic will never separate us

Two weeks had dissolved into a blur of cherry blossoms and whispered truths. By the time the Maryland trees were fully green, Luca found himself navigating the quiet, leafy streets of Silver Spring.

Amelia sat beside him in the car, her hand resting on her five-month-round belly. She looked radiant, though a soft anxiety played in her eyes. "My family... they are a lot, Luca. They protect me fiercely."

Luca reached over, his thumb grazing her knuckles. "I am a surgeon, Amelia. I am used to hearts being guarded. I will be patient."

The house was a classic colonial, the windows glowing with a welcoming, golden light. As they stepped inside, the air was a thick, delicious tapestry of Southern comfort: slow-roasted chicken, collard greens seasoned with smoked turkey, and the sweet, buttery scent of cornbread.

The dinner table was a vibrant, loud, and beautiful chaos. Amelia's father, a man with a grip like iron and eyes that saw everything, sat at the head. Her brothers leaned in, their skepticism slowly melting under Luca's quiet, respectful charm. They talked about Italy, about the train, and about the "madness" of a man flying across the Atlantic for a woman he barely knew.

"So, Doc," Amelia's father said, leaning back as the plates were cleared. "You're heading back to Italy tomorrow. What happens to my daughter when you're ten thousand miles away?"

The table went quiet. Luca didn't blink. He looked at Amelia, then back at her father. "Atlantic will never separate us " Luca said, his voice steady and resonant. "Because my life is no longer in Italia . It is wherever she is. I will be back before the leaves turn red, and I love your daughter sir."

A soft murmur of approval went around the table. The "Italian man" wasn't just a guest anymore; he was becoming an anchor.

Later, as the evening wound down, Luca gathered a stack of plates and followed Amelia's mother, Evelyn, into the kitchen. The room was warm and humid, the sound of the dishwasher humming a domestic rhythm.

Evelyn turned from the sink, wiping her hands on her apron. She looked at Luca not as a doctor, but as a mother searching a man's soul. "You have a good heart, Luca. I can see it. But she's been hurt before. This baby... this is her whole world."

Luca stepped closer, setting the dishes down with careful precision. "Evelyn," he said, his Italian accent softening with sincerity. "I did not come here for a vacation. I came because when I held her in my arms, I realized I had been breathing half-breaths my whole life. I intend to take care of her. I intend to be the man this child looks up to. I am asking for your blessing to come back and make this family my own."

Evelyn's eyes shimmered. She reached out, her hand warm and seasoned by years of love resting on his cheek. "You don't need to ask for what you've already earned, son. Just come back to her. That's all we ask."

She pulled him into a brief, firm embrace the kind of hug that told him he was no longer a stranger. He was home.

The Potomac Promise

The drive to Ronald Reagan National Airport was quiet, the air in the car thick with a heavy, sweet melancholy. Outside, the D.C. morning was bright, but for Luca and Amelia, the sun felt like a spotlight on a ticking clock.

They didn't go inside immediately. Luca pulled his bags from the trunk and then turned to her, the wind from the **Potomac River** ruffling his hair and carrying the scent of jet fuel and salt. He took her hands in his, his thumbs tracing the rhythm of her pulse.

"Look at me, Amelia," Luca said, his voice dropping to that low, melodic Italian register that always made the world around her fade away. He stepped closer, his hands moving from her wrists to frame her face, his touch as light as a prayer.

"I am crossing an ocean, but I am not leaving you. Do you understand? Every heart I monitor in Italy, every surgery I perform it is all just a countdown until I can be back here, in this city, with you and our child."

Amelia's eyes shimmered, a single tear tracing a path down her cheek. Luca caught it with his thumb, pressing it into his skin as if to keep a piece of her with him.

"I will call you before I board," he promised, his intensity fierce. "I will FaceTime you the moment I land in Malpensa. We will live in the quiet spaces of the screen until I can hold you in the flesh again. You are my home now. "

He leaned down, pressing his forehead against hers. "Promise me you won't doubt. Promise me that when the distance feels like a mountain, you remember the way the stars looked over the Zambezi. We survived a years of silence; we will thrive in these months of waiting."

"I promise," she whispered, her voice a fragile thread of hope.

He kissed her then not a goodbye, but a seal. It was a long, slow, desperate kiss that tasted of salt and the inevitable. He lingered against her lips for one heartbeat too long, then finally, with a wrenching effort, he pulled away. He grabbed his suitcase, walking toward the sliding glass doors. He didn't look back; he couldn't. If he looked back, he knew his feet wouldn't move.

Amelia didn't leave. She walked toward the large observation windows of the terminal, finding a quiet spot where the glass met the sky. She sat on the cold bench, her hands resting protectively over her five-month belly, her eyes fixed on the runway.

A few minutes later, she saw it. A massive silver bird, its wings catching the morning light, began its roar down the tarmac. It lifted, defiant and graceful, soaring directly over the shimmering blue of the **Potomac**. She watched until the plane was nothing more than a silver needle stitching through the clouds, heading East, toward the Old World.

She sat there long after the plane had vanished, the vibration of the engines still humming in her chest. The long distance was activated. The Atlantic crossing had begun. But as she watched the river flow beneath the flight path, she didn't feel empty. She felt like a woman holding a secret that the whole world was waiting to hear.

Flight Across the Atlantic

For the past three months, Luca's life had been measured in time zones, battery percentages, and **exhausting weekend flights across the Atlantic just to be with his pregnant girlfriend**. The Atlantic Ocean lay between them, but they had bridged the distance with whispered confessions in the dark, five-hour phone calls that bled into the Italian dawn, and text messages that carried the weight of two healing souls. They had unraveled their secrets layer by layer talking about the pain, the fears of the past, and the quiet hope of the future.

The morning arrived not with the gentle caress of dawn, but with the stark, unflattering reality of a noon sun, finding every crevice of weariness in Amelia's body. She woke to the sound of a chime, a shrill and intrusive noise against the backdrop of her exhausted stillness.

Her limbs felt like pillars of concrete; nine months of building a new life had exacted a heavy, beautiful toll. She was an architecture of motherhood, magnificent but immobilized. The phone screen blazed with his familiar name: **"Perfect Stranger."**

Her throat tightened with an immediate, overwhelming wave of vulnerability. She didn't have the energy for a mask. The sheer physical effort of her condition had scraped her defenses raw. She answered on the second ring, the word a small, broken plea.

"Babe," she started, the sound already wet with tears, "I can't do this... I'm so tired. Everything is hard, Luca. I tried to put my shoes on this morning, and it felt like a marathon. The doctor said if she doesn't make her grand entrance this week, then by Saturday, I have to go under the knife..."

The Atlantic Ocean hummed between them, but the voice that came back was a warm, resonating anchor. It was **Luca's voice**, a low, humble baritone of understanding, wrapping around her fear like a silk scarf.

"*Tesoro mio*," he murmured, the Italian words a sedative on her soul. "Breathe with me, *amore*. You've got this. You are a miracle of strength, and you are making my entire world. Just **breathe**."

He waited for her ragged inhale and exhale before delivering a bombshell wrapped in tenderness. "My three-month sabbatical was approved. Tonight, 8 PM my time, I am on a flight to Dulles."

Amelia went utterly still. The news wasn't just good; it was a detonation of relief and love. She hadn't dared to dream of three uninterrupted months. It wasn't just his presence; it was the **gift of time**, the surrender of his demanding world to her and their daughter. A helpless, beautiful cry rose from her not of pain, but of a joy so profound it was indistinguishable from grief.

Luca, three thousand miles away, mirrored her tears. He could feel the seismic shift of her relief. The Atlantic was a vast, cold divider, yet it was also the canvas for their shared vulnerability.

After the torrent had subsided into a gentle, loving current, Amelia gave a shaky laugh. "Baby, let me go to the restroom. I swear, you haven't seen my belly for only a month, but I feel like I am a **hippo** right now."

Luca's rich, melodious laugh traveled through the line. "If you are a hippo, *bella*, then I must be a hippo, too. But come on, can we find a cuter animal to describe ourselves? How about a **zebra**?" His voice dropped to a conspiratorial, playful register. "You know, a zebra... if I am a zebra, I will have the most... you know what every man needs. And *honeỳ*, have you seen a zebra's backside? Ooh, they can shake that tail."

The laughter they shared was a sacred sound, a testament to the life-giving, buoyant intimacy they had forged across continents. She capitulated with a playful sigh. "Okay, *bello*. You win. I will be your zebra."

The conversation ended, leaving behind a profound stillness, a sense of rightness she hadn't felt in weeks. Slowly, Amelia rose, moving with the heavy, deliberate gait of late-term pregnancy. The walk to the bathroom was an odyssey.

She turned the shower on, letting the water run until the bathroom filled with a thick, purifying steam. She stepped under the cascading stream, not to merely clean her body, but to let the water wash the **stale, cold residue of fear** from her mind. The water was a poet, tracing the curves of her swollen body, warming the chilled marrow of her bones. A prism of light bounced from the window, fracturing into dancing, iridescent colors on the tile wall. Though she couldn't see her own feet, she scrubbed and cleansed, a ritual of preparation for the life-altering Saturday that loomed.

She emerged reborn, wrapped in a plush robe, the scent of lavender and steam clinging to her skin. In the quiet of her kitchen, she cut a thick slice of creamy **cheesecake** and poured herself a tall glass of **milk**, the simplest, purest comforts. Sitting at the table, she looked out the window at the familiar DC street, breathing in the quiet, profound gratitude. *How lucky I am. Thank God for bringing Luca into my life.*

Amelia stared at the glowing screen of her phone, the sent message lingering there like a heavy confession. She had finally told her mother what the doctor said. With a soft sigh, she set the device face down on the table and picked up her fork, finishing the last bite of rich cheesecake. It settled heavily in her stomach, much like the news she had just delivered.

Amelia watched her absorb the update about the potential C-section. There was a pause; it was brief, but loaded with that ancient, fierce parental worry that mothers learn to keep under lock and key.

"It's just a possibility," Amelia murmured, though the silence in the room felt loud.

She looked down at the tight, translucent curve of her belly, her mind echoing with the doctor's clinical tone from earlier that afternoon. *"Amelia, we have to think about second options. If by Friday she is not here, we may have to start talking about a C-section."*

The word "cut" felt sharp, even just as a silent thought. Amelia reached down, her palm cupping the warm underside of her bump as if she could communicate directly with the stubborn life inside.

Baby girl, please, she pleaded silently, *just show up. Show up before they have to come in and get you*

Please, baby girl, she whispered inwardly, *just show up. Show up before they have to come in and get you.*

Amelia phone rings, she picked it up and her mother's call broke the silence, her greeting a gentle, familiar balm: "Good Morning, love."

"And you sound so happy, my baby girl. You were worried sick yesterday and your msg was kinda..... What is this good news, hmm? What's the secret?"

Amelia laughed, a light, genuine sound. "Mama, Luca took three months off to come to help us. Three months! He's flying here tomorrow."

A deep, audible inhale of joy came through the speaker. "Amelia, my heart. This man... he is a keeper, you hear me? You love him and you respect him with all of your heart." Her mother's voice softened further. "He doesn't care if the baby is his blood or not, he is all in, *humble* and *sincere.*"

"I know, Mama," Amelia whispered, her eyes filling again, this time with a deep reverence for the man she loved. "I'm the luckiest woman. She will have his last name, and he already named her **Livia** after his grandmother. He said as soon as she arrives, we will complete the adoption paperwork. He *is* her dad."

Later that afternoon, the phone rang again. It was Luca, not from home, but FaceTime in the luminous chaos of a major international hub. He was at a check-in line, surrounded by the murmur of a dozen languages and the clatter of luggage carts.

"Babe, I thought you said tonight at eight!" she chided, a grin breaking across her face.

Luca winked, adjusting the phone. "*Belle*, when is 7 PM... what time would it be there. I know you don't know time difference." he grinned. " I am waiting to board in a few. I can't wait to see you, *Bella*."

"Don't be a smart rat," she blew him a kiss. "I can't wait, either."

Their banter paused as a call for **Delta One** boarding was announced. Luca leaned in, his voice dropping to a seductive, playful whisper. "You know, when I get there in a few hours, I have to help you bring Livia out. I have a way."

Amelia giggled. "Baby, you're a **cardiologist**, not..."

"Darling, I fix broken hearts," he interrupted, his eyes gleaming. "And sometimes, to help things along, a man has to make love to push things around."

A delicious shudder ran through her. "I am so... **ready**."

He blew a kiss to the screen, his final goodbye for the next seven hours. "I will see you in a few, my love. Say hi to my daughter."

A Vow at Thirty Thousand Feet...

Luca handed over his ticket and stepped past the gate, trading the airport's frantic motion for the hush of the airplane. The cabin was a cocoon of tranquil luxury: **Delta One Business Class**. Deep slate-gray and ivory tones, rich leather seats that promised transformation, and a soft, ambient blue light that seemed to calm the soul.

He settled into the quiet corner of his pod a world away from the hospital floors and the bustling clinics of Tuscany. An air hostess, elegantly dressed in a tailored uniform, approached him with a warm, lemon-scented towel. He wiped his hands, inhaling the momentary peace.

Within minutes, the main door closed. The heavy roar of the engines began, a low-frequency promise of escape. The pilot's voice, a steady, calm presence, announced their imminent departure. As the colossal aircraft surged forward, Luca felt the push of G-force against his seat. The world outside his window tilted, and the thousands of pinpricks of light that defined the city of Tuscany began to blur, then shrink, until the landscape fading into the **midnight black of the night sky**.

The first beverage service began. The flight attendant, a woman with a kind smile, brought him a crisp glass of **Chardonnay** and a small menu. He took a slow, deliberate sip. "Thank you," he said, letting the wine's complexity wash over his palate. "I haven't had a drop of wine in almost four months."

The hostess smiled, intrigued. "Any special reason for the sacrifice?"

A profound, humble pride swelled in Luca's chest. "Solidarity. My **pregnant wife**," he announced, the word *wife* rolling off his tongue with a sudden, beautiful weight. It was the first time he had publicly used it, a silent vow soaring at thirty thousand feet, formalizing a commitment that already lived in the core of his soul.

"I'm heading to DC now. Our little girl will be here by Friday, we think."

The hostess raised her glass in a toast. "To an easy arrival and a happy life. **Cheers**."

She moved on to the next passenger, leaving Luca alone with his thoughts. He pulled out his research folder, but the text was a blur. He stared out into the limitless night sky. Europe was a ghost below the clouds; Washington was a beacon waiting to appear on the horizon. The truth was simple: his professional life, his heart-mending work, was secondary now. He closed the folder.

He reclined the seat into a flat bed, the plush bedding embracing him. There was no surgery, no meeting, no research paper that mattered more than the gentle thunder of Amelia's heart and the tiny, miraculous one beating beneath it. He was in transit, yes, but he wasn't just crossing an ocean; he was crossing a threshold. Luca closed his eyes, his only thought a whispered promise to the dark: *I'm coming, Livia. I'm coming to hold you, to kiss you, and to finally be whole again with your mother.*

The Melody of First Breath

Luca stood vigil, an observer at the edge of creation. The sterile, metallic scent of the delivery room was an unwelcome counterpoint to the rush of adrenaline and fear that had been his constant companion for the past several hours. Amelia's hand, slick with sweat, was gripped so tight in his that their knuckles were **white, merged mountains of bone**. He was the only voice she could hear, a low, constant hum of encouragement, even though his own voice seemed to be swallowed by the high-ceilinged room, unable to travel even the short distance to his own ears.

The world outside their shared, primal space seemed muffled and irrelevant. The Atlantic crossing was forgotten; the dry pasta of the airport cafeteria was a memory from another life. Now, there was only the primal, agonizing rhythm of effort. The only sound that broke through the high tide of their focus was the doctor's steady, non-negotiable instruction: **"Push, Amelia. Push, and pause."**

Amelia's vulnerability was laid bare, raw and beautiful. She was no longer the elegant woman on the Rovos Rail or the independent force in DC; she was pure, elemental force. Luca, the man who fixed broken hearts, was helpless to fix this pain, a profound ache in his chest mirroring the intensity on her face. He kissed her forehead, tasting the salt of her labor, his eyes conveying the endless well of his love and gratitude.

Then, the final, desperate surge.

The air fractured. A sound, ragged and magnificent, tore through the room the first, undeniable sound of **Livia**. It was a cry so loud, so fierce, it felt like it could **chase the birds from the nearest trees, scattering them into the deep sky**.

Luca's vision blurred. The river he was witnessing was no longer the Nile but the quiet, unstoppable flow of his own tears, streaming down his cheeks, a silent, humble overflow of a heart finally given permission to burst.

The doctor, a calm, steady presence, snipped the cord, severing the physical tie but sealing the emotional one. He clapped Luca on the shoulder, his voice bright against the lingering tension: "You are a new member of the Dads' Club, my friend. A girl dad. Congratulations."

Luca barely registered the words. He took his daughter, a tiny, wet, squalling miracle, into his arms. The sudden weight was nothing compared to the enormous weight of responsibility and love that settled in his soul. His tears, hot and unrestricted, continued their flow, running down his stubbled chin, a **river to Khartoum**. He kissed Livia's forehead, a silent, sacred promise, before gently placing her on Amelia's chest.

Amelia looked at her baby for the very first time. Her face was a landscape of exhausted wonder: tears mixed with a triumphant, uncontainable smile. She looked at Luca, her eyes holding every moment of their journey, every whispered promise.

"Thank you, babe," she breathed, her voice raspy. "I love you so much."

Luca kissed her, a long, profound connection that spoke of transit completed and destiny arrived. "I love you, too, babe," he murmured. He paused, looking down at the red, indignant face nestled on her chest. "But I think I love Livia more than anything in this world right now."

A wave of tired, joyful laughter rippled through the medical team, breaking the tension and filling the room with the warm, human sound of life affirmed.

Luca cradled Livia, walking out of the delivery room to show her to the waiting family Amelia's mother and other loved ones a moment of joyous chaos before the baby was whisked away for her initial check-ups. The nurses, gentle and practiced, guided him toward the nursery, a glass-walled sanctuary of tiny, bundled lives. He watched his daughter settle, a silent promise hanging between them: *I'm here now.*

When he returned to Amelia's room, a hush had fallen. She lay utterly still, a warrior finally rested. He approached the bedside, his heart expanding with tenderness. She had fallen asleep in less than three minutes, the effort of 26 hours of labor demanding immediate payment.

He leaned over and whispered a kiss on her cheek, then turned to the family. "I think we should all go to the cafeteria and give her a chance to sleep. She hasn't rested properly in days."

Her mother smiled, a familiar pride in her eyes. "She's stubborn. She made up her mind she was going to do this without the knife, and she did. I know she just fell asleep. She didn't want to give up."

Luca chuckled softly as they walked. "Oh, I know. I told her if she didn't have her by midnight, I was going to make the decision for her."

They entered the cafeteria, an area now quiet and dimly lit, signaling the end of the day. The selection was limited, the steam tables holding only the final, tired remnants of the day's meals. Luca, ever the thoughtful partner, ordered a comforting bowl of soup to go, a restorative tonic for his sleeping woman.

As they sat down to eat their utilitarian meals, Luca joked about the dry, institutional quality of the pasta. Amelia's mother, emboldened by the moment, bragged about her famous **Mac and Cheese**.

"You have to try it, Luca. It's a guaranteed cure for whatever ails you," she insisted.

Luca laughed, the sound warm and genuine. "Ah, *Mama*. Americans. You call it Mac and Cheese. But when Amelia made it for me, I realized it is **Cheese and Macaroni**! The cheese is the star. In Italian food, everything is simple, delicious, and balanced."

They finished their meal, the small talk and laughter a necessary, gentle buffer against the intense drama of the delivery.

Returning to the room, they found Amelia awake, illuminated by the soft, nightlight glow of the room. She was attempting to breastfeed Livia, her face etched with a look of concentration and a slide of private pain.

"Mama," she whispered, her voice laced with disappointment. "There is nothing coming." The sense of failure, though minor, was immediate and sharp after her monumental effort.

Luca moved quickly. He leaned down, a silent communication passing between them. He gently took the baby, already knowing the struggle. "*Bella*," he soothed. "You need to eat before you can give. We can feed her with a bottle for now. You take this soup. You need to fill your own well before you can fill hers."

Amelia continued to enjoy the soup, its warmth spreading through her, a restorative tide. The savory steam tasted like sustenance, but more profoundly, it tasted like **surrender**. She had fought the exhaustion and the fear for so long, and now, with Luca sitting right beside her, she could finally let go. The food was simple, but it carried the **profound, undeniable flavor of being cared for**, the deep knowledge of not being alone in the aftermath.

Her gaze, now softer, turned fully to Luca. He was utterly absorbed. His large, renowned **cardiologist hands, the** hands that fix the complex, ticking machinery of the human heart were now cradling a tiny, perfect life. His thumb, usually resting on a patient's wrist, gently stroked Livia's cheek. His face, weary from the flight and the anxiety, was etched with an adoration so complete, it was its own form of prayer.

The room settled into a profound stillness. The **hospital night** hummed around them a distant rattle of a cart, the soft whisper of the oxygen line but in their small corner, a sanctuary had formed. The only sound that truly mattered was Livia's small, rhythmic **suckling** on the bottle, a tiny, determined sound that was the **new, sacred melody of their lives**.

Luca looked up, sensing her attention. Their eyes met over the crown of their daughter's head. In that gaze, all the turbulence of their long-distance love, the fear of the delivery, and the exhaustion of the journey dissolved. Amelia saw herself reflected in his eyes: vulnerable, spent, and loved beyond measure. He saw his woman, a warrior and a miracle. The silence between them was not an absence of words, but a **saturation of feeling**.

Luca reached out his free hand the one not supporting Livia's perfect weight and found Amelia's, their palms pressing together. Their joined hands rested on the white hospital sheets, a **simple, unbreakable circuit of three**.

In that quiet, incandescent moment, Amelia understood: **Love in Transit** was over. The journey across continents, the anxiety of distance, the physical hardship of bringing life forth it had all been transit. And this, the quiet, humbling presence of their daughter being fed by the man she loved, was the destination.

Livia was their star, newly birthed into the dark sky of their waiting. And as long as they held hands, they knew their light would never fade.

The Blind Alphabet of Love...The Three-Month Sanctuary

The three months vanished like the **flicker of a candle in a high wind**, its light both fierce and fleeting. Livia, now a creature of awareness, had crossed the threshold of her initial fog. She knew her father. Her small eyes, the color of a stormy Atlantic, would **follow Luca's silhouette across the ceiling**, a tiny spotlight of adoration.

He had been the uncomplaining **bedmate of the night**, the first responder to every mew and cry. The rigorous discipline of his cardiology training sleepless nights, absolute focus had been redirected entirely to Livia. He ensured that for these ninety days, Amelia's sole task was healing and recovery. Diaper changes were his architectural projects; early morning feedings were his sacred rituals.

Amelia walked in now, carrying the faint, cold scent of her university office. She had spent the morning preparing for the inevitable return to her teaching career. As she moved to speak, Luca, seated on the worn velvet armchair, raised a hand a silent, imperative sign that Livia was drifting into sleep on his chest.

He carefully settled their daughter into her bassinet, executing a **military-grade tiptoe** out of the living room. The minute the door clicked shut, he was across the room, closing the distance to Amelia with the force of a magnet. His kiss was slow, tender, and deeply relieved the greeting of a man who had missed his lover even while being in the same house.

"How did it go, *Bella*?"

Amelia let her handbag drop to the floor with a sound that felt too loud in the quiet house. She sank onto the sofa, her posture collapsing with the weight of her decision. "Luca, I don't know how I can do this. They need me to take **two undergraduate classes** starting next month. With Livia alone... how will I be able to manage the grading, the lecture prep, and the feeds?"

He didn't offer immediate solutions. Instead, he simply kissed the tension from her brow, a deep, silent act of tenderness. He led her to the kitchen, where he had two bowls of his simple, perfect Italian pasta waiting. The aroma of **slow-simmered tomatoes and fresh basil** filled the room the taste of home he had carried with him.

They ate, the familiar comfort of the carbohydrate grounding them. "*Stranger*," she sighed, a small smile returning, "you have spoiled me. I am falling in love with your pasta more than I am with my man."

Luca laughed, the low sound echoing in the kitchen. Then, he set his fork down, the clatter small but final.

"*Tesoro*, why don't you come with me to Italy? You won't have to work. I will take care of you and Livia. We can be a unit, now."

The idea bloomed in Amelia's mind sunlight and cobblestone streets, his family, a life unburdened by debt or logistical nightmares. Yet, a deep-seated resistance, the ingrained American pride in self-sufficiency, hardened her resolve. She tried to **'man up'**, to find the voice of her former independent self.

"I will be fine, Luca. I have already talked to Mama; she will help with Livia. And you promised to fly back and forth. As soon as the semester closes, and the summer break starts, we will take the first flight to Italy."

Luca leaned in, his voice grave. "I don't want you to feel alone in this. Tomorrow morning is the last of my three months."

A small, playful challenge sparked in his eyes, a familiar fire in the face of impending separation. "Since I am leaving tomorrow, can I get something... a little thing... tonight?"

Amelia's weariness vanished. She laughed, a rich, genuine sound, and leapt onto him. "It has to be quiet, so Livia doesn't get up. And second, it has to be slow. Remember, I am brand new."

They found a quiet sanctuary in the room, away from the nursery door. The air grew thick with a low, burning heat. Luca's fingers began their slow, deliberate journey across her skin, tracing the map of her body like they were **reading Braille the blind alphabet of memory**. He sought not only the Amelia he remembered, but the new landscape of her post-partum body, honoring every curve and stretch mark as a testament to the miracle she had performed. There was no rush, only a tender, almost reverent exploration. It was a communion of two souls confirming their unity before the next forced separation.

Exhaustion claimed them both afterward. They fell into a deep, sated sleep, only to be jolted awake minutes later by the familiar, demanding cry of their daughter. They both reached for her simultaneously, their hands bumping in a moment of **sweet, reflexive chaos**.

Luca won the gentle tussle, scooping up Livia. Amelia stood in the corner, leaning against the cool wall, watching. He changed the diaper with practiced ease, his movements fluid and tender. In that simple, domestic tableau, a fresh wave of doubt washed over her: *Can I really do this alone?* The thought of moving across the ocean, to a life built entirely around his work and their family, felt suddenly less like surrender and more like salvation.

They spent the evening as a devoted unit, the final hours of their three-month sabbatical stretching out like pulled taffy. They fed Livia, bathed her in the small, plastic tub, and marveled at the new sounds she made. Once she was finally asleep, Amelia and Luca curled up on the sofa, watching movie *The Notebook* a quiet, sentimental ritual. Amelia rested her head on his chest, listening to the steady, comforting beat of his heart, the metronome that kept her own life in time. This was the **last uninterrupted night** she would have for a while.

The morning arrived, and Luca, true to his nature, rose early while Amelia was still asleep. He gave Livia her bath, the water warmed to a perfect temperature, and fed her, ensuring she was clean and contented. He tidied the room, erasing the minor chaos of the previous night, then made a **home-style Italian breakfast**: fresh espresso, toasted *pane* with butter, and a scattering of fresh berries.

He carried the tray into the bedroom and set it down. Amelia woke to the scent of **dark roast and warm bread**. Luca sat beside her, kissing her slowly and tenderly.

She looked at him, and the tears came, an immediate, unbidden flow down her cheeks. The reality of the separation was a cold hand gripping her heart.

Luca bent to kiss her tears away. "*Babe*, I don't want you to cry. You know I will be like I haven't left. FaceTime, Zoom, you name it I will be here. You are never alone."

They sat, trying to savor every second, pretending that the gentle sounds of Livia's coos could somehow stop the rotation of the earth. But time was not theirs to keep.

The **Uber notification** on Luca's phone shattered the bubble: *Your ride has arrived.*

The tight hug that followed was a desperate measure to fuse their two bodies. He stood and walked to the bassinet, holding his daughter tightly, kissing her small, sweet head. "*Cuore mio, amore mio*," he whispered in Italian *My heart, my love*. "I will see you soon, darling."

He gently gave Livia back to Amelia and walked outside. Amelia and Livia watched from the window as the black car pulled away, the sight of his retreating figure a familiar, painful echo of the past. Amelia's tears flowed freely, while Livia, nestled in her arms, smiled and played, **blissfully unaware of the geographic tyranny** that ruled her parents' lives.

The taxi door clicks shut with a finality that echoes in his chest. Luca stands on the curb of Dulles, the humid D.C. air sticking to his skin like a layer of grief. He heaves his bag out; it's lighter than when he arrived, or maybe he's just too numb to feel the weight.

As he enters through the sliding glass doors, the transition from the roar of traffic to the sterile hum of the terminal is jarring. Every step across the polished linoleum feels like he's stretching a rubber band connected to a nursery three miles away.

In his mind's eye, the terminal disappears. He's back in the dim amber glow of the bedroom. He sees **Amelia** holding the baby, their silhouettes framed by the window. He feels the phantom sensation of his daughter's velvet-soft cheek against his lips. Three months of "goodnights" a lifetime of tiny breaths and rhythmic heartbeats flash by like a flickering film strip.

A single, hot tear escapes, tracing a path down his cheek. He stops dead in the middle of the crowded floor. Travelers swarm around him like a time-lapse video, but he is a frozen monument to regret.

He catches his reflection on a dark monitor. He looks like a man he doesn't recognize. With a sharp, jagged breath, he wipes his face with the back of his hand, adjusts his collar, and pushes forward to the check-in desk. The mask is back on, but his eyes are dead.

The lounge is an island of luxury that feels like a tomb. Luca sits by the floor-to-ceiling glass, a glass of untouched Scotch sweating on the marble table beside him.

Outside, the silver bellies of planes lift off into the graying sky. He watches them, thinking about the physics of distance, how 900 km/h is fast enough to cross an ocean, but not fast enough to outrun the sound of a baby's cry. He is moving toward his "success" in Italy, but every inch of altitude gained feels like a descent into a deeper loneliness. *"I am flying toward my life, leaving my soul in a crib.*

The intercom cracks to life, a polite, disembodied voice cutting through his trance: *"Delta Flight 419 to Rome is now boarding at Gate B42."* Luca doesn't move at first. He just stares at the runway, realizing that once he steps onto that plane, the "Father" version of him stays behind in D.C., and the "Doctor" version takes over. He stands up, grabs his coat, and walks toward the gate.

The Research of Destiny

This time, the flight back to Italy was a **heavy, joyless passage**. His heart and his focus were left entirely in Washington, D.C.

He settled into his seat, ignoring the menu and the flight attendant. He pulled out his laptop not for work, but for a new, personal research project: **how a European medical professional could practice medicine in the United States.**

He plunged into the complex, multi-layered regulatory environment, his fingers typing furiously.

The Path to Practicing Medicine in the U.S. for Foreign Graduates

For a doctor like Luca, a graduate of an accredited European medical school, the process to practice in the United States involves several key, challenging hurdles:

ECFMG Certification: He must first receive certification from the **Educational Commission for Foreign Medical Graduates (ECFMG)**. This requires passing the rigorous **United States Medical Licensing Examination (USMLE)** Steps 1, 2 Clinical Knowledge (CK), and 2 Clinical Skills (CS).

Residency: Even as an established cardiologist, he would likely need to enter the **National Resident Matching Program (NRMP)** to secure a US-based residency or fellowship position. For a specialist like him, this would mean applying for a **Cardiology Fellowship** or an **Internal Medicine Residency** spot, depending on the state and hospital requirements. Securing one of these positions is highly competitive.

Visa Sponsorship: As an Italian citizen, he would require visa sponsorship, typically a **J-1 or H-1B visa**, which is tied directly to his residency or fellowship program.

State Licensing: After completing his residency/fellowship, he would then apply for specific medical licensure in the state of practice (in this case, Virginia/D.C. area), which involves background checks and further fees.

Luca scrolled through the requirements, the bureaucratic labyrinth daunting. It was both **possible and impossible** at the same time. The path required a monumental sacrifice: years of his life, a pay cut, and the grueling process of re-certification, all for the singular goal of being permanently close to his family.

He stared at the bright, cold screen, the cabin lights dimming around him. The drone of the engines became a lullaby. He fell asleep with his head on the tray table, the complex medical statutes floating in his mind, his last conscious thought a silent vow to his daughter: *I will fix this distance. I will come home to stay.*

The Unfurling of Roots in Tuscany

For the past year, the Atlantic had been a revolving door, with Luca crossing back and forth, unwilling to subject his newborn daughter to a long-haul flight before she was strong. Now, Livia had turned one, and with Amelia's summer break stretching ahead, the transit was finally, gloriously, moving east.

Two days before their arrival, Luca's sister, **Sofia**, drove from Milan to Tuscany. The plan was not just a reunion, but a celebration: Livia's baptism, or **Christening** (known as *Battesimo* in Italian). Since Amelia was not Catholic, Luca, with Sofia's efficient, loving help, was the architect of the event.

They had chosen the location with deep, intentional love: Luca's **grandmother's historic farm and house**, nestled on a rolling hill in the heart of the Tuscan countryside. The old stone walls, warmed by generations of sunlight, and the vista of cypress trees piercing the blue sky, would perfectly frame Livia's welcome into the family and the world.

Sofia checked the antique clock on the mantelpiece, its soft tick a counterpoint to their hurried movements. She looked at Luca, who was securing a final garland of ivy over a stone archway. "Luca, I think you should start to head to the airport now. With the Friday traffic in Florence, you don't want Livia to arrive and you are not there."

Luca agreed, a surge of adrenaline pushing him toward his car. The drive was a familiar pilgrimage, one he'd made countless times, but this time, every detail was magnified by the promise of their reunion.

He accelerated down the long, gravel driveway, the sound of the tires crunching soft as applause. The air was a thick, intoxicating blend of the Italian countryside: the **peppery dust from the road**, the **resinous scent of the cypress trees**, and the **dry, sun-baked earth** that defines Tuscan summer. As he drove through the winding lanes, the vista was a masterwork of light and shadow: fields of golden wheat rippled like velvet, punctuated by the silent, majestic watchfulness of the **cypresses**. The smell of **wild rosemary and heat** wafted through his open window, cleansing his mind of the hospital anxieties and bureaucratic nightmares.

He tasted the anticipation a sharp, sweet metallic tang at the back of his throat. He passed small clusters of old farmhouses, their terracotta roofs glowing like embers, each turn of the road bringing him closer to the end of his self-imposed separation.

He arrived at the airport just as the flight gates opened. He spotted them immediately: Amelia, looking slightly weary but radiant, carrying Livia on her back in a brightly patterned carrier, simultaneously pushing a luggage cart piled high with American comforts.

Luca ran. He didn't just walk; he sprinted, shedding the distance between them. His hug was a desperate, tightening grip, a **mute testament to a months of missed days**. He kissed her a long, slow, public declaration of arrival before taking over the luggage. He guided them to the car, settling Amelia into the front seat.

"I was worried this car seat I bought was too big," he confessed, his hands hovering over Livia, now safely buckled in the back. "But it fits her perfectly."

As Luca drove, turning off the main highway and onto progressively smaller, more winding roads, Amelia looked around, a gentle confusion creasing her brow. This ancient, undulating landscape had never appeared on their FaceTime calls.

Luca sensed it, the silence speaking volumes. "*Bella*, we are going to the farm house. Sofia and I decided Livia's celebration tomorrow should be here, at the same place where my own baptism took place. It is the heart of the family."

Amelia's smile was immediate, luminous. She reached for his hand. He kept one hand firmly on the wheel, the other holding hers so tight their palms became one. Their connection was a perfect loop of electricity, a **tender threat** woven through the fabric of their return.

They arrived to the sight of the old stone house, bathed in the golden, late afternoon light. Sofia emerged, her dark hair pulled back, her welcome immediate and warm. She and Amelia embraced not as in-laws, but as women who shared a deep, protective love for the same man.

Sofia laughed, pulling back. "Do you remember that train ride in South Africa? The Rovos Rail?"

Amelia laughed harder. “I had to run away from your brother because I thought you were his wife!”

Sofia, shaking her head and looking playfully at Luca, joked, “I don’t know what you see in that man, but girl, he is not my type!” The shared laughter was a gentle ceremony, welcoming Amelia into the family’s inner circle.

Sofia showed Amelia to a quiet, sun-dappled room to clean up. When Amelia returned, she found Luca and Sofia already with Livia. “I thought you guys were talking, so I wanted to give Livia a bath and feed her. I know she is tired.”

Sofia and Amelia exchanged a look a silent, shared acknowledgment of the profound, almost comical pride Luca held for their daughter.

As the sun dipped toward the horizon, the cousins, aunts, and friends began to gather outside. The family dinner was a **symphony of Italian celebration**. The air was alive with the deep, melodic rumble of multiple conversations overlaid with sudden, bright bursts of laughter. There was the constant, comforting **clinking of heavy wine glasses**, the rich aroma of **garlic and aged Pecorino cheese**, and the bright, earthy scent of **Chianti** being poured freely.

Above them, the sky deepened to a shade of black velvet, studded with a billion fierce, brilliant stars. Luca held Amelia close, his arm a strong perimeter around her waist.

Sofia, playful and sharp-eyed, called out, "Who ever thought Luca would become *this* Luca?"

The family roared with laughter. One cousin leaned toward Amelia. "You are the luckiest one, *bella*. This one here..."

Luca, sensing the imminent spillage of embarrassing childhood stories, jumped in. "Shhh! Let my woman enjoy the beautiful stars under the sky of Tuscany. This is not a confession booth!"

They all laughed, the sound warm and communal, continuing to savor the rich, familial moment.

After a few hours, Luca saw the subtle slump in Amelia's posture the final wave of transatlantic exhaustion claiming her. "Guys, I have to take my lady to bed," he announced. "I'll see you tomorrow."

They were cheered and waved off with knowing smiles.

As soon as they entered the bedroom, the world narrowed to the two of them. Luca, slow and tender, undressed Amelia, honoring the body that had birthed his child. Their lovemaking was a long, slow conversation each touch, each breath, a silent syllable that connected the deepest parts of their souls, erasing the months of separation. The familiar fire returned, but this time, it was deeper, rooted in the shared life they had built.

Afterward, Luca lay beside her, looking down with a profound, almost prophetic smile. “I think we just made a son, Amelia. I feel it.”

Amelia laughed, then grabbed her phone, opening her period tracker app. She looked at the colorful screen, then up at Luca, whose smile only widened.

The next morning, the family gathered, dressed in their Sunday best the women in elegant dresses, the men in dark suits, their clothes a respectful counterpoint to the ancient stone of the country church. **Catholic baptism** is a sacrament of purification and welcome, and Amelia watched with deep emotion as Livia, swaddled in a white lace garment, was presented at the font. The priest, speaking in clear, sonorous Italian, poured the **holy water** over Livia's forehead, anointing her with the **oil**

of Chrism, formally introducing her to the community of the faithful. Luca and his sister stood as Livia's godparents, making their vows to guide her spiritual life. The moment was one of transcendent beauty, a profound rooting of Livia into the very soil and spirit of her Italian heritage.

After the ceremony, they returned to the farm for a feast of traditional Tuscan dishes, wine, and dancing.

Later that afternoon, Sofia took Livia and her own children to visit a nearby friend, creating a silent, perfect window of opportunity. Luca gently took Amelia's hand and led her outside for a quiet picnic near a small, crystalline stream, sheltered by weeping willows.

"I love this stream of water," Luca told her, his voice low and intimate. "I've been coming here since I was a boy. Whether I was happy or sad, this is the place where my tears and my smiles fell. It is my best place."

Amelia tenderly pushed him down onto the soft, mossy bank, her eyes full of fire and promise. She undressed the bottom half of his body and leaned in, whispering into his ear, **"And this place is where you will plant the seed for your son."**

Once more, they came together, this time under the watchful, silent canopy of the trees, by the **running water that has witnessed generations of Luca's family**.

A while later, they walked back, finding Sofia already in the house. "Lovebirds," Sofia called out with a warm, knowing look. "Amelia, I guess he took you to the water streams."

Amelia, her face flushed with love and wine, played along. "Oh, so is this where he takes all of his women?"

Sofia laughed and looked at Luca. "No, *bella*. This is where he used to cry when he missed our mother."

Amelia's playful smile vanished. She looked at Luca, her eyes instantly filling with empathy, and hugged him tight.

Sofia quickly coughed. "Hey, hey, you two, get a room! I only left for two hours!"

Luca broke the hug, his voice calm and practical. "And speaking of rooms, let's go to sleep. Tomorrow we have to drive to town. "I have surgery in the morning; I need to prepare my mind."

He hugged his sister again and walked to the bedroom. They looked at their daughter, sleeping soundly, a beautiful, peaceful breath in the room. They tiptoed to the bathroom and took a shower together a quick, shared moment of warmth before he held her close, **cradling her against him** as they fell into a deep, dream-filled sleep

The Cooldown

For nearly three months, their lives had been a sun-drenched, dream-spun idyll on the rolling hills of Tuscany. Each day unfolded like a carefully unwrapped gift: mornings began with the scent of Luca's potent espresso and the sweet, yeasty aroma of fresh *cornetti* from the village bakery. Afternoons were spent under the benevolent gaze of the Italian sun, Livia's delighted giggles echoing through ancient olive groves as she chased butterflies the color of faded frescoes. They took long, leisurely drives on winding, dust-red roads, past fields of sunflowers that tracked the sun like golden sentinels, and ancient vineyards heavy with the promise of autumn wine.

The promise had been hanging in the air since the first cicada began its hum in the Tuscan heat. Luca, a man whose hands spent their days mending the literal valves and vessels of human hearts, knew that some wounds couldn't be fixed with a scalpel. Emilia's impending return to the hallowed, brick-lined halls of Howard University in D.C. was a silent countdown they both felt in their marrow.

"Before the Atlantic comes between us again," Luca had said, his voice a low, melodic vow, "we should go south. We go back to the rhythm that started us."

On Thursday night, Florence's Santa Maria Novella station was a blur of hurried commuters and flickering departure boards. Luca looked every bit the Italian doctor on holiday linen shirt sleeves rolled up, a leather weekender bag slung over his shoulder while Emilia balanced one-year-old Livia on her hip. Livia, a perfect, sun-kissed blend of her parents, gripped a stuffed lion, her wide eyes reflecting the station's amber glow.

The Midnight Heartbeat

The sleeper train to Sicily was a nostalgic sanctuary. As they stepped into their cabin, the air was a mix of **faint floor wax and the metallic tang of old electricity.** It wasn't the opulent mahogany of the Rovos Rail where a South African sunset had first bound a doctor from Tuscany to a professor from D.C., but the intimacy was the same.

As the train pulled away, the **clack-clack, clack-clack** of the tracks began to vibrate through the floorboards. Luca sat on the edge of the lower berth, watching Emilia settle Livia.

The carriage swayed with a heavy, hypnotic grace, a rhythmic cradle that made the world outside the window feel like a fleeting dream.

The low hum of the engine and the occasional whistle of the wind against the glass formed a cocoon around them.

"She's asleep," Emilia whispered, brushing a curl from Livia's forehead. She sat beside Luca, their thighs touching, the heat of his skin seeping through her jeans.

"Do you remember the crossing?" Luca asked. Around 2:00 AM, the train was dismantled and rolled onto the massive ferry to cross the Strait of Messina. They stood on the deck, the **biting, salty spray of the midnight sea** misting their faces. The air was thick with the smell of **brine and diesel**, the dark water below churning into white foam. In that moment, suspended between the mainland and the island, the distance to Washington D.C. felt like a lifetime away.

Trapani: Salt and Ancient Light

Friday morning broke in a fever of white light. When they stepped onto the platform in Trapani, the heat was a physical presence a dry, searing weight that smelled of **sun-bleached stone and drying kelp.**

They spent the day in a sensory daze. The salt pans stretched out like a chessboard of mirrors, reflecting a sky so blue it looked bruised. For lunch, Luca led them to a hole-in-the-wall *trattoria* where the walls were stained with decades of sea salt.

Luca and Emilia shared a bowl of **Busiate con il pesto alla trapanese**. Emilia closed her eyes as the flavor hit the **gritty texture of pounded almonds, the sharp, aromatic bite of raw garlic, and the sweetness of cherry tomatoes** that had been blistered by the Sicilian sun.

The table smelled of **torn basil and the crisp, acidic notes of cold Grillo wine**, a sharp contrast to the humid heaviness of the afternoon.

Livia giggled, her tiny fingers exploring a piece of bread, her face smeared with the red gold of the sauce. For a moment, the Howard lecture halls and the sterile hospital corridors of Tuscany didn't exist. There was only the salt and the sea.

The Ascent to the Clouds: Erice

As dusk approached, they hailed a taxi for the climb to **Erice**. The driver, a man who navigated the hairpin turns with a terrifying, one-handed nonchalance, hummed along to the radio as the Mediterranean shriveled into a blue ribbon below them.

With every thousand feet of elevation, the temperature dropped ten degrees. By the time they reached the stone gates of the medieval town, the sweltering heat of Trapani was a memory. Erice was swathed in the *abbraccio di Venere* the "Embrace of Venus" a thick, ethereal fog that made the stone walls sweat. The air was suddenly **cool and damp**, clinging to Emilia's skin like a silk veil. Their footsteps rang out with a hollow **click-clat** against the *basoli* the polished, triangular paving stones that were as slippery as ice.

They ducked into a bakery, the air a warm, heavy cloud of **toasted sugar and lemon peel.** Luca bought a tray of **Genovesi ericine**. Emilia took a bite, the pastry shattering into buttery flakes, the **velvety, warm lemon custard** filling her mouth with a richness that felt like a secret kept for centuries.

That night, they stayed in a room with vaulted ceilings and walls made of cold, grey rock. The wind howled through the narrow mountain passes, a lonely sound that made the warmth inside the room feel sacred.

Luca held Emilia from behind as they looked out the window. The mist had parted for a heartbeat, showing the lights of the world below the flickering pulse of a land they would soon have to leave.

"In my job, I fix the valves so the blood can flow," Luca whispered into her hair, his breath warm against her neck. "But here, with you, on this mountain... it's the only time my own heart beats at the right speed."

Emilia leaned her head back against his chest, watching the steady rise and fall of Livia's chest in the crib nearby. The scent of **damp Earth and almond pastry** lingered in the room. "Then let's not think about the flight, Luca. Let's just be in transit. Just for tonight, the train hasn't reached the station yet."

In the silence of the Sicilian heights, they held onto the moment, a family forged in motion, captured between the salt of the earth and the stars of the south

The two weeks following their descent from the misty heights of Erice had passed in a blur of golden-hour swims and lingering espresso mornings, but the calendar was a cruel, mechanical thing. Despite the prayers they whispered into the cooling Tuscan evenings, the day they had dreaded finally pushed its way through the horizon, unyielding and bright.

The last day of that glorious summer arrived with a clarity that felt almost violent. The sun rose over the vineyards, not with the gentle haze of July, but with the crisp, sharp edges of end of summer a reminder that the earth was turning, and with it, the wheels of a Boeing 747 that would soon put an ocean between them

The mood, once a **fire of untamed joy** from Livia's bright spirit, and the **warm, intimate glow of family gatherings** in the farmhouse, began a slow, agonizing descent. The vibrant hues of the landscape seemed to dim with the fading light of their shared time. An invisible chill permeated the ancient stone walls of the farmhouse, carrying with it the undeniable, harsh truth of their impending separation. The reality of Amelia's return to Washington D.C., to a life without Luca, was now a mere handful of hours away, cooling the sun-warmed earth of their temporary haven with its heavy, sorrowful presence. Each passing minute felt like a grain of sand slipping through fingers, a precious, irreplaceable moment stolen by the relentless march of time. The very air thrummed with the unspoken ache of two souls soon to be cleaved by an ocean once more

Luca, unable to rest, began the quiet, meticulous process of packing the new Italian clothes and small wooden toys for Livia. He handled the tiny garments with a profound, heartbreaking tenderness. Each item he placed into the suitcase was a small, **weighted admission of distance**.

He found Amelia in the kitchen, the light dim, preparing a simple, late-night snack before bed. The warm, comforting scent of **steamed milk and cinnamon** hung in the air, a futile attempt to comfort the underlying anxiety. He walked up silently and wrapped his arms around her from behind, his chin resting on her shoulder, his lips trailing soft kisses on her neck.

Amelia instinctively turned off the stove, the sudden quiet filling the space. She leaned back into his embrace, then twisted in his arms to face him, immediately sensing the gravity that had settled on him. She jumped onto him, wrapping her legs around his waist, holding him with a fierce urgency, their kiss a desperate plea against the ticking clock.

"Are you okay, *bello*?" she whispered into his ear, her voice thick with shared sorrow.

"I am not," Luca replied, his voice a low, raw rumble against her collarbone. "I want you here. I want to wake up with my daughter and my woman in this house, in my country. I cannot pretend I am happy, Amelia."

Amelia tightened her hug, inhaling the familiar, clean scent of his skin. "I know, *babe*. I feel the same crushing weight."

She pulled back slightly, her gaze earnest. "Why don't you move here? You can teach English, *Bella*. The need is huge, and your expertise is top-tier."

Amelia kissed him tenderly, acknowledging the lifeline he offered. "I don't speak Italian, Luca. Not enough to navigate a life. I am learning so hard, I promise. As soon as I can communicate, that will be my next move." She traced the line of his jaw. "If it was easy to practice medicine in America, you would not have to ask me. With my **broken English and Italian accent**, I would already be there waiting for you, doing whatever job I could get."

The reference to his earlier, failed research into practicing medicine in the U.S. hung between them a flash of the **impassable mountain** he was trying to climb for their family. Luca didn't continue the conversation. A quiet sadness moved with him as he walked to the living room, seeking the simple, unadulterated comfort of Livia, now awake and playing with her soft blocks. He picked her up and began to play, his heart fractured between his two loves.

Amelia was left alone in the kitchen, the warmth from the stove fading. She stood there, the reality of the move hitting her with cold clarity. *What if she moves here?* The truth of her hesitation was not entirely the language barrier. Luca had never asked her to marry him. She couldn't uproot her entire life, her career, and her language without knowing what the **next, formal step** in their relationship would be. She paused, then reflected on the sheer, selfless goodness of Luca: the transatlantic flights, the profound care he showed to his daughter.

She walked slowly into the living room and hugged him from behind, wrapping her arms around both him and Livia. "Babe," she whispered, her voice infused with new resolve. "I will ...let me go and figure out how to apply for teaching positions in the universities here, for next year. I will study my Italian like it's my thesis. I want us to be a family, a real one, Luca."

He leaned back into her, pulling her arms tighter around him, Livia giggling between them, an innocent buffer to their pain. It was a hug he wanted to last forever, a final, fierce protest against the separation.

The ride to the Florence airport was cloaked in a **heavy, golden silence**, the kind that only descends when a precious chapter is about to close. The Tuscan landscape, usually so vibrant, now seemed to mirror their mood, fading into hues of soft orange and twilight blue. Luca, his jaw tight with unspoken emotion, kept glancing at **Livia** in the backseat. She was nestled against her car seat, already drifting into a light slumber, her small, perfect profile illuminated by the setting sun oblivious to the vast ocean that would soon separate her parents.

He then turned his gaze to Amelia, his eyes a **dark, fathomless pool of sadness** that mirrored the ache in her own heart. The reality of their impending separation, a chasm of miles and time zones, felt heavier than any medical crisis he'd ever faced.

Amelia leaned over, her touch gentle, and pressed a soft, lingering kiss to his cheek. "She loves you, Luca," she whispered, her voice thick with emotion. "And adore her." She offered a watery, hopeful smile. "I promise, the Atlantic isn't *that* huge. The Pacific is..."

A small, weary laugh escaped Luca, a sound that cracked the tension in the car. "I know, *Bella*," he conceded, the corner of his lips turning up. "I guess I should just change careers and become a pilot. I think for the past year, I've been flying almost every two months."

They both shared a moment of bittersweet laughter, the absurd humor of their situation a fragile shield against the encroaching sadness. In a few hours, the vast, unforgiving waves of the Atlantic Ocean would once again widen, stretching its formidable expanse between them. But this time, it felt different. This time, they carried a child, and a promise, a shared understanding that their love was powerful enough to bridge any distance, even the seemingly infinite miles that lay ahead. The silence that followed was no longer heavy with dread, but with the quiet, unwavering strength of two hearts connected, ready to endure the journey home, no matter how far.

The Scramble Across the Atlantic

Back in Washington D.C., life became a relentless loop of teaching, grading, and the demanding needs of a one-year-old. The long, beautiful summer in Tuscany felt like a dream. Amelia was constantly moving the classroom, the daycare run, the grocery store. She was so focused on managing the logistics that she failed to listen to the quiet rebellion of her own body.

Two months slipped by before the subtle signs became impossible to ignore. Monday morning, after dropping Livia at daycare, Amelia rushed toward her favorite coffee shop. She was a true city dweller, used to eating while walking a deliberate defiance of sitting down when time was a luxury. As she hurried down the sidewalk, savoring the familiar taste of her coffee and banana bread, a sudden, violent wave of nausea hit her. She tried to swallow it down, but the urge was overwhelming. She barely made it to the nearest public trash can, emptying her stomach with a painful heave.

Afterward, she rinsed her mouth with water from her silver bottle, discarded the untouched coffee and bread, and blamed the sudden illness on walking too fast.

She managed to teach her classes, though she felt ill and distracted. On the way home, outside the Metro station, the nausea returned, forcing a second, more humbling stop. Back in the quiet sanctuary of her house, she opened her period tracker app. Her eyes widened. The date was unequivocally missed.

A primal certainty took hold. She walked straight to the nearest drugstore and bought five different pregnancy tests. Rushing home, she took the first one. She didn't believe it. She took a second, a third, until she had used all five. The positive lines stared back, bold and undeniable.

A chaotic mix of joy and terror washed over her. She was having Luca's child, but the Atlantic still separated them. She immediately called Luca.

Luca picked up the phone while walking out of the operating room. He was still wearing his blue scrubs, his face mask dangling below his chin, looking every bit the exhausted but successful cardiac surgeon. The surgery had lasted eight brutal hours.

"Pronto? Darling, how are you?" he answered, his voice low and tired.

Amelia's voice was quiet, almost a whisper, yet it held the weight of their future. "Babe... I think... I am pregnant."

Luca stopped dead in the middle of the crowded corridor. "What?"

"Yes," she said, managing a shaky laugh. "Since I came back, I've been so busy, I didn't realize I missed my period. This morning I vomited twice. I took five tests. They all agree."

Luca's weariness instantly dissolved, replaced by a surge of ecstatic energy. His spirit wanted to transcend the ocean, to be there to hug her, to kiss her belly, to kneel before her. The Atlantic Ocean, the perpetual transit barrier, was now the cruelest presence in their relationship.

The transition was instantaneous. One moment, Luca was a man possessed, shouting at the empty air that he was going to be a father again. The next, the "Switch" occurred.

His eyes snapped back to the glowing screen of his phone, the goofy, manic grin smoothing out into the terrifyingly intense, focused gaze that made him the finest surgeon in his field. He began to scroll not through messages, but through the internal, meticulous calendar he kept for the people who anchored his soul.

"Okay, okay," he said, his voice dropping an octave into that low, melodic 'Doctor Tone' that usually calmed frantic families in waiting rooms. "Darling, let's look at science. Think. When was the last period?"

Across the Atlantic, on streets of D.C. that felt a million miles away, Amelia's voice leaned against the cool line. He could practically see her eyes dancing with that familiar mischief. "Oh, okay, 'Doctor.' Honestly? Between traveling and packing... I think I was too busy to notice. I don't actually remember."

Luca lifted his head. His eyes tracked upward, scanning the air as if reading data points on a transparent screen only he could see. His brain, a machine of precision, began to click.

"You left Italy August 28th," he said, the words coming in a soft, rapid-fire staccato. "The last period was June ...because we missed that anniversary dinner. So, the doctor in me says... .. August... September... October ... should we add July?"

The clinical coldness snapped. The "Doctor" evaporated in a heartbeat, leaving a man completely exposed. The romance radiating from him in that moment was enough to melt the very floor beneath his feet.

"Amelia..." he whispered, the weight of it hitting his lungs. "We're might be in the fourth month. Four months of a life I didn't even know was there. A person, already. A soul, already."

He started panicking.

"Darling, are you okay? Do you need anything? Do you want me to come... right now?"

Amelia laughed, grounding him. "Babe, I am okay. Just pregnant, not sick. We will be fine."

He couldn't contain himself. He spun around, announcing to the passing nurses and doctors, "I am going to be a father again!"

Amelia's laugh followed a bright, musical sound that acted as his North Star. Even through the static of a transcontinental call, he could feel her. He imagined her hand reaching through the phone, cupping the side of his face, her thumb brushing his cheekbone with that devastating tenderness. In his mind, he tasted a kiss quick, deep, and heavy with the promise of a lifetime.

"Babe, I love you, you big-headed genius," she whispered. "Now, let me go pick up Livia before she thinks we've forgotten her. I'll call you the second I'm through the door."

The line went silent. Luca stood there in the sudden vacuum of hospital walls . The "Doctor" had faded entirely, replaced by a "Father" who looked as though he had just seen the sun for the first time. He stared at the dark screen of his phone, watching her voice go in his mind.

The Atlantic Ocean was a vast, salt-heavy chasm, three thousand miles of cold blue deep enough to swallow most things. But it couldn't swallow the sound of Luca's voice.

It had been two months since a flickering digital screen in a D.C. clinic had revealed a second rhythmic pulse a tiny, flickering star on an ultrasound that signaled their family was growing once more. Since that day, Luca had fought the geography of their lives with the precision of a man performing open-heart surgery. If he couldn't breathe the same air as Emilia, he would make sure the air she *did* breathe was filled with him.

In the pre-dawn grey of Washington D.C., before the city's humidity could settle over the Potomac, Emilia's phone would vibrate on the nightstand. It was 6:00 AM for her; 12:00 PM for him in the sterile, white-tiled corridors of the hospital in Tuscany.

"Good morning, *vita mia*," Luca's voice would drift through the speaker, low and honeyed, cutting through her grogginess.

There was always the faint, rhythmic *beep-beep* of a heart monitor or the distant chime of a hospital page in his background, a reminder that while he was saving lives in Italy, his own life was anchored in a bedroom in DC.

"The bottle is on the nightstand, Emilia. The green one. Take it with the water I heard you pour last night." He stayed on the line, listening for the soft *click* of the cap and the swallow, his long-distance vigil ensuring the new life inside her had everything it needed. He didn't just love her; he curated her well-being.

Luca knew that a professor's life at Howard was a whirlwind of lectures and grading, especially with a toddler like Livia running circles around her heels. So, he hijacked the city's infrastructure to reach her.

Every Tuesday, a burst of color would arrive at her door not just any flowers, but **deep orange ranunculus and wild eucalyptus**, the scent of which mimicked the Tuscan hillsides they had wandered.

Emilia would bury her face in the petals, the peppery, clean aroma momentarily erasing the smell of city exhaust and old library books.

On the nights when she was too exhausted to stand at the stove, a notification would chime on her phone: *Uber Eats is five minutes away.* Suddenly, the kitchen would be filled with the scent of **toasted garlic and artisan sourdough**, a meal Luca had hand-picked from a local bistro from five time zones away.

"I cannot cook for you tonight," he'd text, "but I can make sure you are fed."

The true bridge, however, was the data. Luca, ever the doctor, had requested to be copied on every portal update from her OB-GYN.

One rainy Thursday, Emilia opened an email to find a message from Luca before she'd even read the test results herself.

"Your iron levels are slightly low, Love. I have already ordered a delivery of organic spinach and grass-fed steak to the house. And the baby's heart rate? 155 beats per minute. A strong, fast rhythm. Just like mine when I think of you."

The tears usually came in the quiet moments, the "joy-tears" that blurred the screen during their nightly FaceTime.

Livia would press her sticky palms against the iPad, kissing the glass version of her father. "Papa, come out!" she would giggle.

Luca's face would soften, a look of such raw, agonizing adoration that Emilia felt it in her very marrow. "I am right there, Livia. Look at the moon," he would say, his eyes locked on Emilia's. "We are looking at the same one. It's just a very long train ride away, remember?"

When Livia finally fell asleep, the conversation would drop into the low, husky register of lovers who hungered for the tactile.

Emilia would trace the line of his jaw on the screen, her thumb sliding over the pixels as if she could feel the faint stubble of his afternoon shadow.

"I can feel your heartbeat through the phone," she whispered one night, her voice thick with emotion. "It's the same rhythm from the Rovos Rail. It's the same rhythm from the night train to Trapani."

Luca leaned into the camera, his voice a tether of pure silk. "Distance is just a test of how far love can travel without breaking, Emilia. And we? We are a transcontinental express. We don't stop for oceans."

In those moments, their love felt like a blue ribbon tied between two hearts, pulled taut, vibrating with the promise that every departure was simply the prelude to a much grander arrival

The Atlantic Ocean didn't feel like a body of water anymore; it felt like a fragile silk thread connecting two beating hearts. Every call was a lifeline, a bridge built of radio waves and longing. Their **"Different Worlds"** Luca in the sharp, ancient sunlight of Tuscany, where the air smelled of cypress and sterile hospital soap, and Emilia in the humid, bustling rhythm of D.C., where the streets echoed with the heavy bass of transit and the relentless pace of academia. They had learned to trade hours like currency, staying awake until their eyes burned just to hear the sound of a morning yawn or a midnight sigh.

Amelia arrived home late, the weight of a Howard lecture and the humidity of the Potomac settling into her shoulders. She moved through the house with the practiced grace of a mother, shifting a feverish, sleeping Livia from her shoulder to the crib with a breath-held silence.

As she tucked the blanket around her daughter, her phone was wedged between her ear and shoulder. "Thanks, Mama," she whispered into the line to her own mother. "Don't worry about school tomorrow. She's still running a little hot. I think I'll just take her to the pediatrician myself and call out of work. Did she eat?"

"Everything," her mother's voice crackled back, warm and reassuring.

"Thanks, Mama. She's out. Let me get her settled."

Amelia stood for a moment in the nursery, the dim glow of the nightlight casting long shadows against the walls. She felt the heavy, fluttering secret beneath her ribs the new life that was currently a silent passenger in her body, a tiny heartbeat echoing the one she had left behind in Italy. She retreated to the living room, collapsing onto the emerald velvet sofa, her handbag spilling its contents onto the cushions.

Then, the phone vibrated. A low, rhythmic hum that made her pulse spike. She swiped the screen, and the room was suddenly filled with the resonance of a voice that sounded like home.

"**Pronto, bella,**" Luca's voice poured through the speaker. It was low, textured, and undeniably sexy the sound of a man who had spent his entire shift in the cardiac ward waiting just to breathe the same air as her, even if that air was digital.

Amelia's fingers trembled as she touched the unopened email from the doctor. "**Babe... I hope you didn't read it. I know I didn't,**" she confessed, her voice a cocktail of exhaustion and pure adrenaline. "I told the doctor not to say a word. I wanted us to find out together."

"**Open it,**" Luca whispered, his voice thick with an anticipation that seemed to vibrate through the three thousand miles of cable. "Right now. I'm right here with you, Emilia. I am holding your hand."

With shaking fingers, she clicked the attachment. The digital chime of the download felt like a thunderclap in the quiet room. Her eyes scanned the clinical, medical print, bypassing the charts and the blood counts until they hit the word.

Her breath hitched. A sob bright, jagged, and beautiful broke from her throat.

"**Luca...**" she choked out, the happy tears finally spilling over her dark cheeks. "**Babe... we're having a son.**"

Across the world, in a room overlooking the waking streets of Italy, Luca's joyful shout echoed off the marble walls. "**A son! Emilia, thank you... Grazie, amore mio!**" He sounded breathless, as if he had just run a marathon to get to her. "I love you so much. *Dio*, I wish I was there to wrap my arms around you. I wish I could feel him move."

They stayed on the line for hours as the sun began to bleed over the Tuscan hills and the moon hung high over D.C. The conversation drifted from the logistics of a blue-painted nursery to the poetry of a name, their voices weaving a cocoon of intimacy that defied the map. Luca began to speak to her belly through the phone, his Italian vowels a low, guttural vibration that seemed to soothe the very air around her.

Slowly, the silence of the D.C. night began to win. Amelia's responses grew shorter, her breathing deeper, until she finally drifted off right there on the sofa, the phone still pressed to the pillow near her ear.

Luca didn't hang up. He listened to the rhythm of her sleep, the soft, rhythmic puff of air that told him she was safe. He sat in the Italian dawn, thousands of miles away, but his soul was anchored to that velvet sofa in Washington.

"**I love you,**" he whispered into the silence, his voice a ghost in her ear. "**Rest now, my love.**"

He stayed on the line for another minute, watching the gray light hit the vineyards outside his window, counting the seconds until the world finally brought them back to the same time zone, and the same bed

At six months pregnant, Amelia felt a sharp, sudden pain one evening after work, just outside the Metro station near Chinatown. She stopped and felt a distressing warmth. She quickly found a nearby restroom and was horrified to discover she was bleeding.

She immediately called her doctor, who told her to go to the hospital emergency room, and then called Luca. They spoke the entire drive to the hospital, his voice a low, steady anchor of professional calm, guiding her until he could speak directly to the doctor handling her case.

She was lucky. It was a scare, not a miscarriage. The bleeding was due to a minor tear, and the baby was safe.

As soon as he hung up, Luca was already moving. He rushed to the Florence airport, trying to book the first flight. He could only secure an economy seat on a flight to New York that was about to board. He didn't hesitate. He took the ticket and, seven hours later, landed in New York, instantly catching a connecting domestic flight to D.C. His phone remained off for hours during the transatlantic flight.

Amelia spent a long, anxious night in the hospital, trying to reach him, assuming he was in surgery or busy. By morning, she was feeling much better. Livia was safe with Amelia's mother, allowing her to focus on healing.

At around 10:00 a.m., she heard a quiet knock on her hospital room door. She walked slowly and opened it. She stood frozen for a beat, then collapsed into Luca's tight embrace. He was unshaven, exhausted, and wearing the same clothes he'd rushed out in, but he was there.

After the embrace, they talked softly, privately, reclaiming the intimacy that distance had stolen. Luca took a quick shower in the hospital room, returning to a breakfast tray Amelia had ordered.

"No, babe. I don't want you to lift a finger," he insisted, though he devoured the food.

"Sweetie, I am not sick," she reassured him. "It was just a little blood. All the checkups were good. Our son is fine. I am okay. Don't worry."

After they ate, they took a taxi to Amelia's mother's house to pick up Livia. Her mother was shocked to see Luca.

"I didn't know you were coming!" she exclaimed.

"I didn't either," Luca replied, hugging her mother. "She called me, bleeding. I wanted to be here for my son, for her. I couldn't sleep if I didn't come."

Her mother hugged him and sighed, "Well, since you're here, here is your daughter. I was about to take her to Kindercare."

Luca laughed, taking Livia. "She is not going to daycare. Papa is here."

The week that followed was a masterclass in devotion, a period where the frantic pulse of the hospital scare settled into a deep, domestic hum. Luca didn't just inhabit the house in D.C.; he fortified it. He moved through the space with the quiet, efficient energy of a man who had spent his life in sterile rooms, now obsessed with making sure this particular room was a sanctuary.

Luca was a man of action, and in D.C., his mission was singular: total restoration for Emilia. Every morning, before the sun had even cleared the top of the Washington Monument, Luca was already up. Emilia would wake to the sound of him whispering to Livia in Italian, dressing her in soft layers for school.

When he returned from the school run, he was a whirlwind of care. He'd find Emilia trying to reach for a glass or a book, and he'd be there instantly. "No, *amore*," he'd say, his large, surgeon's hands gently pressing her back into the cushions. "Stay. The world can wait for you."

He turned the D.C. kitchen into a makeshift Tuscan trattoria. The house began to smell less like city life and more like **simmering San Marzano tomatoes, fresh basil, and the earthy, toasted scent of garlic.**

He didn't just cook; he engineered her nutrition. He prepared plates of iron-rich greens and perfectly seared proteins, bringing them to her on a tray as if she were royalty. Every evening ended the same way. He would sit at the edge of the bed, the scent of **lavender and cooling peppermint oil** filling the room as he took her swollen feet into his lap. His thumbs, strong and precise, worked away the tension of the city and the pregnancy.

"Luca, sweetie," Emilia would laugh, her voice a mix of adoration and slight exasperation as he hovered with a third pillow for her back. "I am not an invalid. I am just pregnant. I can actually walk to the kitchen by myself, I promise."

Luca would pause, his unshaven face softening into a weary, lopsided grin. He'd lean down, pressing a lingering kiss to the crown of her head, his breath warm against her hair. "In the hospital, I fix the hearts of strangers. Here, in this house, I am protecting *my* heart. You and our son. Let me be the doctor for once who doesn't have to leave."

The sight of the tall, strikingly handsome Italian doctor at Livia's preschool became the talk of the morning drop-off. He'd carry Livia on his shoulders, her tiny hands gripped in his dark hair, both of them laughing in a private language of "Ciao" and "Baci." For that one week, the Atlantic didn't exist. There was no "long-distance," no "time zones," and no "waiting for the phone to vibrate."

There was only the weight of his daughter on his shoulders, the secret of his son growing beneath Emilia's heart, and the quiet, fierce joy of a man who had crossed an ocean just to make sure his family could finally breathe easy

The unavoidable separation returned. By 5:00 p.m., Luca had to leave for the airport. While Livia was taking her afternoon nap, Luca began massaging Amelia's feet, his touch slow and restorative.

"Babe, I can't do this anymore," he murmured, his hands working magic on her tired ankles. "I talked to your doctor. I explained the situation and my professional opinion. He agreed with me: **you need to be on bedrest** for three months. No more teaching, no more stress."

He looked up at her, his eyes earnest. "So, for these next three months, I want to take care of you. I want you to be with me."

Amelia was tired of fighting. She was tired of the distance and the anxiety. She wanted the authority of his presence. "Okay, I will stay home," she softly uttered, surrendering the last vestiges of her independent resolve.

"Okay, then you and Livia will come to Italy," he continued. "I can buy you first-class tickets, so you will be comfortable and fine."

Amelia lifted his chin, forcing him to meet her gaze. "Darling, business is okay, but you have two children and a wife who is temporarily without a job. You have to be careful with your money." They both laughed, sharing an intimate embrace.

"Babe, do you think a week will be enough for you to be ready?" he asked, his voice low, tinged with a desperate hope that she might say *yes*, even though they both knew the complexity of her life at Howard.

Emilia looked at him, her eyes tracing the tired lines around his mouth the marks of a man who had flown across the world on a heartbeat's notice. She didn't answer immediately. She felt the heavy, rhythmic kick of their son against her ribs, a reminder of the life they were co-authoring in two different languages.

Luca saw the hesitation and moved toward her, his surgeon's instinct for decisive action taking over. "Okay, how about the 20th?" he said, his hands coming to rest on her shoulders. "That will give you more days. I've put insurance on the tickets so we can add more if you need them. But mind the clock, *amore* most airlines won't let you fly after seven months."

They shared a small, bittersweet laugh, a fragile shield against the reality of the calendar. But the laughter didn't reach their eyes.

The next morning arrived with a cold, grey light that felt far removed from the golden sun of Tuscany. The house was silent, save for the rhythmic hum of the refrigerator and the soft, shallow breathing of a sleeping toddler.

Luca moved like a shadow. He had packed his bag the night before, a task he performed with a heavy heart. He stood in the doorway of the nursery, watching Livia. She was sprawled across her bed, a tangle of dark curls and patterned pajamas, her favorite stuffed lion tucked under one arm.

He knelt by the crib, the scent of **baby powder and laundry detergent** filling his senses. He leaned in, pressing a ghost of a kiss to her small, perfect head. He moved with agonizing slowness, terrified of triggering her new habit the frantic, desperate clinging that had characterized their week together. Every time he had so much as put on his shoes lately, Livia had latched onto his leg, her tears a visceral protest against the ocean that always took her Papa away.

He retreated from the room, his chest tight, and found Emilia waiting in the hallway.

He pulled her into a fierce, wordless embrace. He buried his face in the crook of her neck, inhaling the **sweet, citrus scent of her hair**.

Emilia felt the scratch of his morning stubble against her skin and the solid, grounding pressure of his arms. She felt the son between them move, a restless stirring as if the baby, too, knew the departure was imminent.

"I will be counting the minutes until the 20th," he whispered, his voice cracking. "Don't lift anything. Don't stress. Just grow our boy."

He didn't look back as he stepped out into the humid D.C. morning. He couldn't. He climbed into the waiting car, the sound of the door closing echoing like a finality. As the taxi pulled away from the curb, Luca watched the house disappear in the rearview mirror, already mourning the warmth of the bed he had just left, his heart already halfway across the Atlantic, waiting for the 20th to bring the pieces of his soul back together.

The air in D.C. had turned crisp, carrying that specific end-of-fall scent: a mix of damp earth, dried oak leaves, and the faint, metallic chill of the Potomac River. The sky was a brilliant, bruised blue, and the Lincoln Memorial stood like a bone-white sentinel against the horizon.

Amelia walked slowly, her gait now a heavy, rhythmic sway. At almost seven months, her belly was a proud, high curve that seemed to announce her future before she even arrived. Beside her, the stroller clicked over the uneven joints of the sidewalk, pushed by her mother's steady hands. Inside, Livia was a bundle of pink fleece and soft snores.

They stopped at a vendor, the scent of sugary waffle cones and cold dairy cutting through the autumn chill. Amelia licked at her ice cream, the cold sweetness a brief distraction from the dull ache in her lower back.

"I'm going to miss my granddaughter," her mother said, her voice catching on the wind.

Amelia reached over, squeezing her mother's arm. "I know, Mama. But Italy and the U.S. aren't the separate planets they used to be. It's a seven-hour flight. That's shorter than a workday."

Her mother sighed, eyes fixed on the horizon where the Washington Monument pierced the sky. "And your boss? What is his attitude about you just... leaving?"

"I took my paid leave first," Amelia said, a small, mischievous laugh bubbling up. "When the government money runs out, I'll take leave without pay. He told me he'd hold my spot for a year, medical leave, family leave, whatever we have to call it. He's working with me."

Her mother stopped walking, her face tightening into the expression Amelia knew all too well. "You know your father. He doesn't like this. Moving thousands of miles to stay with a man you aren't even married to."

Amelia stopped, too. She turned, the weight of the baby shifting inside her like a restless sea. "How lucky I am, Mama," she said, her voice dropping into a low, fierce register. "He loves me. He loves Livia. Tell me, Mama, which man would do that? He wants to be closer to his family, yes, but he's built a place for us in the center of it."

She looked down at the stroller where Livia slept, oblivious to the borders being crossed for her sake. "Luca has never asked me "the question" never talked about the ring!, but he asked to be the father of my daughter. Tell me who does that? He loves her as if she were his own blood."

Her mother's eyes snapped toward her, sharp and piercing as a winter frost. "Don't you ever say that," she commanded, her voice trembling with sudden authority. "He adopted her. Livia *is* his. Do not break that boy's heart, Amelia. The world is full of sperm donors, but it is starving for real fathers."

The weight of the words hung in the air, heavier than the marble monuments surrounding them. A wave of nausea suddenly rolled through Amelia's stomach, the familiar, dizzying protest of a body that was no longer hers.

"Mama, wait," she gasped, tossing the remainder of her ice cream into a nearby wire bin. "Let's sit. I feel like I'm going to vomit."

Her mother quickly adjusted the blanket over Livia and guided Amelia to a stone bench. They sat in silence for a moment, watching the kaleidoscope of tourists. People from every corner of the globe were laughing, posing with peace signs in front of Lincoln's giant, stoic feet, and capturing memories they could take home in their pockets.

Amelia watched a young couple take a selfie, their joy radiating through the cold air. She felt a sudden, sharp pang of nostalgia for the city that had raised her the grand scale of it, the history carved into every stone.

"Oh, boy," she whispered, a watery laugh breaking through her nausea. "I am surely going to miss D.C."

Her mother let out a short, dry chuckle, bumping her shoulder against Amelia's. "Oh, well. Like you said... it's only seven hours from Italy."

They both laughed then, a shared, breathy sound that dissolved the tension. They leaned into each other, a huddle of three generations against the autumn wind, hugging tightly as the sun began to dip behind the Great Emancipator, casting long, golden shadows over the life they were about to leave behind.

Leonardo

Amelia arrived in Italy as the last amber leaves of autumn were being swept from the cobblestones by a sharp, northern wind. But inside the home Luca had prepared for them, the air was perpetually warm, smelling of beeswax candles and the faint, citrusy top-notes of his cologne.

By the time the December frost began to lace the window-panes, Amelia didn't just look pregnant; she looked monumental. At nearly seven months, her belly was a high, tight curve that seemed to defy gravity, making her appear as though she were "about to pop" weeks ahead of schedule. But it wasn't just the size, it was the **glow**. Her skin held a luminous, pearlescent quality, as if the new life inside her was a lamp she was carrying through the dim Tuscany winter. Her hair was thicker, her dark eyes brighter, and even the way she moved had changed a slow, regal sway that commanded the space around her.

The three months that followed were a blur of domestic grace. Luca, the man who had once lived for the adrenaline of the operating theater, began to perform a different kind of surgery: he carved out a life that put them first.

Every morning, the blue-gray light of the Roman winter would bleed through the shutters. Luca was always up first. Amelia would wake to the rhythmic hiss of the moka pot and the low, muffled sound of Luca coaxing Livia into her school coat. He didn't just "help"; he took over with a quiet, fierce devotion. He would press a kiss to Amelia's forehead, a lingering, warm seal that tasted of espresso and promise before whisking Livia away to school. Amelia would watch from the window as his tall, athletic frame stooped to hold the toddler's hand, the two of them navigating the narrow, winding *vicolo* like a scene from an old film.

Evenings were sacred choreography. Luca would return early, shedding his doctor's coat for an apron, his hands usually reserved for the precision of a scalpel now moving with the same grace over garlic and herbs. He refused to let Amelia stand for long.

"Just the tomatoes, *bella*," he would murmur, his voice vibrating against her spine as he pulled her into the curve of his chest.

She would sit on a high stool, her magnificent belly resting against the edge of the marble island, dicing San Marzano tomatoes while he stirred a reduction of olive oil and basil. The kitchen would fill with the intoxicating aroma of *Sugo* rich, herbaceous, and ancient. Sometimes, the cooking would stop entirely because a kiss would deepen, turning into a slow, swaying dance to the muffled sound of a neighbor's radio playing Italian jazz.

Then came December, and Italy transformed. The city didn't just decorate; it glowed.

Their first Italian Christmas was a tapestry of tradition. They walked through the *Piazza Navona*, the air thick with the smell of *frittelle* and roasted chestnuts crackling over open coals. Luca bought Livia a handmade wooden figurine from a stall, his eyes shining with a pride that had nothing to do with his medical degree and everything to do with the little girl calling him *Papà*.

On Christmas Eve, at the *Vigilia*, they enjoyed the Feast of the Seven Fishes. The table was a crowded masterpiece of salted cod, calamari, and linguine. As the bells of a nearby basilica began to toll for midnight mass, echoing through the heavy stone walls of the city, Luca sat behind Amelia on the sofa. He wrapped his large surgeon's hands over the mountain of her belly, his fingers spreading wide to encompass the life within. He felt the rhythmic, sturdy kicks of his unborn son, a frantic, joyful Morse code.

"He's restless," Luca whispered into the crook of her neck, his breath hitching. "He knows he's home."

Amelia leaned back, closing her eyes. The distance of D.C., the fear of her father's judgment, and the coldness of the airport all evaporated. There was only the taste of Panettone on her tongue, the sound of Livia's soft breathing in the next room, and the steady, unbreakable heartbeat of the man who had claimed them all.

Their world was no longer divided by an ocean. It was contained entirely within the four walls of an Italian home, blooming in the quiet, silver light of a winter that felt exactly like spring.

The Tuscany Oven

The Tuscan air was turning sweet with the first breath of spring, but for Amelia, time had slowed to a grueling crawl. At nine months, her body felt like a beautiful, overstretched instrument. Every step was a negotiation with gravity, and her "glow" had deepened into a flushed, weary heat.

Luca didn't want her going to the final clinic alone. He had called her from the hospital, his voice a mix of professional steel and paternal anxiety, asking her to push the appointment back for hours. He had a heart to repair one last valve to stitch before he could focus entirely on the new heart beating inside his love.

When he finally burst through the front door, still smelling of sterile scrub soap and the ghost of the hospital, he found her sitting on the edge of the sofa. She looked exhausted, her eyes rimmed with the red of unshed tears.

Luca dropped to his knees before her. He didn't say a word at first; he simply leaned his forehead against the mountain of her belly, closing his eyes to listen to the frantic, healthy thrum of his son. He reached up, his large, warm palms cupping her face as if checking for a fever.

"Bella... What is going on? Are you okay?"

A single tear tracked down Amelia's cheek. "I'm just so tired, Luca. I can't do anything. By my math, he was supposed to be here last week. I feel like I'm failing at the finish line."

Luca didn't offer a medical lecture. He leaned in, pressing a soft, lingering kiss to her lips, and used his thumb to wipe the salt from her skin. "My love, look at me," he whispered. "The best cakes are baked slowly, with the most care..."

Before he could finish the metaphor, Amelia let out a watery, jagged laugh. "So that's it? I'm just an oven now?"

Luca's bark of a laugh filled the room. With the effortless strength of a man who spent his days lifting the weight of the world, he scooped her up. He lifted her belly and all as if she weighed nothing, his broad shoulders easily supporting her.

"No," he grinned, his eyes dancing with a wicked Italian charm. "You are not *anyone's* oven. You are *my* oven. How about that?"

He carried her to the bed, laying her back against the pillows as if she were made of glass. He spent the next twenty minutes massaging her swollen feet, his surgeon's thumbs finding every point of tension until her breathing leveled out and a smile finally touched her lips. He kissed her one last time, grabbed his bag, and whispered, "I will see you as soon as I fix this heart."

Amelia slept for two hours, a heavy, dreamless slumber. When she woke, she moved through the house in a daze, pulling on a light coat to walk the short distance to Livia's school.

The walk back was a blur of discomfort. Livia skipped beside her, her voice a "sewing machine" of frantic energy, stitching together Italian and English in a way that only a two-year-old could. "Look, Mamma! *Il sole!* The sun is big like your belly!" Amelia could only manage a strained, "Yes, baby. Okay."

Inside the house, Livia immediately looked around, her lower lip pouting. "Where is Dad?" "He'll be here soon, honey," Amelia promised, handing her a snack.

Just then, the door swung open. Luca stood there, looking triumphant, holding a bouquet of wild Tuscan flowers in one hand and a thermal container in the other.

"Flowers for the lady," he announced, handing the blooms to Amelia, "and for my little princess..." he produced a tub of cream-colored bliss.

“Luca Ice cream! Bella too much sugar" Amelia doesn't approve of the ice cream moment.

Luca wagged a finger, his hand moving in that classic, rhythmic Italian gesture. "Bella, this is not 'ice cream.' This is *Gelato*. We are in Italy now. We enjoy our food; our food is art, not poison!"

They both laughed, the tension of the day dissolving as they watched Livia dive into the gelato with messy, joyful abandon. Luca caught Amelia’s eye, his expression softening. "Don't worry about the delay. I called the doctor; he’s waiting for us. I was running a bit late with the surgery, which is why I didn't answer your messages. I didn't want to talk until I knew the patient was safe."

The departure was a practiced routine. Luca buckled Livia into the back of the car, double-checking the straps with a father’s obsessive care, before opening the passenger door for Amelia with a courtly bow.

As he slid into the driver’s seat, he glanced into the rearview mirror. "Are you ready, Livia? Ready to go see your brother on the big screen?" "*Sì, Papà! Andiamo!*" Livia shouted.

They began to chatter in rapid-fire Italian, the musical syllables filling the car. Amelia sat back, a mock-pout on her lips as she looked at them. "Excuse me? Do you see the American sitting right here? I’m being left out of the loop."

Luca threw her a wink as he shifted the car into gear, the tires crunching over the gravel driveway. "Too bad, darling. You better learn fast, or soon we will be three people speaking the language of music and one... *Americano.*"

The car moved onto the winding Tuscan road, flanked by cypress trees and the golden light of the setting sun. They laughed, their voices weaving together two languages, one family moving toward the final heartbeat of their journey.

The Tuscan sun was a lazy, golden coin slipping behind the cypress trees as they did their fifth lap around the villa's stone perimeter. Emilia was eight days past her due date, and her son seemed perfectly content to remain nestled within her, cocooned away from the world.

"Walking is supposed to be the trick, Emilia," Luca said, his arm hooked firmly around her waist, serving as a steady, human railing. "Gravity is a doctor's best friend."

Emilia let out a heavy, theatrical sigh, her hand resting on the magnificent, low-hanging swell of her belly. The gravel crunched rhythmically beneath her feet. "Luca, honey, this walking is doing nothing but making my ankles vanish into thin air. You know..." She glanced at him with a mischievous, tired glint in her eyes. "I read in a medical journal one of the fancy ones you keep on your nightstand that we could just go upstairs and make love. Hard. They say that's the *real* way to jumpstart the heart."

Luca let out a rich, booming laugh that echoed off the ancient stone walls of the farmhouse. "Mmm, nooo," he teased, holding up his hands in mock retreat. "I feel like I would be touching my son's forehead. I am a cardiothoracic surgeon, *bella*, but even I have boundaries."

"Coward," she joked, leaning into his warmth.

They paused by the outdoor table where a bowl of **tart lemon granita** sat melting.

The icy crystals felt like lightning on her tongue, sharp and refreshing against the lingering afternoon heat.

The air was thick with the aroma of **crushed rosemary and dry earth**, the quintessential perfume of a Tuscan evening.

Luca took a bite of the ice, his expression suddenly turning wistful. "I miss Livia. It's only been three days since Sofia took her, but the house feels... hollow."

Emilia snorted, leaning her head on his shoulder. "Trust me, she doesn't miss us for a second. With Auntie Sofia, that child is probably diving headfirst into gelato and staying up until the moon is high. She's living her best life while we're out here dragging our feet."

They started toward the car for a short drive to the village, but Emilia stopped dead. Her hand gripped Luca's forearm with a strength that made him wince. A sharp, jagged line of pain radiated across her lower back, a tightening that felt final.

"Emilia? *Cara?*" Luca was instantly in 'Doctor Mode,' his hand sliding to her pulse point, his eyes scanning her face for the signs of true labor.

She waited for the wave to pass, her eyes locked onto his, fierce and unyielding. "By the way," she gritted out as the contraction subsided, "no matter what happens tonight or tomorrow... I don't want to have him by the knife. No C-section unless it's a total emergency, Luca. I want to feel him come into this world on his own terms."

Luca started to nod, his professional mind already calculating the variables of a late-term delivery. "Well, as a doctor, if the fetal distress levels"

"No," she interrupted, pointing a firm finger at his chest, a weary but defiant smile on her face. "Don't answer me as a doctor. Answer me as *my man*."

Luca paused, the setting sun catching the silver at his temples and the raw adoration in his gaze. He laughed softly, pulling her hand to his lips and kissing her knuckles. "Okay, okay. I hear you. I promise. I hope we wouldn't get there anyway this boy is a fighter, just like his mother."

He guided her toward the car, opening the door with a flourish and helping her navigate the seat with the tenderness of someone handling a priceless relic. As they drove back up the winding, poppy-lined driveway, the sky bled into a spectacular display of violet and burnt orange. It was a promising Tuscan sun seta sky that looked ready to welcome a new life into the fold.

The Contract of Trust

The delivery room, once filled with the soft hum of anticipation and Italian lullabies, had suddenly turned cold and clinical. The rhythmic *thump-thump* of the fetal monitor, the sound that had been their North Star for nine months had begun to stutter. It was no longer a gallop; it was a fading echo.

Amelia lay gripped by a contraction that felt like a tectonic shift in her spine. Sweat soaked her hair, plastering it to her forehead in dark, jagged streaks. She looked up at Luca, her eyes wild with a mixture of pain and a haunting memory.

"Babe," she gasped, her fingers digging into his hand so hard her knuckles turned white. "Remember... Remember Livia? We waited. They told me then, too... but we waited, and she came. I can do this. I don't want the surgery. Don't let them cut me, Luca. Please."

Luca didn't look at the nurses. He didn't look at the attending physician. His eyes were locked on the monitor, his surgical brain involuntarily calculating the decelerations in the baby's heart rate. The "Doctor" in him saw the danger; the "Man" in him felt his soul fracturing.

He leaned down, his face inches from hers, his own eyes brimming with hot, silent tears.

"Amelia, look at me," he whispered, his voice trembling but anchored by a terrifying certainty. "I need you to listen. I need you in my life. I need Livia to have her mother, and I need this boy to have his breath."

"I can push," she cried out, a jagged, desperate sound. "Just one more hour, Luca. Give me an hour!"

"We don't have an hour," Luca said, and for the first time, his voice carried the absolute authority of the operating theater. "The baby's heart is slowing, Amelia. If we wait, I lose both of you. I am your man, and he is your doctor, and we will never do anything that isn't right for your soul. But right now... I am signing the papers."

"No... Luca, no," she sobbed, but her protest was drowned out by a fresh wave of agony. She felt like she was being torn apart from the inside. "I want to push! I have to push!"

"Do not push!"

The command came from both Luca and the attending doctor in a sharp, simultaneous bark. They both stared at the monitor. The green line was dipping a valley that didn't want to become a mountain again. The baby was tired. The cord was likely compressed.

"Get her prepped! Now!" the doctor shouted.

The room exploded into motion. The brakes on the bed were kicked loose with a metallic *clack*. Nurses swarmed, moving with the practiced, lethal efficiency of an emergency team.

"I'm sorry, *Mama Livia*," Luca whispered, leaning over her as the bed began to roll toward the double doors of the emergency theater. He was already reaching for a surgical mask, his face a mask of grief and duty. "I'm so sorry, but I have to save you. I will be right there. I will protect you. Just trust me. Trust your doctor."

Amelia's scream echoed down the sterile hallway, a raw, primal sound of a mother fighting for a chance she wasn't being given. As the bright, unforgiving lights of the operating room swallowed her, the last thing she saw was Luca, the man who loved her enough to break her heart so he could keep her alive.

Leonardo was born *"sotto il coltello"* under the knife a necessary C-section.

Exhaustion defined the room. When the doctor lifted their son, Luca looked at the boy, his face alight with wonder, and called his name: "Leonardo... **Leo**. Son, welcome to Italy." He then turned to Amelia, who was pale and spent.

As he reached for her, Luca noticed something was wrong. Amelia avoided his gaze. Her tears were not tears of joy, but of profound, deep depletion.

"Amelia," Luca asked, his voice low, the professional doctor emerging through the husband's fear. "Tell me how exactly you feel."

"I am not a bad mother," she cried out, the pain of the long, failed labor overwhelming her. "After all that pain, I don't want to see him. I can't."

Luca understood immediately. The long labor, the emergency surgery, the exhaustion she was suffering from the devastating onset of **postpartum psychosis**, a raw severance from reality and her child.

He gently hugged her. "I am here. You don't have to do anything you don't want to do. You have to heal. Every step, I will be with you."

After three days, they came home. Luca was suddenly faced with the immense challenge of juggling two young children, a demanding surgical career, and a wife who was emotionally incapacitated. He made the only call he could.

"Sofia, if you would help me with Livia for a couple of weeks, until Amelia feels better, I will appreciate it, *sorella*," he pleaded. Sofia promised she would be there the next morning.

Through intensive therapy for Amelia and endless hours of gentle, constant love from Luca, she slowly began the agonizing process of healing and reconnection. Sofia drove down every weekend, bringing Livia to play with her brother, deepening the family bond.

The two months following Leonardo's birth had been a long, silent winter inside the stone walls of their Tuscan villa. Outside, the world was waking up to a vibrant spring, but inside, the air was heavy with the clinical scent of antiseptic and the unsaid weight of a mother's distant heart.

Luca moved through the house with a ghost-like precision. He was a man who lived by the rhythm of heartbeats, but the one he was currently monitoring was the most fragile he had ever encountered. He walked a razor-thin line, a tightrope stretched between being the world-class surgeon who understood the chemical storm in his mother of his kids's mind, and the lover who just wanted to see a spark of the woman who had captivated him on a train in South Africa.

Every morning, Luca would sit in the armchair across from the bed, watching Emilia. She wasn't the professor from Howard who could command a room with a single sentence; she was a pale shadow, her eyes fixed on the distant hills.

In the quiet hours of the night, while he fed Leo a bottle and listened to the baby's soft, greedy gulps, Luca's mind would betray him. He played the scene in the delivery room over and over like a surgical reel. *Did I move too fast? Did I break her spirit to save her body?* The doctor knew the C-section was necessary, but the man felt like a traitor. He blamed himself for the "knife" that had severed the primal connection between Emilia and her son.

He curated her life with obsessive care. He didn't just bring her medication; he brought it with a sprig of fresh jasmine and a glass of water from the mountain spring. He didn't push her to hold Leo. He didn't guilt her. He protected her from the pressure of "motherhood" as if it were an infection.

"Babe," he whispered one evening, kneeling by her feet. The sun was dipping, casting long, amber shadows across the terracotta floor. He took her hands once so expressive, now so still and pressed them to his face.

"Don't rush," he murmured, his voice a low vibration. "The world isn't going anywhere. We are not going anywhere. Leo... he is safe. He is growing. He is waiting for you, but he is in no hurry. And neither am I."

He began to massage her hands, his fingers finding the tension points he had memorized. He wanted to ground her back into her body, to remind her that she was still there, beneath the fog of the psychosis.

Luca had stopped wearing his hospital scrubs at home, opting instead for the soft cashmere sweaters she used to love. He wanted to smell like *her* Luca, not the man who had authorized the surgery.

The challenge was the "Zero." Leo would cry in the next room, a healthy, vigorous sound, and Emilia wouldn't even flinch. To the world, it looked like coldness; to Luca, it looked like a wound.

"Luca," she said, her voice finally breaking the silence, dry and hollow. "You should have let me push. You took him from me before I could say goodbye to the version of me that was a good mother."

He felt a sharp, jagged pain in his chest, the kind no surgery could fix. " I had to, so I wouldn't have to say goodbye to you, Emilia," he replied, his eyes filling with a fierce, protective light. "I am the doctor, remember? And your heart is just bruised. It isn't broken. We are just in a long tunnel, but the train is still moving."

He leaned in and kissed her forehead, a lingering, sacred touch. He would carry the weight of both children, the house, and his career until her legs were strong enough to stand again. He would be the bridge over the Atlantic of her mind, waiting patiently for the day she could finally reach out and pull her son to her breast. He was her man first, her doctor second, and her anchor always even when the sea was at its darkest

The Hollow Echo

The Tuscany hills were mocking her. They rolled out in endless waves of emerald and gold, blooming with a vibrant life that Amelia felt she could no longer touch.

She was driving the small silver car too fast, the winding roads blurred by a film of tears she couldn't stop. She finally pulled over at a high scenic overlook, a "heel" of a hill that looked out over a valley of olive groves. She killed the engine, and the silence that rushed into the car was deafening.

Then, she broke.

It wasn't a soft cry; it was a jagged, primal mourning. She leaned her forehead against the steering wheel, the horn letting out a short, pathetic beep that vanished into the wind. She felt like a house that had been hollowed out, leaving only the structural beams.

With trembling hands, she dialed the only person who had known her before she was "Mamma."

"Mama?" her voice was a broken whisper.

"Amelia?, what is it?"

"I don't know how to do this," Amelia sobbed into the phone, her eyes fixed on the distant horizon. "I look at Leo... he's beautiful, Mama. He has Luca's eyes. But when I hold him, I feel like I'm holding a stranger. I don't hate him... God, I could never hate him but I can't find the bridge to love him. It's like there's a wall of glass between us."

She took a shuddering breath, the bitterness finally leaking out. "And I blame Luca. I look at the scar on my stomach and I see his signature. He forced me, Mama. He took the one thing I had left my choice. He played the doctor when I needed my best friend, and now I feel like I'm broken in two."

There was a long silence on the other end of the line. Then, her mother's voice came through, steady and thick with a different kind of wisdom.

"Amelia, listen to me. You are standing in a dark room, but you are not alone. You think that scar is a mark of failure? It is a mark of a man who loved you enough to take the blame so you could stay alive. Look at what he does, *my daughter*. He works all day, he comes home and holds Livia, he changes Leo, he cooks, he watches you sleep with eyes that would melt stone. He is loving you through your silence. He is holding the roof up while you are down in the cellar."

Amelia leaned back, the cool air from the open window hitting her damp face. "He's too perfect, Mama. It makes me feel even more disappeared."

"You haven't disappeared," her mother whispered. "You are just resting. Give yourself grace. The love isn't gone; it's just under the snow. Wait for the thaw."

They talked for a long time, the sun beginning to dip and cast long, violet shadows over the vines. When she hung up, Amelia stepped out of the car. Her legs felt heavy, but she began to walk. She picked a few wild poppies, their red petals as bright as blood, and said a quiet *"Buongiorno"* to an elderly couple walking a golden retriever. They smiled back a simple, human connection that felt like a stitch in her heart.

She got back into the car and turned the radio up. A soaring Italian ballad filled the cabin. Amelia began to sing loud, off-key, and butcher the lyrics, her voice cracking. She started to laugh through her tears, a manic, beautiful sound that echoed her mother's strength.

She looked at herself in the side mirror. Her eyes were red, her hair a mess, and her soul was bruised. But she looked at her reflection and made a silent, fierce vow.

"I will find my way back," she whispered to the woman in the glass. "I will find the bridge."

She shifted into gear and drove toward home, the music screaming into the Tuscan twilight, a woman fighting her way out of the dark.

The Nursery Door

The rain was a rhythmic, drumming melancholy against the glass, blurring the Tuscan landscape into a smear of grey and deep emerald. Inside the villa, the air was cool and smelled of damp earth and old stone. Luca was slumped in a deep, exhausted sleep beside her, his chest rising and falling with the heavy cadence of a man who had been carrying the weight of three lives on his shoulders for sixty days.

Amelia sat up slowly, her eyes tracking the droplets as they raced down the pane, drip by drip. The silence in her mind was louder than the rain. She felt hollow, a vessel that had been emptied and forgotten.

Then, the silence was pierced.

From the room across the hall came a thin, sharp wail. **Leo.**

Amelia looked at Luca. He didn't stir; his body remained anchored by a fatigue that bordered on a trance. For the first time in two months, Amelia didn't wait for him to wake up. . She stood up, her feet cold against the terracotta floor, and drifted toward the nursery like a ghost.

She stood at the threshold, her hand hovering near the frame. The room was dim, lit only by a tiny amber nightlight. She watched the small, rhythmic struggle of her son the way he tried to turn his head, his tiny fists bunching up against the air as he cried for a comfort he hadn't yet truly known from her.

He looked so small in the center of the large crib. Fragile. In the shadows, his skin glowed with a terrifying, beautiful purity. The air in the room was sweet **warm milk and baby skin** a scent that usually triggered a primal rush, but for her, it had felt like a threat. Until tonight.

She walked closer, her breath catching in her throat. Every instinct told her to turn back to the safety of her numbness, but the sound of his crying was beginning to grate against the wall she had built.

She reached for the bottle on the warmer. Her movements were stiff, clinical. She leaned over the crib and positioned the nipple in his mouth, careful desperately careful not to let her skin touch his. She didn't want to feel the heat of him; she wasn't ready for the electricity of a son's touch.

Leo latched on. The room fell silent, save for the rhythmic **gulp-pause-gulp** of his feeding.

As she held the bottle, watching his long lashes flutter against his cheeks, a jagged, painful emotion began to push through the soil of her heart. It wasn't joy not yet but it was **pity**. A profound, aching sorrow for this innocent creature who had been born "under the knife" into a world where his mother was a stranger. He was so pure, so unaware of the tragedy of his arrival.

The seed was planted. It was a tiny, sharp thing, drawing blood as it took root.

Once he fell back into a milk-drunk stupor, his tiny mouth falling open in a sigh, Amelia pulled the bottle away and backed out of the room. She didn't look back.

She climbed back into bed beside the still-sleeping Luca. She closed her eyes, and for the first time since the surgery, the rain didn't sound like a warning. It sounded like a beginning. She drifted into a sleep that felt, for the very first time, like rest

The next day Amelia returned from a therapy session. The house was quiet. She found Luca asleep on the sofa, utterly exhausted, with Leo nestled softly asleep on his chest.

Amelia paused in the doorway. A wave of unexpected, unbidden emotion a profound **strike of love** entered her soul for the first time since Leo was born. She saw not a demanding infant, but her son, protected by the man she loved.

She quietly moved to the sofa, gently lifting Leo from his father's chest. For the past two months, she had done little more than breastfeed him, but now, as she held him, **rocking him slowly**, she felt an intense, immediate bond.

Luca woke, his eyes heavy with sleep. He blinked once, twice, before realizing what he was seeing: Amelia holding their son, truly holding him, with love. He offered to take Leo. "I can take him, babe."

Amelia kissed Leo's head, tears of true, pure joy finally tracing paths down her cheeks. "It's okay. I felt something I have never felt. And I want it to last forever. Leo, I am sorry, love. I love you."

Luca's own tears came then, silent and profound, watching his wife finally connect with the boy he had named "Lion." It was the first time he had seen his son held by his mother with such deep, maternal love. The long night of fear and separation was finally over.

The Slow Thaw: A Season of Small Victories

The spring rains had given way to a Tuscan summer that felt earned rather than merely arrived. The time the brutal Italian August arrived, the Tuscan hills were bleached gold by the sun. It had been exactly a year since Leo's traumatic entrance in February, and the calendar was ticking toward August 15th Ferragosto (*a major italian national holiday celebrated on his birthday, that marking the peak of summer and the catholic feast of the assumption of Mary*), which was also Luca's 40th birthday.

The villa had been a place of quiet, careful restoration a long, slow climb out of a valley that had once seemed bottomless. Healing, they discovered, didn't happen in a sudden burst of sunlight; it happened in the quiet, mundane moments where the "seed" Amelia planted on that rainy night finally began to push through the soil.

Leo a sturdy, bright-eyed boy with Luca's defiant chin and Amelia's soulful, deep-set eyes. The "Zero" had slowly evolved into a "One." It started with a tentative touch, then a shared bath, and finally, the morning Emilia woke up and reached for him before Luca could even get out of bed.

Seeing Leo perched on a blanket in the grass, his chubby legs kicking at the clover, no longer felt like a reminder of a trauma. He was a person now, not just a clinical outcome. The house was no longer a tomb of whispered conversations. It was filled with the rhythmic **jingle-clack** of baby toys and the high-pitched, melodic babble of a boy discovering his own voice.

As Amelia reclaimed her strength and her bond with Leo, the "Doctor" in Luca finally began to step back, allowing the "Man" to breathe again. The hyper-vigilance that had carved hollows beneath his eyes started to fade. For the first time since the "knife," Luca felt he could leave the villa for more than an hour without the world collapsing.

On Saturday afternoons, the scent of **freshly cut grass and leather cleats** replaced the smell of medicinal lavender.

Luca returned to the local soccer pitch with his old friends. He threw himself into the game with a primal intensity, the sweat stinging his eyes and the physical exertion acting as a purge for the months of stored-up anxiety.

Standing on the pitch, his lungs burning and his shins bruised, he felt like a human being again not just a protector, not just a surgeon, but a man who was allowed to play, to laugh, and to miss his family from a distance of a few miles rather than a few rooms.

When he would return home, dusty and smelling of the outdoors, he'd find Amelia on the terrace. She was usually reading a book on African-American history, with Leo napping in a bassinet beside her, his small hand occasionally twitching in his sleep.

"How was the game, *calciatore*?" she'd ask, her voice warm, the shadows in her eyes finally retreating.

"We lost," Luca would laugh, leaning over to kiss her a French kiss, one that tasted of salt and returning life. "But I think I'm winning at home."

They were no longer just survivors of a crisis; they were a family in a new kind of transit moving toward a horizon that didn't feel like a threat. With Sofia taking Livia to her house more frequently and the rhythm of their life stabilizing, the heavy weight of the past year began to feel like a story they had survived together.

But as the calendar turned toward the end of the month, Luca realized another milestone was approaching one that felt heavier and more significant than any soccer match or medical checkup. His own birthday was on the horizon, the first one he would celebrate as a father of two, in a house that finally felt like it belonged to them all.

Amelia, a full-time mother, had embraced the *dolce vita*. She continued her therapy sessions, but the easy rhythm of life in Italy was a powerful balm. She'd picked up enough Italian to navigate the local *mercato* alone, a small victory that filled her with pride. She filled her quiet moments with a new passion: writing a culinary book she jokingly called *Not So Italian*. Luca would laugh at the title, yet he meticulously read every page, becoming her unofficial, unpaid editor. The family was whole, knit together by the quiet fabric of shared days and nights.

The FaceTime call flickered to life, the screen filling with Sofia's mischievous grin and the backdrop of a sleek Milanese apartment. On the other side, Amelia sat on the terrace in Tuscany, the late afternoon sun casting a warm, honeyed glow over her face. In the background, the soft, rhythmic sound of Leo's babbling served as a gentle soundtrack to their conspiracy.

"Sofia, I need your brain," Amelia started, leaning into the camera. "Luca's big day is approaching, and after the year we've had... I want to give him something that isn't a doctor's pager or a medical journal. What would your brother truly love?"

Sofia leaned back, swirling a glass of deep red wine that caught the light like a ruby. "The big day is in ten days. **Ferragosto**. The peak of the Italian summer. To get the 'Doctor' to his own surprise party without him realizing the whole family is already there? That is the trick."

She didn't hesitate. "He loves our grandmother's farmhouse, the *nonna's* old place in the hills. He spent his summers there as a boy, skinning his knees and climbing olive trees. He will be happiest there, where the air smells of wild thyme and woodsmoke. Do you want me to help you arrange a surprise?"

Amelia's face lit up, the first spark of genuine excitement she'd felt in months. "Yes. Let's do it."

For the next forty-eight hours, the two women became architects of a beautiful deception. Their FaceTime calls were hushed, clandestine meetings woven across phone lines between Milan and the Tuscan hills. While Luca was at the hospital, his mind occupied with valves and vessels, Amelia and Sofia were coordinating catering, secret arrivals, and the delicate art of the "lure."

They decided on a plan that played on Luca's greatest weakness: his fierce, protective devotion to his family.

The following evening, as Luca sat on the patio trying to unwind with a glass of sparkling water, his phone buzzed. It was Sofia.

Amelia watched from the kitchen, holding her breath as she overheard the "distress" in Sofia's voice.

"Luca, *fratello*, I am in a complete bind," Sofia feigned a panicked sigh. "A massive customer a buyer from a boutique in Rome is coming to the farmhouse tomorrow to collect a huge order of the private reserve olive oil. I'm stuck here in Milan with a broken-down car and a meeting I can't leave. I can't make the drive. Please, could you go? Just to unlock the cellar and oversee the hand-off?"

Luca rubbed his temple, his professional exhaustion battling his sense of duty. "Sofia, tomorrow?

"Please, Luca. It's the grandmother's legacy. I can't lose this account."

Amelia stepped out, playing her part with an Oscar-worthy nonchalance. "Babe, go. It's a beautiful drive, and the farmhouse air will do you good. Take the morning off. I'll be fine here with Leo."

Luca looked from his sister's desperate face on the screen to his wife's encouraging smile. He had no idea that at that very moment, his cousins were already icing down the Prosecco .

"Fine," Luca sighed, a small smile finally breaking through. "I'll go. For the oil. And for *nonna*."

Sofia winked at the camera just before the line went dead. The trap was set. The "Doctor" was heading home, and he had no idea that the heart he was about to encounter wasn't on a surgical table it was the beating, joyous heart of the family he had fought so hard to keep together.

While in the kitchen Amelia called Sofia for the laugh. Amelia smiled, a genuine spark finally touching her eyes. "He thinks we are having a quiet dinner for two at the villa in the hills. Here is the plan: I'll tell him I'm taking the kids to your house early that afternoon so we can 'test out' some new toys you bought for them. You pick us up at 2:00 PM."

"And then?" Sofia prompted.

"Then, you keep the kids at your place while a private car picks me up from your house to take me to the venue," Amelia explained. "Luca will drive himself from our house, thinking he's meeting me there for a romantic date. After the party, we'll all pile into his car to drive home together. He won't suspect a thing if he thinks the kids are already settled with you for the night."

Sofia toasted her glass against Amelia's. "Perfect. The 'Americano' is becoming a master of Italian shadows."

On his birthday Sofia called " hi bro, Just a reminder, the buys will be there by 10:30 am"

"Sof, you know it's my birthday," Luca complained, "I just want to sleep and be home with my kids. can they come after lunch?"

Sofia adopted a tone of near-defeat. "I don't know what to do anymore. I think we should just sell the farm house. You're never there, and I can't keep up with the work."

"Hey! Hey, hey!" Luca immediately relented. "It's okay. I will go and deal with the oil. How about that?"

Sofia, hiding a triumphant smile, quickly hung up and called Amelia. The plan was afoot.

Next day Luca woke to find no fanfare, no special breakfast Amelia simply kissed him and handed him his usual cup of coffee. He was instantly disappointed, though he tried to rationalize it: *Two kids, a new baby, and all the house work... she's tired.*

He kissed her goodbye, leaving without even a "Happy Birthday" from his *Bella*. All the way through the winding Tuscan roads, Sofia called him.

"What now?" he snapped, his voice tight with disappointment. "I'm driving there."

"Brother," Sofia asked, her voice careful, "are you okay? Do you want the truth or a lie?"

"Truth, Sofia," he sighed.

"I know this is childish, but it's my birthday, and Amelia just... forgot."

Sofia pretended to sound indifferent. "Oh, well. You're a father of two now. There are lots of things more important than your birthday." She smoothly transitioned. "By the way, can you please stop at the store and pick up some light bulbs? A few don't work in the main house."

"Sof, are you kidding me, ?" he groaned.

"Nope. Call me when you get there."

"Tell your people I wouldn't make there by 10:30"

"Do not worry, they will understand, drive safe thanks"

Luca put on his favorite music, a sweeping Italian opera, and settled into the drive. The sadness lingered, but the sheer beauty of the landscape was an antidote. The drive moved slowly, transitioning from the bustling city traffic to the **slow, majestic curves of the mountains**, whose ancient forms held the story of his family. The air was rich with the scent of **pine and sun-drenched stone**.

As soon as he arrived, he parked and walked toward the stone farmhouse. He opened the main door and stopped dead.

The ancient, **sun-baked stone farmhouse**, usually a haven of quiet reflection, now thrummed with a suppressed, electric energy. Luca, pulling up the winding gravel path, noticed nothing amiss, his mind still clouded by Amelia's apparent forgetfulness. The scent of **wild rosemary and distant woodsmoke** hung in the air, a familiar comfort. He parked, the car engine ticking softly in the stillness, and walked toward the heavy oak door. His heart felt a peculiar mix of longing for his family and the dull throb of disappointment.

He pushed the door open, stepping from the quiet afternoon light into a sudden, blinding burst of sound and color.

"**SURPRISE!**"

The roar was instantaneous and overwhelming, a joyous cacophony of voices that seemed to shake the very rafters of the old farmhouse. His entire family was there cousins he hadn't seen in months, boisterous aunts whose laughter was like music, dignified uncles, and then, his eyes found them: **Livia, a tiny whirlwind in a bright dress**, clapping her hands, and **Sofia, radiant with mischief**, her arm linked with Amelia's.

Luca froze on the threshold, a man utterly undone. The world spun for a beat, the sadness of his drive utterly vaporized, replaced by a wave so potent it stole his breath. He simply sat down on the ancient, cool stone, a **gasp of pure, unadulterated joy** leaving his chest, his eyes wide, glistening, taking in every single beaming face. The room was festooned with simple, rustic decorations garlands of fresh olive branches and white paper lanterns casting a soft glow. The long wooden tables were laden with the feast of a thousand mothers: platters of **cured Tuscan meats, bowls of vibrant green pasta salads, crusty bread, and pitchers of local red wine**.

He finally stood, his legs a little unsteady from the emotional shock, his gaze locking onto Amelia. She looked breathtaking, her eyes sparkling with triumphant love. He walked straight to her, oblivious to anyone else, and pulled her into a long, possessive hug, a fierce embrace that communicated months of unspoken affection and gratitude. His lips met hers in a **profound, soul-deep kiss**, erasing every moment of doubt, every mile of separation.

When they finally broke apart, both breathless, Luca chuckled, a joyous, disbelieving sound. "Darling," he confessed, leaning his forehead against hers, "I called Sofia on the way here to complain that you didn't care about my day!" He turned to his sister, still laughing, a newfound lightness in his voice. "Sof, why didn't you tell me? You let me suffer!"

Sofia, her face alight with the satisfaction of a perfectly executed plan, simply smiled brightly. "I was waiting for this exact moment, brother. Every single reaction was worth it." The warmth of her gaze wrapped around them all, a testament to the enduring, unbreakable bonds of their Italian family. The celebration had truly begun.

They enjoyed a long, beautiful day together, filled with the **rich, comforting cacophony of an Italian family gathering**. As evening descended, they drove back to the city, the farm house lit only by the distant wash of starlight. Sofia and her husband stayed behind, promising to enjoy the country air for a few more days.

The Stars of Forever

As they drove away from the farmhouse, the vibrant, joyous waves of family laughter slowly faded, swallowed by the deepening twilight. The boisterous energy of the birthday party receded, replaced by the soft, **peaceful hum of the road** and the quiet, contented sighs of their sleeping children in the backseats. Luca glanced into the rearview mirror, his gaze sweeping over his son and daughter, their small faces serene in slumber. Livia's hand was curled near her cheek, a delicate petal; Leo's was a tiny, innocent fist near his mouth.

He reached for Amelia's hand, lacing his fingers through hers, the warmth of her touch a grounding anchor in the rush of his emotions. The car began to climb, winding through the **ancient Tuscan hills**, leaving the last distant lights of the village behind. The air grew cooler, carrying the elusive scent of **cypress, damp earth, and night-blooming jasmine**. Above them, the sky deepened to an inky velvet, and then, as if a celestial curtain had been pulled back, a **million brilliant stars** exploded into view, scattered across the vast expanse like scattered diamonds. They were utterly alone, suspended between the silent earth and the shimmering cosmos.

Luca pulled the car over, not quite to the side of the road, but deliberately into a small, secluded turn-off, nestled under the protective silhouette of a cluster of **gnarled olive trees**. He cut the engine. The sudden silence was profound, broken only by the gentle chirping of crickets and the distant hoot of an owl.

He turned to Amelia, his eyes, usually so intense, now glistening with unshed tears, reflecting the starlight. The raw emotion was a palpable thing, **racking his strong frame**.

"Amelia," he began, his voice low, trembling, filled with a vulnerability she had rarely witnessed. "My **Perfect Stranger**." He took a deep, shuddering breath. "You have stolen my heart, *Bella*. I have no control over it. You came into my life like a storm and a sunrise all at once, and you made me change." He squeezed her hand, his confession pouring out under the vast, silent sky. "Before you, I was a mess, a lost boy using women as a temporary port, never truly docking. I was a bad boy, living a life of surface connections."

He looked directly into her soul, his gaze unwavering. "You are my **Love in Transit**," he whispered, "and my last stop, my only destination, is finally you."

He paused, then unbuckled his seatbelt. "Wait here," he murmured, his voice husky.

He stepped out of the car, his silhouette momentarily blocking the starlight, and walked to one of the ancient olive trees. With a deliberate, tender hand, he plucked two fresh, silvery-green leaves. Back at the car door, he knelt on one knee, opening the door for Amelia, and with trembling fingers, he began to intertwine the pliable olive leaves, shaping them into a simple, beautiful circlet.

"Amelia," he asked, his voice thick with emotion, holding out the ephemeral, organic ring, "will you marry me, please? Make me the happiest man in this world, under these Tuscan stars?"

Amelia's eyes, already glistening, swept first over her sleeping children in the back, then settled on his face the weary, honest, profoundly beautiful face of the man who had fought distance, fear, and his own past for their family. The olive leaf ring, though fragile, felt more powerful than any diamond. It was a promise rooted in ancient earth, under eternal stars, just like their love.

"Darling," she replied, her voice soft with tears and absolute love, "you were my husband before those two arrived. **Yes. I will marry you, darling.**"

He slid the delicate olive leaf ring onto her finger, a fleeting, tender symbol of their unbreakable bond, before pulling her into a fierce, joyful embrace. The new chapter of their life had just opened, and under the silent, witnessing stars of Tuscany, they were finally, irrevocably, ready to walk the line together, forever bound to this earth and to each other.

The Passing of the Seasons

They had not yet set a wedding date, but the unspoken truth of their commitment vibrated in the air around them, a certainty deeper than any calendar. Luca had gifted Amelia a massive, deep blue **Tanzanite** a stone closer to her heart than any traditional diamond. Its oceanic hue perfectly mirrored the vast waters that had so often divided and ultimately united them, a silent testament to the journey their love had weathered.

Amelia had embarked on a personal quest: to master Italian. She believed, with a conviction as potent as Nelson Mandela's wisdom, that while speaking to someone in a language they *understand* reaches their brain, speaking to them in their *mother tongue* speaks directly to their heart. She yearned to speak her vows to Luca, not in her native English, but in the lyrical, passionate language of his soul, his heritage, and their future. This was her ultimate gesture of belonging, a promise whispered in the very cadence of his ancestry.

The decision to extend their engagement wasn't born of hesitation, but of a profound, protective devotion. Luca watched the woman he loved transform, and he found himself unwilling to interrupt the sacred quiet of their healing with the frantic noise of wedding logistics.

Luca recognized that Amelia was finally breathing truly breathing for the first time in long time. To press her into the whirlwind of floral arrangements, guest lists, and seating charts felt like an intrusion on her peace. He wanted her to wake up every morning without a "to-do" list hanging over her head, allowing her the luxury of simply **being**. By slowing the clock, Luca gave Amelia the one thing money couldn't buy: a season of life where her only responsibility was to be happy.

Perhaps the greatest catalyst for the delay was the blossoming relationship between Amelia and Leo. Luca found himself mesmerized by the shift in the house. The tentative glances had turned into shared laughter; the distance had dissolved into a bond that felt ancient and soul-deep.

One afternoon, Luca returned home early, the heavy oak doors muffling his footsteps. He stopped in the hallway, his breath catching in his throat. In the sun-drenched center of the rug, Amelia was on her hands and knees, her hair falling in loose waves over her shoulders as she chased Leo.

The boy's giggles were bright and infectious, a sound that felt like sunlight turned into audio. When Amelia caught him, pulling him into a gentle tackle and showering his face with kisses, Leo's tiny arms wrapped fiercely around her neck.

Luca leaned against the doorframe, his heart aching with a pride so sharp it was almost physical. He realized then that he didn't just want a wife; he wanted this version of Amelia the one who was whole, radiant, and deeply connected to their children. To rush the wedding was to rush this precious, formative era of their family.

Amelia's dream became their shared North Star. She envisioned a day where the ceremony wasn't just a union of two people, but a celebration of a completed circle.

Livia, with her growing grace, standing tall and proud.

Leo, sturdy on his feet, his hand tucked firmly into Amelia's.

She wanted them to remember the day not as a blurry childhood memory, but as the moment they officially walked their mother toward the future they had all built together. Luca agreed with every fiber of his being. Their love didn't need a deadline; it was a living thing, growing stronger in the "slow" moments, proving that the best things in life are never rushed, but meticulously nurtured until they are perfect

The Language of Belonging

Amelia's commitment to Italian was more than an academic pursuit; it was an act of profound love, a bridge she meticulously built towards Luca's soul and the heart of her adopted home. Her days became a beautiful, immersive symphony of language acquisition. She enrolled in cooking classes held by formidable **nonnas** in sun-drenched Tuscan kitchens women whose hands spoke volumes more than their Italian, and who understood not a single word of English.

With flour dusting her apron and the rich aroma of simmering *ragù* filling the air, Amelia learned not just to make pasta from scratch, but to read the unspoken cues of Italian life: the emphatic hand gestures, the melodic inflections, the way food was an extension of love. Each perfectly rolled *gnocchi* and every carefully braided loaf of bread was a triumph, a word added to her expanding vocabulary of belonging. This practical, sensory immersion proved more effective than any textbook.

Her intellectual curiosity, too, began to bloom in this fertile ground. She diligently researched the requirements to become a **sub-lecturer** at the local university. For an American to teach English or an English-based course in Italy, especially part-time, often involved securing positions as Lecturers or Foreign Language Assistants. While a full professorship demanded navigating a complex and competitive system of public examinations (*concorsi*), part-time and contract roles were frequently available for native speakers with advanced degrees. This allowed her to pursue a meaningful, limited workload perhaps teaching Business English, American Literature, or a communications elective a way to honor her career while prioritizing her burgeoning family life. It was a conscious choice, an act of balancing her ambition with the quiet, profound joy of her domestic world.

Amelia herself, once hesitant and reserved, now found herself gesticulating naturally as she spoke, her hands expressing emotions as fluidly as her words. She was no longer a visitor; she was finally *at home*. Amidst this beautiful chaos, she had also diligently finished her manuscript, **"Not So Italian,"** a charming, self-deprecating cooking book that chronicled her culinary adventures and misadventures. Luca, her most devoted champion, had celebrated its publication on Amazon with immense pride, a small, proud victory that resonated deeply within their walls. Their life was a testament to love, patience, and the beautiful, intricate art of building a home across cultures.

The seasons in Tuscany didn't just change; they danced by, marked by the lengthening shadows of the cypresses and the steady, miraculous growth of the children. What was once a house of quiet recovery had transformed into a villa overflowing with the beautiful, chaotic noise of a life fully lived.

Time seemed to accelerate, fueled by the boundless energy of two children who were no longer babies, but small people with distinct, vibrant souls. The "someday" of their wedding was drawing closer, not because they were rushing, but because the children were finally becoming the pillars of the ceremony Amelia had always envisioned.

Leo, now nearly two, had traded his tentative crawls for a "wobbly" confidence that kept the entire household on their toes. He was a whirlwind of discovery, his sturdy legs carrying him into every corner of the vineyard.

His speech was a linguistic masterpiece of "baby-babble," a seamless, melodic bridge between his two worlds. One moment he'd shout for a "ball," and the next he'd be demanding *"acqua,"* his accent a perfect, unintentional mimicry of the Italian sun.

The shy, hesitant boy had vanished, replaced by a toddler who navigated the world with wide-eyed wonder and a laugh that echoed through the stone hallways of the villa.

At nearly four, Livia had blossomed into a true *bambina* of Italy, though her heart remained large enough to hold two continents.

Recent visits to Washington, D.C., to see her grandmother and father had become cherished adventures. She returned to Tuscany with stories of the Potomac and the bright lights of the city, her suitcase filled with American storybooks that she insisted Luca read to her at night.

Back home, she was Luca's "delightful shadow." Whether he was checking the garden or sitting in his office, Livia was there, her hand often tucked into his. She had started singing classes in the village, and her voice was a constant, "rapid-fire" radio of joy. She blended English and Italian phrases with an untamed, rhythmic flair, often making up songs about the Tuscan hills and her "Papa Luca."

The rhythm of their home life was now a vibrant, joyous scene. The quiet, heavy air of the past had been replaced by the sound of Livia's melodic chatter and the thud of Leo's footsteps on the terracotta floors.

Luca would often catch Amelia's eye across the dinner table, a silent communication passing between them. They didn't need words to acknowledge the miracle. The engagement had been long, yes, but in that time, they hadn't just planned a wedding they had built a sanctuary. They had watched their children's "tiny hands" grow stronger, more capable of holding onto the dream that was now just a heartbeat away from becoming a reality

A Tuscan Christmas Glow

The Tuscan winter had a way of making the villa feel like a fortress of ancient stone and warm light. Outside, the December air was a sharp, silver blade, smelling of pressed olives and the distant, smoky tang of wood-burning stoves in the valley. But inside, the house was a sanctuary.

It was Leo's second Christmas on this earth, his second year of being the golden boy of the house and the villa was draped in a shimmering, ethereal blanket of holiday magic.

The afternoon was bleeding into a deep, violet dusk when the heavy oak door groaned open. Luca stepped into the foyer, his silhouette framed by the flickering amber lights of the courtyard. He looked every bit the exhausted hero, his shoulders slumped under the weight of a twelve-hour surgical shift and an hour at the gym.

"¡Bella! I'm home!" he called out, his Italian baritone vibrating through the hallway. "I'm a mess, sticky, tired, and probably smelling like a locker room. I'm heading for the shower. Where are my lions?"

Amelia's voice drifted from the kitchen, sweet and steady. "Lilian took them to the park to catch the last of the sun. They'll be back before the lamb is out of the oven."

Luca didn't need to be told twice. He disappeared into the master suite, the sound of the rainfall showerhead soon filling the room with a rhythmic, percussive hiss.

The Steam and the Soul Amelia checked the oven, the savory aroma of herb-crusted lamb and roasted rosemary potatoes already beginning to bloom. She wiped her hands on her apron, but as she heard the low, resonant sound of Luca singing a soulful, gravelly Italian ballad that vibrated through the walls she felt a familiar, magnetic pull.

She walked into the bathroom, where the air was already a thick, white velvet of steam. Through the frosted glass, she could see the blurred, powerful outline of her man. She stripped away her clothes, her skin prickling in the humid heat, and stepped into the spray.

The water was scalding and perfect. Luca didn't hear her at first over the roar of the water. Amelia stepped into his space, her small, cool hands sliding around his damp waist, her front pressing into the broad, wet expanse of his back.

Luca let out a low, ragged growl of surprise that quickly turned into a purr of recognition. He turned in the downpour, his eyes dark and heavy with a sudden, scorching hunger. He pulled her flush against him, his large surgeon's hands capable of such terrifying precision now moving with a desperate, primal tenderness.

He tilted her head back, his mouth finding hers in a kiss that tasted of peppermint and heat. It wasn't just a kiss; it was a conversation. It was the way they spoke when the kids were sleeping and the world was quiet. The water sluiced over them, a private waterfall that washed away the stress of the hospital and the fatigue of the day. In the roar of that shower, there were no patients, no schedules, no pasts, only the slick friction of skin on skin and the steady, racing beat of two hearts in perfect, thundering sync.

When the water finally ran cool, Luca lifted Amelia effortlessly, her legs locking around his waist. He carried her out into the bedroom, the cool air hitting their damp skin like a shock. He stood her on the bed and began to dry her with a plush, oversized towel, his movements slow and reverent, as if he were tending to something fragile and holy.

"We have the medical association gala Saturday night," he whispered, his voice a low rasp as he began to massage a thick, fragrant lotion into her back. "A reunion. A night for us to be something other than exhausted parents."

Amelia leaned her head back against his shoulder, closing her eyes as his thumbs found the knots in her shoulder blades. "I think I have just the dress to make them all jealous."

Just as they were finishing Luca looking devastating in a crisp white shirt that accentuated his tan, and Amelia glowing in her buttercup-green silk the doorbell rang. It was a frantic, joyful chime.

Luca sprinted to the door, swinging it open to a rush of cold winter air. Livia and Leo practically tackled him. He caught them both, one on each hip, his bicep bulging under his shirt as he hoisted the "Italian army" into the air.

"Papà! The trees have lights! Big ones!" Livia shouted, her cheeks two bright winter apples. Leo just giggled, tugging on Luca's ear with a gummy, joyful grin.

"I see, I see!" Luca laughed, kissing their cold noses before nodding to Lilian. "Thank you, Lilian. You've saved us again."

"Of course, Signor," Lilian smiled, looking at the pair of them. "You two look like you just stepped off a Milan runway. Have a wonderful night."

Amelia emerged, looking like a vision of sophisticated grace. "Lilian, stay for dinner? It's enough for a village."

"I wish I could, but I have a date with some mulled wine and my grandmother," Lilian laughed, waving goodbye.

As the door clicked shut, the house settled into its sacred evening ritual. They gathered in the dining room, the table a masterpiece of Italian tradition. The amber glow of the Christmas tree reflected in the wine glasses, and the scent of the lamb filled the room.

Amelia plated the food, her silk dress shimmering like liquid gold in the candlelight. They ate, laughed, and watched Leo try to feed his mashed potatoes to the imaginary dog under the table. It was a symphony of domestic perfection, a tapestry woven so tightly that as they prepared to head to the party, Amelia truly believed nothing could ever fray the edges of their life.

The Gilded Gala

The Grand Ballroom of the Villa Medici was a cathedral of light and sound. It was exactly **8:00 PM** when the heavy gilded doors swung open for Luca and Amelia to enter.

The air was thick with the scent of expensive lilies, aged Franciacorta, and the crisp, ozone-coolness of a Tuscan winter night clinging to the guests' furs. Crystal chandeliers hung like frozen rain from the frescoed ceilings, casting a thousand dancing diamonds across the floor.

As Luca and Amelia stepped into the room, the low hum of conversation faltered for a heartbeat. They were, quite simply, the sun. Luca, in a tailored midnight-blue tuxedo that made his surgeon's frame look like sculpted granite, held Amelia's hand with a possessive, grounded strength. She, in her buttercup-yellow silk, was a burst of summer in the middle of a winter gala.

They were making their way toward the head table when Luca suddenly stiffened a microscopic hitch in his stride that only Amelia, who knew the rhythm of his heart, could feel.

Seated at a small, intimate table near the dance floor was **Isabella**. She looked like a portrait in charcoal and silk dressed in a floor-length black gown that clung to her like a second skin. Beside her sat a tall, sharp-featured man, an architect from Milan, but her eyes were nowhere near her date.

"Isabella?" Luca's voice was a blend of shock and forced politeness.

She stood slowly, a predator rising from the tall grass. Her smile was slow, her red lips gleaming. "Luca. I didn't think the Great Surgeon stepped out of the theater for anything less than a heart transplant." Her gaze flickered to Amelia, sharp as a scalpel. " the... *Americano*."

"My love, Amelia," Luca corrected, his voice dropping an octave into a protective growl. He kept his arm firmly around Amelia's waist. "I didn't think I'd see you here. When did you leave the south? How is Trapani?"

"Trapani... I don't know ... I have been here since September Luca," she purred, her eyes never leaving him. "I've taken a position here in Florence. Surgery. Just like the old days."

"Good for you," Luca said, his tone final. "Enjoy the evening."

The Golden Hours They moved to their table, the encounter seemingly dismissed. From 9:00 PM to 11:00 PM, the night was a blur of high-society magic. The dinner was a masterpiece truffle risotto that melted on the tongue and wine that tasted of sun-drenched earth.

Luca was the star of the room, but he only had eyes for one person. He leaned into Amelia, his breath warm against her ear, whispering jokes about the hospital board members. He looked at her with a pride so profound it was almost tangible, a man who had survived the storm and found his harbor.

When the orchestra began a slow, sweeping Italian waltz, he led her to the floor. They moved in perfect sync, her yellow silk swirling around his dark trousers like a flame. For those minutes, the world was just the scent of her hair and the heat of his hand on the small of her back.

But from the edges of the room, the shadow watched. Every time Amelia laughed, she could feel Isabella's gaze, a cold, heavy weight from across the ballroom. Isabella didn't dance; she sat, sipping dark wine, her eyes tracking Luca's every move with a hunger that was terrifyingly patient.

The clock on the velvet-lined wall ticked toward **11:40 PM**. The room was warm, the wine had flowed freely, and the atmosphere was thick with the beautiful exhaustion of a perfect party.

Luca leaned in, his thumb tracing the line of Amelia's jaw. His eyes were soft, clouded with a mixture of wine and deep, uncomplicated love.

"I have to use the restroom, *bellissima*," he whispered, his voice a low, intimate rasp. "Don't go anywhere. When I get back, I'm taking my woman home and reminding her why I love her."

He leaned down and kissed her with a long, lingering press of lips that tasted of black cherries and promise. It was a kiss of absolute fidelity, a seal on their night.

"I'll be there in two minutes," he promised.

Amelia watched him walk away, his tall frame cutting through the crowd. She felt like the luckiest woman in Tuscany. She smoothed her yellow silk, took a sip of her water, and waited.

She didn't see Isabella stand up. She didn't see the black dress slip into the shadows of the hallway just seconds after Luca. She only saw the clock hit **11:42**, and decided, with a playful smile, that two minutes was too long to be away from him.

She stood up, following the golden light toward the hallway, walking straight into the heart of the wreck.

The hallway leading to the restrooms was a narrow artery of stone and shadows, away from the clinking crystal and laughter of the party. Amelia walked slowly, her heels clicking a rhythmic, anxious beat. Luca had been gone too long. The "Doctor" was usually a man of precision, but the "Father" was exhausted, and she had gone to find him, perhaps to steal a quiet kiss to cheer him up .

Then, she rounded the corner and the world stopped.

The hallway was a narrow artery of cool stone, a sanctuary away from the clatter of the Ferragosto party. When Luca emerged from the restroom, he expected to see the dim, quiet corridor. Instead, he saw her.

Isabella stood there, leaned against the ancient masonry as if she had been waiting for him for a decade. Their eyes met, and for a split second, they spoke a silent, jagged language that only a first love understands a dialect of shared secrets and old scars.

She walked closer, her heels clicking a slow, predatory rhythm. Her smile was sharp, and the deep crimson of her lipstick seemed to catch the amber light, hypnotizing him for a heartbeat.

"I thought you didn't see me," she purred, her voice a low, melodic rasp. "Or perhaps your eyes are blinded by the... *Americano*."

Luca stiffened, the mention of Amelia acting like a splash of cold water. He tried to pull on his professional mask, the one that had performed a thousand successful surgeries.

"I loved your speech, Isabella. Truly. You've still got that fire," he said, his voice forced into a casual, distant register. He tried to pivot the conversation, to push her back into the "Colleague" category. "How is Trapani? I can see that Sicily is still in your blood."

Isabella laughed, a sound like dry silk, and moved into his personal space. The scent of something dark, like neroli and expensive tobacco hit him, a phantom memory of medical school nights.

"Well, I haven't seen you since the funeral," she said, her eyes tracing the line of his jaw. "Did Sofia ever give you my message?"

Luca let out a short, dry laugh. "You know Sofia. She hated us then, and she hates that I 'stole' her best friend. Besides... She is very close with my lady now. No, she will never tell me anything from you."

Isabella didn't flinch. She became predatory, her body leaning closer until he could feel the heat radiating off her. She knew that while his heart might be legally taken, a piece of his soul would always respond to the girl who had survived the trenches of residency with him.

"She is protective," Isabella whispered, her hand rising to brush a microscopic speck of dust from his lapel. "But she cannot erase what is written in the bone, Luca."

She looked at him with a gaze that promised a return to the "old fantasy," a time before kids, before C-sections, before the heavy gravity of real life. Before Luca could find the words to dismiss her, before the "Doctor" could reassert control, she lunged.

She leaned in, a swift, possessive movement, and pressed her lips to his. It was a claim, a sudden, desperate attempt to overwrite the last year of his life with a single, crushing memory.

And in that exact, horrifying second, Amelia rounded the corner

The Standstill Amelia froze. Ten feet away, bathed in the dim amber glow of a wall sconce, Luca wasn't alone. He was pinned against the stone wall, and Isabella, the woman from the funeral, the " sofia's best friend" with the haunting eyes had her hands threaded through his dark hair. They were kissing. It wasn't the tentative kiss of a stranger; it was the hungry, practiced embrace of two people who knew the map of each other's mouths by heart.

Amelia's lungs felt like they had filled with concrete. She couldn't move. She couldn't scream. Instead, the sight of them acted like a key in a lock, and the heavy door of her memory swung wide, dragging her backward.

The Flashback: The Farmhouse (first time she came to Italy) The image of their locked lips blurred, replaced by the flickering candlelight of the family farmhouse. She remembered the wine-soaked laughter of Luca's cousin, the way he had leaned in to whisper about "The One Who Got Away." *Isabella.* Amelia saw a mental montage she hadn't realized she was building: Luca and this woman, years ago, riding vintage bicycles through these very hills, their lab coats draped over the handles. She heard the phantom roar of a motorcycle on a road trip to the Mediterranean, Isabella's arms wrapped around Luca's waist. She saw them in the sterile halls of medical school, two brilliant minds destined to be one.

The Flashback: The Funeral (Last Year) The memory shifted to the gray rain of Isabella's father's funeral. She saw Isabella again, draped in black lace, collapsing into Luca's chest. Amelia had stood back, moved by the "friendship," watching Luca stroke Isabella's hair to calm her.

Then, the most painful ghost surfaced: the night at the farmhouse after the burial. Amelia had looked out toward the moonlit ridge and seen two silhouettes Luca and Isabella standing so close they looked like a single shadow. She had told herself it was grief. Now, watching them in the hallway, she realized it was a homecoming.

Back in the present, Amelia watched Luca's hands. They had been at his sides, stiff with shock, but then she saw the slow, involuntary rise. His fingers splayed across Isabella's waist, a reflex of a decade of muscle memory.

Amelia didn't just see a kiss; she saw a conspiracy.

As she stood paralyzed in the shadows of the hallway, a new, sharper memory cut through the fog. She remembered a quiet afternoon months ago, shortly after she arrived, when she had pointed to a name on a guest list. *Isabella.* She had asked Luca about her then, her intuition already prickling.

Luca had barely looked up from his medical journals. He had brushed it off with a casual wave of his hand, his voice smooth and dismissive. "Just Sofia's friend from school, *Bella*. A family acquaintance. Nothing more."

Even Sofia, her friend, her sister in law , the woman she had bared her soul to had maintained the same calculated silence. "She's just my best friend, Amelia. Don't worry your big head over her."

The betrayal boiled in Amelia's blood, hotter than the Tuscan sun. It wasn't just Luca. It was the cousins at the farmhouse who had whispered in Italian when she walked into the room. It was the aunts who had redirected the conversation every time the "First Love" was mentioned. The entire family had been a fortress, protecting this ghost, keeping the truth tucked away in the cellar like an old, potent wine they didn't want her to taste.

This woman had been a ghost she was told didn't exist, yet here she was, solid and breathing, her hands tangled in Luca's hair.

Amelia's heart didn't just break; it felt like it was melting into a pool of lead. If they all lied to protect this, was it really just a "past" relationship? Or was she, just a mother of his kids, just a temporary inhabitant of a heart that still belonged to the woman in the hallway?

Is he still in love with her? The question didn't just haunt her; it erased her. She looked at them one last time, the "Doctor" and the "Woman who stole his heart " and realized she wasn't part of this story. She was just a footnote in a language she would never truly master.

She turned and fled, the weight of a thousand family secrets pressing down on her shoulders as she ran toward the night.

The jealousy wasn't a fire; it was a cold, drowning wave. She looked at the man who had forced her into a C-section to "save" her, the man who had watched her struggle with their son, and she realized that while she was drowning in the dark, he was breathing the air of a past life.

She didn't wait for him to open his eyes. She didn't wait for the excuses.

The amber glow of the hallway shattered. The vision of Luca's hands, those surgeon's hands she trusted with her life resting on Isabella's waist was a physical blow that knocked the air from Amelia's lungs.

She didn't scream. She didn't cause a scene. The humiliation was too cold for that. Instead, she turned, the buttercup-yellow silk of her dress whipping around her legs like a dying flame. She ran.

She was a modern-day Cinderella fleeing a ball that had turned into a wake. Her heels clicked a frantic, jagged rhythm against the marble, past the startled faces of Florence's elite, past the shimmering Christmas trees that now looked like jagged glass. Behind her, she heard the heavy, rhythmic thud of Luca's dress shoes and his voice, raw and desperate, cutting through the orchestral music.

"Amelia! *Aspetta!* Wait!"

She burst through the heavy oak doors into the freezing Tuscan night. The shock of the cold hit her lungs, but she didn't stop. A lone taxi was idling near the fountain, its yellow light a beacon of escape. She reached for the door, her fingers trembling, but before she could slide inside, a large, warm hand slammed the door shut.

"Go," Luca barked at the driver, his face pale, his breath hitching in the frigid air. "Go now!"

The taxi pulled away, leaving them standing in the glow of the villa's lanterns. Behind them, in the shadow of the doorway, Isabella stood. She didn't move. She simply watched, a dark silhouette of triumph, her red lips curved into a ghost of a smile as she watched the "Americano" dream unravel on the cobblestones.

The Cold Ride Home Luca's valet pulled the black Maserati to the curb, the engine idling with a low, predatory growl. Luca opened the door, his eyes pleading. "Get in the car, Amelia. Please. Don't do this here."

She got in, but she pressed herself against the passenger door as if the leather seats were made of thorns. The car lurched forward, tearing through the winding, moonlit streets of Florence toward their villa.

Inside the cabin, the tension was a living thing. The passing streetlights flickered across Luca's face in rhythmic flashes light, dark, light, dark revealing the agony in his eyes.

"It wasn't what you saw," he started, his voice a low, urgent rasp. He was driving with one hand, the other reaching out toward her, though he didn't dare touch her. "Amelia, listen to me. I didn't kiss her. She trapped me. She kissed me, and for a horrifying second I was just in shock. My brain didn't register it until I saw you."

"Your hands moved, Luca!" she screamed, the sound tearing from her throat like a jagged piece of metal. "I saw your fingers! You didn't push her away. You held her! You held the woman who 'broke your heart' while I was standing ten feet away in the dress you told me made me look like art!"

"I was paralyzed!" he roared back, his Italian temper finally snapping under the weight of his guilt. "It was ten years of history hitting me in the face in a dark hallway! It meant nothing! She is a ghost, Amelia! You are my life! You are the mother of my kids!"

"Don't you dare bring kids into this!" she sobbed, her head falling into her hands. "Don't use our son or daughter to cover up the fact that you still want her. I saw the way you looked at her at the table. You were surprised? No, Luca. You were haunted."

The car screeched to a halt in the driveway of their villa. Amelia didn't wait for him to kill the engine. She threw the door open and sprinted inside, the warmth of the house feeling like an insult.

She reached the bedroom first. She didn't stop to take off the yellow dress. She grabbed the extra pillow from her side of the bed, the one she usually tucked under her arm when he was on call and marched back to the doorway.

Luca was standing in the hall, his tuxedo jacket discarded, his tie hanging loose around his neck. He looked broken, a man who had just lost the most important surgery of his career.

"Amelia, please Bella lets talk!!!"

She didn't let him finish. She hurled the pillow at his chest with a strength born of pure, unadulterated rage.

"Sleep in the living room, Luca," she whispered, her voice suddenly, terrifyingly quiet. "Sleep with your memories. Sleep with Isabella. But do not think for one second that you are sleeping with me."

She slammed the heavy oak door, the sound echoing through the stone hallways of the villa like a gunshot. She turned the lock with a definitive *click*.

On the other side of the door, Luca sank to his knees, his forehead resting against the wood. Inside, Amelia collapsed against the bedpost, the buttercup-yellow silk pooling around her as she wept for a Christmas that had ended before the clock even struck midnight.

The Coldest Winter Rose

The winter that descended upon Tuscany was the harshest anyone could remember, but the frost outside the villa was nothing compared to the glacial silence that had taken root within its walls. It was the season of **The Coldest Winter Rose**, a time when the beauty of their life should have been blooming, yet felt frozen in a single, jagged moment of betrayal.

The holiday season, once a beacon of warmth, had become the backdrop for Amelia's undoing. The images played on a relentless, agonizing loop in her mind: the scent of pine and expensive champagne, the soft glow of fairy lights, and then the sight that shattered it all.

Luca. His arms wrapped around her, but his lips pressed against his ex-partner.

Every time Amelia closed her eyes, she was back in that hallway, feeling the air leave her lungs. The betrayal wasn't just a kiss; it was the theft of the safety she had spent years building. The man who had been her anchor had suddenly become the storm.

For the sake of the children, they performed a domestic play that left Amelia feeling hollowed out. During the day, they shared the same space. They handed toys to Leo and applauded Livia's singing performances, their smiles practiced and brittle.

As soon as the children's bedroom doors clicked shut, the mask fell. Luca had been relegated to the sofa, a silent, brooding presence in the dark. The grand master bed felt like an island where Amelia lay awake, staring at the ceiling, shivering despite the heavy duvets.

A New Year Without a Promise, New Year's Eve had passed not with a bang, but with a deafening silence. As the clock struck midnight and fireworks erupted over the distant hills, there was no celebratory toast, no whispered vows for the future.

There was no New Year's Eve kiss.

While the rest of Italy welcomed the new year with hope, Amelia felt trapped in the old one. She watched the frost creep across the windowpane, tracing the shape of a rose that would never bloom. She looked at Luca the man who was her best friend, her protector, and now her stranger and wondered if the "interwoven world" they had built was strong enough to survive the ice that was now cracking the very foundation of their home

February is here , the Tuscan sky outside the farmhouse wept a soft, chilling rain, mirroring the internal tempest that had raged for days. Luca arrived home after a grueling, endless day of surgeries, the sterile scent of the hospital still clinging to his clothes. He pushed open the heavy oak door, seeking the solace of his home, but instead, his breath hitched. Two sets of luggage, stark and unforgiving, stood like sentinels by the front door packed. His heart, usually a steady drum, **seized in a vise of pure panic.**

He walked into the kitchen, the familiar warmth of the space now feeling alien, and looked at Amelia. Her eyes, once soft pools of deep affection, were now **hardened by the relentless days of emotional isolation**, like cold, polished stones. "Whose bags are those?" he asked, his voice barely a whisper, dread coiling in his gut.

"Ours," Amelia stated, her voice flat, devoid of the melody he cherished, drained of all warmth. "We are leaving, Next week, we will be gone"

"No!" Luca cried out, the denial ripped from his chest, his voice cracking, raw with disbelief and terror. "You are leaving, but my kids are staying here! Livia is in school here! This is their home!"

Without a word, Luca gripped the handles of her suitcases, his knuckles white against the leather. He didn't just move them; he hauled them back inside, the heavy thud of the luggage against the floor sounding like a gavel bringing a trial to order.

He pulled his phone from his pocket, the blue light of the screen illuminating the harsh lines of his face. His thumbs moved with brutal efficiency. He opened the airline app the one they had used so many times to plan their joyous futures and with a few cold taps, he canceled the tickets. The flight to the USA, the escape to her mother, the chance to put an ocean between her and the image of his betrayal all of it vanished into the digital void.

He looked up at her, his eyes burning with an "angry look" that was fueled by a terrifying mix of desperation and possessiveness.

"You aren't running, Amelia," he rasped, his voice vibrating with a dangerous edge. "We are going to fight either we fight for this, or we fight each other. But it is **us**, even if it's us against the world. It is never you against me."

The ultimatum hung in the air, a heavy, suffocating weight. He refused to let her vanish into the night; he was forcing her to stand in the wreckage of what they had become.

Amelia didn't scream. She didn't plead. The betrayal had left her too hollow for a public explosion. She didn't say a single word. Instead, she turned away from him, her posture stiff and regal despite the trembling in her hands.

She retreated up the grand staircase, the rhythm of her footsteps the only sound in the cavernous hall. When she reached her bedroom the sanctuary that had become a prison she stepped inside and closed the door. The click of the lock was a final, sharp punctuation mark, leaving Luca alone in the hallway with the ghosts of his mistakes and the canceled remains of her departure.

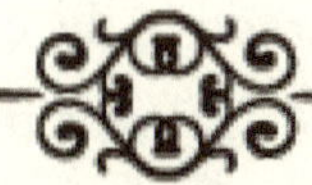

The Stone in the Bed

For days the villa had been a tomb of marble and silence. The air, once sweet with the scent of *pasta* and jazz, was now thick with the metallic tang of resentment. Luca had moved his life into the nursery, sleeping on a narrow cot surrounded by stuffed animals and the rhythmic, mocking breathing of his children. He was a man performing a penance, trying to "fix" the air with flowers bouquets of lilies and peonies that filled every vase but to Amelia, they smelled like a funeral.

She was sliding back into the gray, viscous deep of her depression, her body moving through the house like a ghost haunting its own life.

One Tuesday evening, the tension finally snapped. Luca returned from the hospital, his face etched with the exhaustion of a twelve-hour shift. He found the kitchen dark. No stove was lit; no table was set. Without a word, he shifted into the role he had played for months. He tucked a sleepy Leo into his crib, spent twenty minutes on the floor fixing the broken wheel of Livia's favorite wooden truck, and then set to work over the stove.

By the time the smell of sautéed garlic filled the room, Amelia drifted in. She didn't look like the woman in the yellow sundress. Her hair was tangled, her eyes sunken and rimmed with a hard, unforgiving red.

Luca plated the pasta, sitting Livia down and setting a small bowl for Leo. He didn't look up when Amelia entered. "Do you want a plate, Bella?"

Amelia didn't sit. She stood in the center of the kitchen, her shadow long and jagged. "I just want answers, Luca."

Luca's hand paused, his fork hovering. He glanced at the children Livia was watching them with wide, knowing eyes. "Not here, Amelia. I won't do this in front of them."

"Then when?" she snapped, pulling a chair back with a screech that made Livia flinch. "Do you still love her? Is she still the 'First Love'? Why am I the only person in this country who didn't know who she was?"

Luca put his fork down with a slow, deliberate click. The "Doctor" was gone. There was only the man, cornered and bleeding. "I will answer whatever you want. What do you need to hear, Amelia? Tell me."

"Do you still love her?" Her voice was a whip, cracking in the quiet room.

Luca's face hardened. He looked her dead in the eye, his voice dropping into a low, terrifyingly honest register. "Do you want the truth? Fine. Yes. I will always love her."

Amelia felt the floor drop away. Her heart didn't just break; it shattered into a million pieces of ice. She turned, stumbling toward the bedroom, but Luca was faster. He caught up to her in the hallway, his hand blocking the door.

"You asked, I answered!" he roared, his chest heaving. "She was my first love, Amelia! My best friend for a decade! I cannot reach into my chest and cut out the years we spent in the trenches together. I will never go back and change the past."

He stepped closer, his shadow looming over her. "But listen to me if I had met you before her, I would never have even looked at her. I am *in* love with you. She is the girl I *used* to love. Her name is carved into my history, and I can't change that, but I moved on. I chose you. I chose this."

"You lied!" Amelia wept, her voice high and thin. "At the funeral... Everyone played me for a fool. Your cousins, Sofia, the aunts... they all looked at me and saw the 'Americano' replacement while they protected her!"

"No one played you!" Luca shouted back. "What would have changed back then? To tell you I once loved the woman who was mourning her father? It was irrelevant, Amelia! I didn't kiss her. She kissed me. Period."

Before she could scream back, a sharp, terrifying wail pierced the air.

"PAPÀ! Leo fell! He hit his head!" Livia's scream was frantic from the kitchen.

The war between them stopped instantly. They both ran. Leo was on the floor, a bright, angry knot already forming on his forehead where he had caught the edge of the chair. Luca didn't hesitate. He scooped his son up, his large hands moving with clinical precision, checking the baby's pupils, his touch urgent and tender.

"Get me ice," Luca commanded, his voice cold.

Amelia stood frozen in the doorway. She watched Luca go to the freezer, wrap ice in a cloth, and sit on the floor, cradling Leo against his chest. He whispered to the boy in rapid, soothing Italian, his back turned completely to Amelia. At that moment, he ignored her so thoroughly it felt like she had been erased from the room.

She looked at Leo, the boy she struggled to love, the boy who looked exactly like the man who had just admitted to loving another woman and the sharp, crippling pain of the PPD surged back. She saw the child as part of the problem, a physical tie to a man who lived in a past she couldn't enter.

Without a word, Amelia turned and walked back to the bedroom, closing the door softly.

In the kitchen, Livia didn't follow her mother. She stood by her father's side, leaning her small head against his leg, watching him tend to her brother. The house was quiet again, but the foundation had finally crumbled. Amelia sat in the dark, her suitcases staring at her from the corner of the room, and she knew.

Italy was his home. Isabella was his history. And she was just a guest who had stayed too long.

The clock on the home office wall ticked toward midnight, the sound echoing like a heartbeat in the oppressive silence. Luca sat hunched over his desk, the harsh desk lamp illuminating anatomical charts and surgical diagrams. He was deep into his preparations for the next morning's surgery, burying his soul in the cold, objective logic of medicine. In the sterile world of nerves and tendons, there was no room for the haunting image of the Christmas party or the look of shattered glass in Amelia's eyes.

Then, a sound broke his concentration a sharp, pained cry from Leo's room.

Luca was a surgeon, but in the dark of night, he was simply a father. He found Leo flushed and sweating, his forehead radiating a heat that made Luca's chest tighten. It was a fever, sudden and fierce. With practiced, gentle hands, Luca fetched the medicine from the cabinet, whispering soothing Italian nonsense as he coaxed the toddler to swallow. He stayed by the bedside, his large hand resting on Leo's small back, feeling the frantic rhythm of the boy's breathing slow into the steady cadence of sleep.

He waited until the room was perfectly still before he tip-toed out, closing the door with the precision of a thief.

As the latch clicked, he turned to find Amelia standing there. In the dim moonlight, she looked like a ghost, her face pale and her eyes dark hollows of unresolved grief.

"We need to talk," she whispered, her voice a jagged blade.

Luca felt a wave of exhaustion hit him that no amount of coffee could cure. He was tired of the loops, tired of the accusations, and tired of defending himself against a ghost he couldn't kill.

"Amelia, I can't be in the ring fighting the wind anymore," he said, his voice flat and weary. "We both have to fight for this family, together. But if you can't see that... if you're already gone..."

He straightened his shoulders, a cold, hard attitude settling over him like armor. "Then go ahead. Do whatever you want. I am done."

The words felt final, a bridge burning in real-time. "I'm going home," he added sharply, referring to the solitude of his office or perhaps the distance he was now putting between their hearts.

Luca looked at her, a bitter, "angry smile" tugging at the corner of his mouth. "Good," he snapped.

He didn't wait for her retort. He turned his back on her and walked out toward the balcony, the glass doors groaning as he shoved them open. The freezing Tuscan night air rushed in, biting at his skin, but he welcomed the sting. He stood at the railing, staring out at the dark silhouettes of the olive trees, his breath blooming in white clouds before him. He was a man who saved lives for a living, yet as he stood there in the coldest winter, he had never felt more powerless to save his own

The Roots of the Olive Tree

The morning light that filtered through the villa windows was grey and uninviting, lacking the golden warmth that usually defined their Tuscan home. Inside, the air was just as thin.

Luca moved through the kitchen with a mechanical, practiced efficiency. He finished feeding the kids their breakfast, wiping Leo's messy face and helping Livia into her heavy winter coat. There was no music playing today, no playful banter between father and daughter. Just the clink of silverware and the rustle of fabric.

When the children were ready, Luca gathered them up. He held his babies close, his movements protective and firm, and walked toward the bedroom where Amelia was still buried under the covers.

He didn't lean over to kiss her forehead. He didn't whisper a morning greeting against her skin. He stood by the foot of the bed, his presence looming and distant.

"Amelia."

The sound of her name was startling. Luca almost never called her just *Amelia*. It had always Bella, been *cara*, *amore*, or a whispered endearment that felt like a caress. Now, it was just a word dry, flat, and stripped of every ounce of affection. It sounded like a stranger calling out to a stranger.

"I am taking the kids to meet Sofia at the farm," he said, his voice devoid of emotion. "Leo needs to say goodbye to his auntie "

Amelia shifted, her heart hammering against her ribs. She opened her mouth to speak, to ask a question or perhaps to protest the coldness in his tone, but she never got the chance. Before she could utter a single word, the kids distracted him Livia tugging at his hand and Leo babbling about the horses. With a final, indifferent glance toward the bed, Luca turned and led them out of the room.

The silence that followed was deafening. Amelia sat up slowly, the pain in her chest sharpening into something jagged. It wasn't just Luca's coldness that hurt; it was the realization that in their excitement, the children hadn't even looked back. They hadn't noticed her silence or her sadness. To them, Luca was still the center of the universe the hero who fed them and dressed them while she felt like a fading shadow in the corner.

She dragged herself to the window, pulling the curtain back just enough to see. Below, in the driveway, Luca was settling the kids into their car seats. He didn't look up at her window. He didn't hesitate. He simply closed the doors, climbed into the driver's seat, and drove away, leaving nothing behind but the faint tracks of tires on the cold, frosted gravel

The drive to the family farmhouse was a journey through a landscape of silver-green leaves and ancient dust. Luca drove in silence, the only sound the rhythmic snoring of Leo in the back and Livia hum-singing a song she had learned at school.

When they arrived, the air smelled of pressed fruit and sun-baked earth. Sofia was in the cool shadows of the barn, her hair tied back, her hands stained with the work of the harvest. She was labeling the new batch of extra virgin olive oil the liquid gold of their ancestors.

"You look like you've worked a double shift at the hospital," Sofia said, wiping her brow as she pulled Luca into a tight hug.

Luca rolled up his sleeves, his surgeon's forearms exposed as he began to help her hoist the heavy crates. "Sis, I know you love this place, but you're doing this alone. I'm not much help these days. If you want to sell the groves... it's okay. I won't hold it against you."

Sofia slammed a bottle onto the wooden table, her eyes flashing with a sudden, ancestral fire. "Sell it? Luca, if I stop this, it's like burying our parents all over again. You know what this meant to Papa? This wasn't just a business. It was the pride of our grandfather, and his father before him. This" she gestured to the rows of amber glass "this belongs to Livia and Leo. This isn't just oil. It's their heritage. It's their blood."

Luca bowed his head, humbled by her fierce loyalty. "Understood. I won't mention it again."

The Walk Through the Grove After the crates were stacked, they wandered out into the grove. The Great Aunt was sitting on a stone bench, laughing as she handed Livia and Leo small cones of lemon gelato. The children were sticky and glowing, their laughter ringing out under the canopy of ancient trees.

"Can we walk, Sof?" Luca asked, his voice cracking.

As they moved deeper into the trees, away from the children's ears, Sofia turned to him. "Okay. No more games. Tell me what is burning your heart."

"She's taking Leo," Luca said, the words falling like lead.

Sofia stopped dead, her face turning pale. "What? What do you mean she is taking him? Where is my nephew going?"

Amelia says she needs a break. D.C. I don't know if it's a break or the end," Luca whispered, leaning his forehead against the rough bark of an olive tree. "We had a final fight last week. I'm tired, Sof. I'm tired of fighting for someone who won't even step into the ring. She's just... blank. She won't talk. She won't eat. She's fading away right in front of me.

"I tried to call her," Sofia admitted, her voice soft. "She was so cold. I thought it was just the... the depression."

"I want my kids with me," Luca choked out, his eyes filling.

"And Livia?" Sofia asked. "That girl lives for you. She will be destroyed."

Luca's jaw set into a hard, stubborn line the look of a man who would go to war. "Livia isn't going anywhere. She's in school here. She's integrated. On top of that... she is mine. She may not be my biological blood, but I met her when she was a heartbeat in her mother's belly. I gave her my name. I was the first one to hold her. I adopted her legally, Sof. No one, not the law, not Amelia will ever tell me she isn't mine."

Sofia hugged her brother, her head resting on his chest. "She is yours. She is my first niece, and we will figure this out. If I have to drive back and forth every day to help you, I will. We are a fortress, Luca."

"I feel sorry for Leo," Luca murmured, looking toward the kids. "She loves him, but the bond... it's not the same. And look at him, Sof. He's full of life. He's like a painting of me. I know every time she looks at him in America, she will see the man she's trying to leave behind."

Sofia pulled back, her expression darkening. "By the way, Isabella called. She asked about you again. I told her to stop. I told her next time, I'm going to go off on her. She said you blocked her number? And her email?"

Luca shook his head, a flash of pure anger in his eyes. "If she hadn't kissed me, we wouldn't even be talking about my son moving to America. Yes, I blocked her. I want nothing. She walked away from me years ago; I didn't walk away from her. That chapter is a tomb. She just refuses to stay buried."

The Memory A shout of joy broke through the tension. Livia and Leo were sprinting through the trees, the Great Aunt "chasing" them with a slow, theatrical waddle. Leo was the last in the line, his chubby legs working hard to keep up, his face split in a wide, gummy grin.

Luca's heart melted. He ran toward them, scooping Leo up and tossing him into the air until the baby shrieked with delight. For a few beautiful, golden minutes under the Tuscan sun, they weren't a broken family or a legal dispute. They were just a father and his children, playing among the trees that had watched their ancestors do the same for a hundred years.

The smell of the hospital antiseptic and exhaustion clung to Luca's skin as he pushed through the heavy front doors. He had spent the night in the operating theater, his hands steady while his mind was a battlefield. But as he stepped into the foyer, his heart didn't just race; it plummeted.

There, lined up like tombstones near the door, were the bags. They were packed, zipped, and ready to go.

A surge of desperate adrenaline hit him. He wasn't a surgeon in this moment; he was a drowning man reaching for a lifeline. He climbed the stairs, his footsteps heavy, and entered the bedroom. Amelia was there, her back to him, dressing with a methodical, cold precision.

Luca watched her, his throat tightening until it ached. His eyes were glassy, "almost tearing" as he took in the sight of the woman who was his entire world preparing to exit it.

"Bella..." his voice cracked, the old endearment slipping out like a reflex. "Are you sure you want to do this?"

Amelia didn't flinch. She turned, her expression "sharp like a razor," her resolve hardened by weeks of icy silence. "Yes," she snapped. "And please, can we stop this back and forth? We have already talked. I think we have nothing to talk about anymore."

Luca's breath hitched, a jagged, "hard breathe" that shook his chest. "No, Bella," he pleaded, stepping closer. "You have nothing to talk about, but I still have so much to tell you. I have so much to ask you... to ask you to forgive me. Please. Do not take my kids."

Amelia let out a sharp, "angry laugh" that sounded more like a sob. "Wow. So it's all about the kids, ha? Never me. It's always about what you're losing, Luca, never what you broke in me."

She turned back to her mirror, her voice dropping to a low, dangerous whisper. "Do not make it harder, please."

The rejection hit him with more force than the sleepless night ever could. Luca stood there for a moment, his head bowed, before he slowly "shook his head." The fight was leaking out of him, replaced by a hollow, numb obedience.

Without another word, he walked into the bathroom. He turned the shower to a punishing heat, trying to wash away the scent of the hospital and the sting of her words. When he emerged, he didn't go back to her. He didn't try to argue again. Instead, he walked straight into the children's room.

The air was softer there, smelling of sleep and lavender. He sat on the edge of Livia's bed and began to "prepare her for school," his fingers trembling slightly as he brushed her hair, focusing on the only part of his world that hadn't yet turned to ice

Every gesture was a testament to his shattered heart. As he was ready to drop Livia to school , he stopped in the kitchen where Amelia was preparing a last, silent breakfast, the clinking of cutlery echoing in the oppressive quiet.

"Say goodbye to Mama," he told Livia, his voice hollow, devoid of any warmth, a chilling pronouncement. "When you get home, she will be gone to America."

Livia, her bright, innocent eyes wide with childlike wonder, oblivious to the profound, existential crisis tearing her parents apart, simply waved. "Bye, Mama! Say hi to America!" Her utter innocence was the sharpest, most unbearable stab of all, a wound that went deeper than any shouting could inflict. They left the house as it was a normal day.

The drive back from Livia's school had felt like a funeral procession. When Luca stepped back into the villa, the silence was no longer heavy it was final. He found them in the sunroom: Leo, dressed in his tiny travel coat, his boots already buckled, standing beside Amelia.

The sight of the boy ready to leave hit Luca like a physical blow. He didn't ask permission; he simply crossed the room and swept Leo into his arms. He held him "so tight," burying his face in the toddler's neck, breathing in the scent of home and innocence one last time. He squeezed his eyes shut, his tall frame trembling with the effort of holding back a sob.

Amelia stood a few feet away, watching the scene with a gaze that remained disturbingly detached. She watched his knuckles turn white as he gripped the boy, wondering why Luca felt "so much pain to let it go." In her mind, the pain was a consequence of his own making, a debt he was finally forced to pay. She saw his suffering, but it felt miles away, blocked by the wall of ice she had built around her heart.

Finally, Luca pulled back, his eyes red-rimmed but his expression hardening into a mask of grim resignation. He set Leo down and looked at Amelia. He didn't plead again. He didn't use her name.

"Well," he said, his voice sandpaper-dry. "Whenever you are ready, let me know. I can start to take the bags to the car."

He stood there, a man offering to carry the very weights that would crush him, waiting for her to give the word.

Amelia didn't even look up. She continued to zip a small side pocket on her handbag, her movements fluid and indifferent. "Sure," she said, the word falling flat and cold between them. She didn't pause, she didn't waver; she simply continued "to do her things," moving through the room as if he were nothing more than a piece of the furniture she was leaving behind

The drive to the airport was a hollow experience. The only sound was the "cricket" silence of two adults who had run out of words, punctuated only by **Leo**. He was a tiny island of innocence in a sea of grief, completely unaware that his world was being bifurcated. He sat in his car seat, babbling to his own toes, his cheerful, nonsensical chatter making the heavy atmosphere feel even more suffocating. Luca gripped the steering wheel until his leather gloves groaned, his face a "mask of grief" that refused to crack until the engine finally cut out at the terminal.

At the airport, every movement felt like it was performed underwater. Luca operated on a painful instinct, doing "everything a loving man could do" for the family he was losing. He hauled the suitcases onto the cart, his movements mechanical and heavy, pushing them toward the gate with the solemnity of a pallbearer.

When they reached the final security threshold, the mask shattered.

Luca scooped **Leonardo** up, burying his face in the boy's soft neck. He held him "so impossibly tight," his large, surgeon's frame convulsing with "silent, racking sobs." It was a primal, agonizing separation; he was memorizing the weight of his son, the scent of his hair, and the warmth of his skin, knowing that in mere minutes, this tactile reality would become a haunting memory.

Without a single word, Luca handed the boy back to Amelia. He couldn't look at her to meet her eyes was to invite a total collapse. He was "colder than ice cream in an Alaskan winter," his heart not just broken, but "encased in a block of ice" to prevent it from bleeding out right there on the terminal floor.

He turned and walked away. His back was a rigid line of agony, his shoulders shaking with the force of his grief. He didn't look back. He couldn't. To turn around was to beg, and he had nothing left to offer but his departure. He walked away from half his soul, leaving a piece of himself "irrevocably severed" on the polished airport tiles.

Amelia stood frozen, the weight of Leo in her arms suddenly feeling like lead. As she watched Luca's retreating back, her heart "seized in her chest." The razor-sharp certainty that had guided her all morning suddenly blunted into a "wave of profound, agonizing doubt."

Was she making the right decision? Could she have believed his pleas? Could she have fought harder?

The questions roared in her mind, but it was too late. There was no goodbye kiss, no final look of understanding. There was only the sight of the man she loved disappearing into the crowd, leaving her standing in the terminal, shivering in the wake of the coldest winter she had ever known.

Her phone rang, shattering her agonizing thoughts, pulling her back to the harsh present. It was her mother. "Amelia, are you sure you want to do that? He's just a man, yes, but I know that boy loves you. You're making a mistake."

Her mother's voice continued, a desperate, loving attempt to be the voice of reason, as Amelia moved through the motions of checking in her bags, her mind numb.

Now seated at the gate, waiting for the final boarding call, Amelia felt the tears come again, hot and stinging against her cold cheeks. "Mama, Luca was cold. He didn't even look at me," she choked out, the pain raw and exposed.

"Wake up and smell the coffee," her mother countered, her voice firm, siding with Luca even across continents. "That boy loves you, Amelia. He's hurting, too."

Before her mother could finish, Amelia's boarding group was called. "Mama, we are starting to board. In seven hours, we will be all yours. Bye, Mama."

She turned off her phone, burying it deep in her handbag, and stepped onto the plane. She sunk into the plush seat of the first-class cabin an unexpected upgrade Luca had purchased, a final, silent, searing protest against the separation, a last act of protection for his son. He didn't want his son flying economy.

She wept silently, the vast, empty seat beside her a testament to the gaping void in her life, a void that echoed the one in her arms. The untouched rubber of the tires seemed to mock her, poised for a journey she never wanted to take. "Here, America, we come," she whispered into the cold, silent air, her voice a desolate plea, a love like a rose in the middle of winter, its petals now falling, frozen, dead.

The Return of the Shadow

The flight back to America was an eerie contrast to the storm they had left behind in Tuscany. Leo, as if sensing the exhaustion in his mother's soul, was an angel. He slept for hours, his small head resting on her lap, and spent his waking moments quietly captivated by his movies. He didn't cry for his father; he didn't ask for the villa. He was simply a passenger in a life he no longer controlled.

When they touched down at **Reagan National Airport**, the humid D.C. air felt thick and heavy compared to the crisp **Tuscan breeze** Waiting at the gate were Amelia's parents, their faces etched with a mixture of relief and profound worry.

The reunion was a bittersweet masterpiece. Her mother's embrace was a sanctuary, and her father's firm hug felt like the only thing keeping her upright. Leo, blinking away the sleep of a ten-hour flight, looked around the bustling terminal with wide, uncertain eyes. He didn't recognize the marble floors or the English chatter, but when his grandfather scooped him up, pouring out a lifetime of bottled-up love, the boy simply "went with the flow," resting his head on a shoulder that smelled of home.

Her father pulled back, looking at the boy's dark curls and the set of his jaw. He smiled sadly. "Amelia, this boy is a **photocopy of Luca**."

The comment hit her like a "sharp, sliding pain." It was a physical reminder that she could fly across an ocean, but she could never truly leave Luca behind. He was written into the very DNA of the child she held. Amelia flinched internally, but she donned her mask, nodding with a practiced, hollow smile as if the name didn't taste like ash in her mouth.

The first night back in her childhood home was a "huge memorial" of the life she used to lead. The house was filled with the scent of a home-cooked dinner and the voices of cousins who had rushed over to see her. They laughed and ate, but Amelia felt like an observer watching a movie of her own life.

By midnight, the house finally fell into a restless quiet. Amelia retreated to her old bedroom. It had been meticulously prepared, but stepping inside felt like stepping into a time capsule. She looked around at the walls the same posters of **2Pac** she had hung as a teenager were still there, staring back at her with a defiance she no longer felt.

She sat on the edge of the twin bed, the mattress too small and the air too familiar. A jagged, painful laugh escaped her lips.

"I went 60 steps ahead," she whispered to the empty room, "only to take 80 steps back."

She felt the crushing weight of the regression. She had left as a woman building a dynasty in Italy, and she had returned as a broken girl hiding in her parents' house.

She turned her gaze to the side, where **Leo** lay sleeping peacefully. He was sprawled out, his breathing deep and rhythmic, completely oblivious to the fact that he had woken up in a "new world." He was the only beautiful thing she had brought back from the wreckage, a silent witness to a journey that had led her right back to where she began only this time, she was carrying the ghost of a man who looked exactly like the child in the bed

A week of agonizing, absolute silence stretched between continents, each day a new layer of ice forming over her heart. Luca, across the ocean, nursed a wounded pride colder than the Alaskan winter he had mentally invoked, hardening his resolve. He meticulously avoided Amelia's attempts to call, burying himself in the operating room. There, the precise, demanding work of reconstructing damaged hearts was a better distraction than any bar, any comfort, any memory. It was easier to mend physical wounds than the chasm he felt in his soul.

Three weeks in Washington, D.C., had felt like three lifetimes. The initial comfort of her parents' home had curdled into a restless, aching homesickness that Amelia hadn't expected. She spent her afternoons taking long, solitary walks through the city, her boots crunching on the cold pavement of the National Mall or winding through the historic streets of Georgetown.

She desperately wanted the monuments, the familiar skyline, and the rhythm of the capital to remind her that this was where she belonged. She looked at the Potomac and tried to feel the connection of her youth, but her soul remained stubbornly tethered to the rolling hills of Tuscany. The "soul" of her life was still trapped in a land of olive groves and terracotta, no matter how many miles she put between them.

The silence from Italy was a different kind of cold a surgical, precise freezing out that Luca had mastered. He was killing her with a lack of presence, a void where his voice used to be.

Whenever Amelia called , the connection was sterile. Luca would answer the phone, his voice a flat, unrecognizable monotone. He didn't ask how she was; he didn't mention the weather or the house. He simply handed the phone directly to **Livia**, the transition so fast it felt like he was afraid her voice might contaminate him.

Every long, heartfelt message she sent the ones where she tried to explain her pain, or the ones where she just missed him remained met with a deafening void. He never replied. He didn't argue, he didn't shout; he simply chose to act as though she no longer existed in his world.

Every time she hung up the phone after hearing Livia's melodic Italian-English chatter, Amelia would look at Leo. The boy was thriving in the attention of his grandparents, but the way he tilted his head when he was confused, or the way his eyes crinkled when he laughed, was a constant, haunting "photocopy" of the man who refused to speak to her.

She had expected a fight. She had prepared for his anger, his pleading, or even his desperate arrival at her doorstep. She hadn't prepared for this the total erasure of their "interwoven world."

Standing on a corner in D.C., watching the gray sun set over the city, Amelia realized that Luca's heart hadn't just stayed in Italy; it had turned into a fortress. He wasn't just letting her go; he was teaching her what it felt like to be truly alone, proving that the "coldest winter" wasn't a season in Tuscany, but the space where his love used to be.

As she turned to walk back to her parents' house, the irony tasted like copper in her mouth. She had run away to find herself, to escape the image of his betrayal, yet she found herself wandering a city she no longer recognized, desperately checking a phone that refused to ring.

She was 3,000 miles away from the man who broke her heart, only to realize that the silence he was giving her was louder than any shout, and more painful than any goodbye they had ever shared at the gate.

How long could she stay in this "backwards step" before the silence from Italy became the permanent soundtrack of her life?

The vibrant energy Amelia once had for the D.C. streets began to flicker and die. The days grew shorter, not just because of the winter solstice, but because Amelia began to surrender to the shadows. The adrenaline of the escape had worn off, leaving behind a hollowed-out void where her spirit used to be.

The "backwards steps" she had joked about were now a free fall. The heavy, suffocating blanket of **postpartum depression**, combined with the trauma of her broken engagement, began to pull her under.

The Withdrawal: Amelia, once a woman of fire and grace, became a ghost in her parents' home. She stayed in her room for days on end, the posters of 2Pac watching over a woman who no longer recognized herself.

She stopped eating. The shower remained dry. Most heartbreakingly, she began to push **Leo** away. The boy who was a "photocopy of Luca" became too painful to look at. His laughter felt like an accusation, and his needs felt like mountains she couldn't climb.

Her parents watched in a state of mounting terror. This wasn't the daughter who had conquered Italy; this was a stranger who had simply given up on living.

Amelia's mother, watching her daughter sleep through the afternoon, felt a chilling realization. She was now experiencing exactly what Luca had endured the wall of silence, the unreachable soul, the feeling of loving someone who was physically there but spiritually gone.

The house, once filled with the joy of Leo's arrival, was now heavy with the scent of unwashed laundry and the sound of muffled sobs coming from behind a locked bedroom door.

One night, after a quiet, tension-filled dinner where Amelia's chair sat empty for the third time that week, her mother looked across the table at her husband. The light in the dining room felt dim, reflecting the exhaustion in their eyes.

"We are losing her," her mother whispered, her voice trembling. "She isn't opening up. She won't let us in, and she's pulling away from her own son."

Her father stared at his plate, his heart breaking for his little girl. He knew they were out of options.

"Tomorrow morning," her mother said with a sudden, firm resolve, "I am going to **call Luca**. I know they are at war. I know he hurts her. But I feel like we can't handle this alone. He is the only one who knows the woman she became in Italy, and he's the only one who might be able to reach her before she's gone for good."

The decision hung in the air a desperate bridge being built back toward the man who had stayed silent, a plea for help from the only person who might still hold the key to Amelia's frozen heart.

The Tuscan evening was bleeding into a deep, bruised purple, the kind of sunset that usually brought Luca peace. Inside the villa, the warmth of the hearth battled the chill of the "Coldest Winter Rose" that still clung to the stone walls.

Luca was sat at the heavy oak table, his large hand gently guiding **Livia's** smaller one as she labored over her drawing homework. Livia was a "tiny, cheerful melody" in the quiet house, her voice a "delightful, non-stop mashup" of two worlds. *"Guarda, Papa! The sun is yellow, like the limoni!"* she chirped, her accent a perfect, lyrical blend of her mother's D.C. roots and her father's Italian heritage. Luca smiled, but it was a tired ghost of a smile that didn't reach his eyes.

Suddenly, the vibration of his phone against the wood sounded like a gunshot in the silent room. He looked down. The caller ID read: **Amelia's Mother.**

His breath hitched. For forty three days, he had built a fortress of silence, using his anger as mortar to keep the pain out. His finger hovered over the glass. Part of him the proud, wounded part wanted to let it ring until it died. But then, a sharp, piercing thought of **Leo** shredded his resolve. *Is he okay? Is he hurt?*

He swiped to answer, his voice a gravelly rasp. "Pronto?"

"Son," Amelia's mother began. Her voice was "warm, yet heavy with a care that transcended continents." It wasn't the voice of an accuser; it was the voice of a woman who had seen the rise and fall of a thousand tides. "How are you, Luca?"

The simple kindness of the word "son" cracked the dam. Luca, the stoic surgeon who could steady his hands through a ten-hour heart transplant, began to crumble. The exhaustion and the "bitter regret" poured out of him in a desperate torrent. He told her everything the suffocating weight of that Christmas party, the way Isabella had forced that kiss, and his immediate, visceral rejection of the woman who had tried to ruin his life. He spoke of the "final, crushing decision" to let Amelia take Leo, a choice that had felt like amputating his own limb without anesthesia.

Amelia's mother listened with a "palpable wisdom," absorbing his agony through the static of the satellite delay. When he finally fell silent, gasping for air, she spoke in a "low, poetic hum."

"Luca," she said softly. "I believe you. I know my daughter. She trusts you with her very soul, but you must understand she saw her nightmare made real. Her love for you is fierce, but her fear of betrayal is a **monstrous, deep-seated shadow**."

Her words were a "balm." Hearing the mother of the woman who hated him say the words *I believe you* caused a "fragile crack" to appear in the wall of ice around his heart. For the first time in weeks, he didn't feel like a villain; he felt like a man who was simply, tragically human.

But then, the tone shifted. He heard her take a "sharp, audible breath," a sound so heavy with worry it seemed to vibrate the phone in his hand.

"Luca," she whispered, the lightness vanishing. " Son, I just called you...to tell you... the mother of your kids... has not gotten up from the bed for three days."

An "electric jolt" a pain "more piercing than any scalpel" ripped through Luca's chest. The air was sucked out of the room. He felt the blood drain from his face as the image of Amelia, paralyzed by the darkness of **postpartum depression**, flooded his mind. He remembered the blankness in her eyes after Leo was born, the terrifying "suffocating fear" of her slipping away into that void. He had vowed to be her lighthouse, yet his own pride had turned off the light.

His anger didn't just fade; it evaporated. He realized with "devastating clarity" that his silent treatment hadn't been a lesson it had been a "cruel mirror" reflecting her deepest terror. He had left her alone in the dark when she was already drowning.

"How is Leo?" he asked, his voice "strangled and raw." The fear for his son was a physical weight, a primal agony that made his hands shake.

"Leo is fine," she answered, her voice flickering with a "forced lightness" that didn't fool him. "He's a handsome little fellow who doesn't realize his mama is being a stubborn fool."

But the tremor in her voice told the real story. Leo was fine for now, but the foundation of his world was crumbling. Luca looked at Livia, who was still coloring her yellow sun, oblivious to the storm on the other end of the line. The "rose of his love" was bruised, battered by the frost of betrayal and distance, but in that moment, he felt it fighting for life. He wasn't a man at war anymore; he was a man who needed to save the woman who held his heart captive across the sea.

The Unbroken Thread

The walk from the living room to the bedroom felt like a journey across a thousand miles of jagged ice. Behind the door, Amelia lay in a silence that had once been her suffocating cage, but as the soft padding of her mother's footsteps approached, the atmosphere shifted, thick with an unspoken, electric tension.

Thousands of miles away, Luca sat in the hollow quiet of the villa, his heart drumming against his ribs a frantic, rhythmic count of every step his mother-in-law took toward that bedroom door. He closed his eyes, his mind racing to the child he had handed over at the gate.

A new, sharper fear began to claw at him. He thought of **Leo**, the "photocopy" of himself. He wondered, with a sickening twist of guilt, if his son was being caught in the crossfire of a "blame game" he was too young to understand. Did Amelia look at Leo's dark curls and see the man who had betrayed her? Did she look into the boy's eyes and find only reminders of the winter rose that had withered?

Luca gripped the phone so hard the plastic groaned. He wanted to leap through the static, to reach across the ocean and pull her into his arms. He wanted to whisper into her hair that she would be okay, that he was coming for her, that the darkness didn't have to win.

In D.C., the bedroom door creaked open. Amelia didn't move; she remained curled into a tight knot under the blankets, her eyes fixed on a faded pattern on the wallpaper. She had heard the "gentle murmur" of her mother's voice from the other room, a low frequency she couldn't quite decipher but that felt like a lifeline being cast into a storm.

As her mother entered, the room felt smaller, the air heavier with the weight of what was about to be revealed. Amelia sensed the change the way the "suffocating cage" of her depression was being breached by a force she wasn't sure she was ready to face.

She didn't know that on the other end of a satellite signal, the man she was trying to forget was holding his breath, his soul hovering at the foot of her bed, waiting for the first sign of life from the woman who had taken half his world with her.

"Amelia" her mother said, her voice tender, a warm embrace in itself, extending the phone. "Luca wants to talk to you."

Amelia took the phone, her hand trembling, a tremor that ran through her entire body. She didn't speak; she couldn't. Her throat was constricted by days of unshed tears, her mind a tangled mess of guilt, pain, and the overwhelming fear that he, her Luca, truly hated her.

Then, Luca's voice came through the receiver. It was no longer the cold, cutting sound of the airport, nor the terse anger of his earlier silence. It was a low, guttural, **passionate confession**, a sound that felt as if it had been **boiled in the hot, unyielding Tuscan sun**, distilled to its raw, essential truth.

"*Bella*," he whispered, the sound of her name a plea, a lifeline thrown across the vast ocean. "When you are hurt, truly hurt, I am shattered. My world implodes. I love you, Amelia. My God, I need you. I need you to be better, not just for you, but for our kids. *For me*. I am not strong enough to raise these two incredible, demanding humans we created alone."

He was no longer the imposing cardiac surgeon, the man of unflappable control and precise decisions. He was a broken man, confessing his deepest weakness, his profound, unvarnished need. His admission that he **needed her strength**, that his formidable self was incomplete without her was the unexpected, powerful key that unlocked her floodgates.

Amelia didn't speak. She only began to weep, a deep, rattling cry that shook her entire body, a primal release of the guilt, the sorrow, the crushing burden she had bottled up since she walked out of that ballroom. It was a weeping born of relief, of pain recognized, of love reaffirmed. Her mother, sensing the sacred, infinite, soundproof space they now occupied, quietly walked out of the room, gently closing the door behind her.

After the torrent of tears receded, leaving her breathless, raw, and utterly spent, Amelia finally spoke, her voice still trembling but infused with a fragile, dawning hope. "I am so sorry, baby. I love you."

They talked for a long, immeasurable time, the familiar rhythm of their voices weaving a tender, **unbroken thread** across the vast, dark Atlantic. He told her about Livia's latest school drawing, a charming mess of sunflowers and olive trees.

He spoke of Sofia, of the terrifying emptiness of the bed next to him, of the aching void in his arms where Leo should be. He told her of his own fears, his shame for letting his pride wound her, for abandoning her in her deepest need.

Then, a flicker of his old teasing self, a spark of the Luca she adored, returned. His voice, softer now, took on a playful command. "Girl, get up and take a shower. Mama told me you haven't left the bed for days. Something there must smell like fish."

Amelia let out a wet, genuine laugh a choked, raw sound, but undeniably the first sound of true joy in a while. The despair that had held her captive began to recede like a tide. In that single, miraculous moment, the **electronic current of the phone line** was stronger than the combined, formidable force of the waves, the doubt, and the distance. Luca and Amelia were connected again, bound by a love that could be tested to its very limits, wounded, but never, ever severed. The winter had passed; the rose was ready to bloom.

Amelia asked for space, not because she doubted him, but because she needed to be a whole woman for her husband and her children. She didn't want Luca to see the blank, shadowed version of herself she had been after Leo's birth. She began to anchor herself in the present, starting with Yoga and specialized breathing classes, reclaiming the mind-body connection that labor and trauma had stolen.

Morning and night calls became the new, sacred rhythm of their long-distance love. Thanks to the magic of technology, the WhatsApp call needed no currency, only commitment. The Atlantic was no longer a vast, isolating barrier; it was a backdrop, an ocean they crossed twice daily with their voices. They would talk for hours, sharing Livia's latest hilarious bilingual anecdote or Leo's newest tooth. The tenderness of their separation was a deliberate choice, fueling their recovery and strengthening their eventual union

The Compass of the Heart

The phone call with Luca hadn't been a debate; it had been a bloodline, a steady, pulsing drip of life-sustaining warmth that flowed directly into Amelia's depleted veins. There had been no "you did this" or "I did that." Through the static of the transatlantic line, they had stripped away the armor of their pride. It was a raw realization that they weren't just two people in a relationship, but two halves of a single, breathing ecosystem. Luca's voice, thick with a love that had survived the frost, reminded her that while the winter had been long, the roots of their life were still deep and intertwined.

The next morning, the heavy, suffocating grey of the past few weeks lifted. Amelia woke before the sun, her body moving not with the lethargy of depression, but with a renewed, quiet purpose.

She took a long, steaming shower, feeling the hot water wash away the salt of old tears and the scent of a bed she had inhabited for far too long. In the kitchen, the air soon filled with the domestic symphony of a family being nurtured: the sizzle of bacon, the aroma of fresh coffee, and the clinking of plates.

When her mother walked into the kitchen, she froze in the doorway. She didn't see the ghost who had been hiding under the covers. She saw her daughter "blossoming like the cherry blossoms on Lincoln Memorial" vibrant, pink-cheeked, and radiant against the morning light. They sat together, the silence finally replaced by a long, honest talk and the simple, profound joy of a homemade breakfast.

After breakfast, Amelia didn't retreat. She strapped **Leo** into his jogging stroller, kissed his forehead no longer seeing a painful reminder of Luca, but a beautiful promise of their future and headed out into the crisp D.C. air.

For the first time since she had landed at Reagan, Amelia actually *saw* the city. Since her arrival, Washington had been a graveyard of "buildings without souls," a collection of cold marble and meaningless monuments. But as she ran, her lungs burning with the cold, fresh air, the city roared back to life.

The Senses: She breathed in the distinct, earthy smell of the D.C. trees. She heard the rhythmic, underground thrum of the Metro the distinct "sound of the Blue, Yellow, Silver, and Red lines" pulsing beneath the streets like the city's own heartbeat.

She saw the people the commuters, the tourists, the runners and felt a thread of connection to the world again.

As she pushed the stroller, her pace steady and strong, she realized she was finally *here*. She was in D.C., but she wasn't a girl hiding from a mistake. She was a woman who had "walked through fire" and emerged on the other side with her soul intact.

She looked at the monuments in the distance and realized that she didn't need the city to tell her who she was. She only needed the memory of Luca's voice and the strength in her own legs to remind her of her worth. She was a woman worthy of being loved, a woman who had built a life across an ocean, and a woman who was finally ready to stop running and start living whether the sun was rising over the Potomac or the rolling hills of Tuscany.

The following weeks became a digital sanctuary, a bridge of data and light that spanned the vastness of the Atlantic. No longer was the ocean a cold chasm of separation; it had become a "living, breathing connection." Through the magic of FaceTime and WhatsApp, the thousands of miles between Washington, D.C. and Tuscany dissolved into the glow of a smartphone screen.

Their days were anchored by the "endless flow of their re-united voices." They moved beyond the silence, replacing it with long, soul-baring Zoom calls and fervent whispers late into the night.

They didn't just talk about the weather or the children; they mapped out the architecture of their future. They spoke about the fracture that had occurred, but this time, they weren't examining the break they were admiring the strength of the weld.

Luca would walk through the vineyard, holding his phone out so Amelia could see the vines, while she would show him the sunset over the Potomac. These "pixelated faces" were their lifelines, a constant reminder that their love was a living thing, thriving in the digital ether.

During one particularly quiet Zoom call, Luca looked at her with a depth of tenderness that made her breath hitch. He didn't demand her return. He didn't set a deadline or issue an ultimatum.

"Take your time, Bella," he whispered, his eyes soft and steady. "Stay until you feel the ground solid beneath your feet again. The door is open. It will always be open. Whenever you are ready to come back to Italy... I will be here."

This was the ultimate gift of his love: the freedom to choose him all over again. Amelia understood then that it was no longer a question of *if* she would return, but *when*. The "backwards steps" she had feared were actually the momentum she needed for the leap back home.

Their love, once "battered and bruised" by the frost of betrayal and the ice of silence, was officially in transit. But this journey was different from the one she had taken at the airport. This wasn't about finding a path back to one another; they had already found it. It was about "confirming that the destination" was, and had always been, "irrevocably each other's hearts."

As Amelia walked the streets of D.C., she felt the weight of the ocean, but it no longer felt heavy. It felt like a tether. Every WhatsApp notification, every chime of a video call, was a heartbeat. They were two souls, separated by a sea but unified by a promise, waiting for the moment when the digital whispers would once again become a physical embrace under the Tuscan sun.

Days turned into a hopeful rhythm of reconnection. Luca, dedicated as ever, emerged from a long, complex day in the operating room, his mind still replaying the successful rhythm of a mended heart. He had just finished talking to a patient, newly awakened from medication-induced sleep, her eyes clear and grateful. As he walked down the gleaming hospital corridor, his phone rang. It was his boss, a rare, direct call. A flicker of apprehension, then curiosity.

"Luca," his boss's voice was unusually formal, yet tinged with an unfamiliar excitement. "Can you come to my office?"

A few minutes later, Luca entered the spacious, wood-paneled office. His boss, a man of few words, handed him a crisp, official-looking letter. Luca's eyes scanned the words: "Doctors Without Borders... Global Health Initiative..." The air in the room seemed to thicken with unspoken possibility. His gaze finally settled on the project details: "We got the funding... a three-year program to run clinics in Zimbabwe, Algeria, Peru, and Burma..." His boss looked at him, a knowing smile playing on his lips. "Where do you want to go, Luca?"

For a second, Luca's heart stopped. The world outside the elegant office seemed to fade, replaced by a vivid, almost hallucinatory image: the thunderous spray of Victoria Falls, the deep crimson of an African sunset, the ancient trees, the very soil where he had scattered his father's ashes. His heart returned, not to the familiar clinical hum of the hospital, but to the same vast, star-dusted sky where he had made love for the first time under African stars with Amelia, now the mother of his children. Without thinking, without saying a single word, he merely uttered one name, a whisper of destiny.

"Zimbabwe."

His boss blinked, clearly shocked. "Dude, are you okay?"

Luca looked at him, his eyes alight with a fire that surprised even himself. "Zimbabwe," he repeated, his voice firm, resolute. "It's where my Dad is, where I met love of my life, where my heart truly found its home. I will be happy to go there."

His boss, still reeling but impressed by the fierce conviction, shook his hand. "Only bad news, Spadoni: you only have two months to get ready."

Luca laughed, a sound of pure, unadulterated joy. "Even tomorrow, I will head there!" The words were light, playful, yet held the immense weight of a dream finally articulated.

Driving home that evening, the familiar Italian landscape seemed transformed, shimmering with new meaning. He could picture everything: the dusty red roads, the vibrant markets, the smiling faces of the children he would serve. A profound realization blossomed in his chest, so clear it felt like a prophecy: *this* was where he wanted to get married. Not in some grand Italian cathedral, but under the vast, untamed sky of the land that had witnessed the rebirth of his soul and the genesis of his love. He couldn't call Amelia; it was far too late in D.C., and she would be sleeping, dreaming their mending dreams. This news was too big for a phone call.

The Secret Preparations

The sun had not yet touched the Potomac when the phone vibrated against Amelia's nightstand. She reached for it through a fog of sleep, her eyes fluttering open to the soft glow of the screen. It was 6:00 AM.

"Pronto," she croaked, her voice thick with sleep. "Babe... is everyone okay? It's 6:00 AM. I'm not training for a marathon today."

A low, rich chuckle vibrated through the speaker, a sound that felt like a warm hand on her cheek. "Darling, I was waiting for the light to brighten your sky before I called," Luca said, his voice brimming with a boyish excitement she hadn't heard in months. "I have news. Incredible news. I got the job, Amelia. Doctors Without Borders."

Amelia sat bolt upright, a shout of pure, unadulterated joy escaping her. She knew the late nights he'd spent studying, the passion he had for bringing his surgical skill to those who needed it most. "Oh my god, Luca! I'm so proud of you!" But then she paused, her heart skipping a beat. "Wait... where? Where are they sending you?"

"Africa," Luca said, the smile evident in his tone. "Guess wh ere..."

"Uganda?" she guessed, her mind racing. "Is it where your father did his research?"

"Yes and no," Luca replied. "He was in Uganda, but we... we got **Zimbabwe**."

The air in the room seemed to shift, filling with the scent of rain on red earth and the roar of distant water. "Zimbabwe!" Amelia cried. "Luca, I can't wait. I can't wait for Leo to see the waterfalls you know how much he loves water. And Livia... she's finally going to see a zebra in real life. It's her favorite animal!"

They bubbled over with plans for a few more minutes, the transatlantic distance feeling like nothing more than a thin veil. But the reality of Luca's world broke in; a sharp beep signaled another line. "Bella, I have to go. I'm on call today and the hospital is paging. Get up, start your day. I love you. Bye."

The click of the end-call was the starting gun for Luca. The next few days were a whirlwind of "secret preparations," conducted with a focus that rivaled his most complex surgical procedures. He moved through the villa like a man possessed, his mind a map of logistics and longing.

His first call was the most important one. He dialed the number for **Rovos Rail**, the "Pride of Africa." As the line connected, a hopeful tremor vibrated in his voice a rare moment of vulnerability for the stoic surgeon.

"Do you offer wedding packages?" he asked, holding his breath.

The answer from the other end was a resounding, enthusiastic *yes*.

A jolt of pure exhilaration shot through him. He leaned back in his leather chair, looking out at the Tuscan pines but seeing the vast, golden savannah. The train the very one that had once carried him through the depths of his despair and eventually back toward hope would now become the vessel for their ultimate union. It wouldn't just be a journey through a continent; it would be the final leg of the journey back to each other. He wasn't just planning a wedding; he was engineering a masterpiece of redemption

He called Sofia next, his sister's familiar voice a comforting anchor. He poured out the news: the Doctors Without Borders offer, his choice of Zimbabwe, and his audacious plan to get married in Africa. Sofia, ever the pragmatist, was momentarily sad to hear he would move to Africa for three years, remembering their own childhood sojourn in Uganda with their father, researching the "monkey kingdom." But her sadness quickly transformed into fierce determination. "Of course, I'll help you arrange everything," she declared, her enthusiasm infectious. "Consider me your African wedding planner!"

He knew he couldn't deliver such monumental news to Amelia over the phone. This was a moment that demanded his physical presence, the tangible warmth of his hand, the honesty in his eyes. In a matter of days, he bought a ticket and flew to the USA.

The frost of the "Coldest Winter Rose" began to thaw under the weight of a plan so bold it could only be fueled by desperate, enduring love. Luca realized news is deserves face to face; he needed to be the antidote. Without a word to Amelia, he secured two tickets, packed Livia's small bags, and crossed the Atlantic.

When the doorbell rang in the quiet D.C. suburb. Amelia pulled the door open, expecting a delivery or a neighbor, but the world seemed to tilt on its axis.

There stood Livia, beaming and jumping with a "tiny, cheerful melody" of a greeting, and behind her looming like a solid, immovable mountain of hope was Luca. Amelia almost faint-ed, her knees buckling as the "love of her life" caught her gaze. The reunion was a "tender, lingering ache," a flood of tears and whispered apologies that washed away the weeks of icy silence. For seven days, they lived in a bubble of domestic restoration, Luca rebuilding the fractured trust brick by brick, his hands once again finding their place in hers.

Two days into the visit, Luca invited Amelia's father for coffee. They sat in a small, quiet cafe, the steam rising from their cups like a prayer. Luca looked at the man who had raised the woman who held his soul and spoke with a raw, humble honesty.

"I haven't told Amelia yet," Luca confessed, his voice steadying. "But I want to marry her where the sun is constant. I want to take her to Africa. I am asking for your blessing first, as a man who owes you everything for the gift of your daughter."

Amelia's father, a man of "quiet strength," didn't hesitate. He stood, his chair scraping against the floor, and pulled Luca into a fierce, masculine embrace. "I will never stand to block the blessing God brought to our doorstep," he whispered, his eyes "shining with understanding."

That evening, the air in the kitchen was thick with emotion as Luca met with both parents. The blessing was absolute, a sacred seal placed upon their future. Later, when the house had settled into a peaceful quiet, Luca found Amelia in the dim light of their room. He leaned in, his lips brushing her temple, his voice a low, vibrating promise.

"I have your father's blessing, Bella," he whispered, watching her eyes widen. If you say yes,...again!! you will make me the happiest man alive."

The answer was written in the way she clung to him, a silent, tearful surrender to the future.

With the "Yes" finally anchored in her heart, the transition from the coldest winter to the warmth of a Safari sun began. Luca, ever the "meticulous planner," threw himself into the logistics with surgical precision.

A wedding under the vast, golden canopy of the African sky. A blissful honeymoon safari where the only sounds would be the wild calls of the savannah and the laughter of Livia and Leo. To savor every heartbeat of their reunited family before the demanding rhythm of his surgical career called him back.

He was't just planning a trip; he was orchestrating a rebirth. The pain of the past was being replaced by the "meticulous rhythm" of a love that had survived the frost and was now ready to bloom in the wild, untamed beauty of the African plains.

After a few days of joyful, whirlwind planning in the States, they packed to head back to Italy. On the plane, the quiet hum of the engines was a counterpoint to the anticipation buzzing between them. Their children, Livia and Leo, were sound asleep in their first-class seats an indulgence Luca insisted upon, a silent promise that their family, once separated, would always travel in comfort and together.

Luca looked at Amelia, his heart swelling with the secret joy of his carefully laid plans. "Will you be mad," he began, a playful glint in his eyes, "if we get married in Africa?"

Amelia's eyes, already bright with the joy of their reunion, lit up even further. "Please, don't even start!" she teased, her voice bubbling with delight. Then, a mischievous thought sparked in her mind, her own audacious dream taking flight. "How about...

how about if we get married on the train we met on? That would be dope!"

Luca leaned in, his lips finding hers, a soft, tender kiss that sealed their unspoken understanding. "Darling," he whispered against her mouth, "our souls speak the same language." He pulled back, his eyes dancing with triumph. "Okay, yes, we are going to Italy. But in three weeks we will be heading to Africa. The end of this month, *mia bella*, we are getting married." He confessed, a joyous tremor in his voice, "I have planned everything. I was just hoping you would say yes."

They kissed tenderly, a profound, soul-deep communion. They savored the moment of their united future, suspended high above the very ocean that had always kept them apart, yet tonight was the same ocean that now bound them irrevocably together, a silent, powerful testament to their enduring, triumphant love.

The Cathedral of Thunder

The few final days in Italy were a **blur of emotional velocity**, a concentrated mix of gratitude, giddy anticipation, and the sweet pang of goodbyes. The farmhouse, usually a sanctuary of simple domesticity, now hummed with an almost palpable excitement, feeling less like a home and more like a **staging ground** for an epic adventure. Suitcases lay open, half-packed, spilling over with clothes, maps, and the vibrant African print fabrics Amelia had already begun collecting.

Sofia, with her sharp intellect and even sharper love for her brother, became the quiet architect of Amelia's peace. Having witnessed Luca's anguish the raw, visceral fear of loss that had driven him to tears not so long ago she felt a profound, almost sacred responsibility to ensure Amelia's happiness was absolute, unblemished, and breathtaking.

Her first decree, delivered with a mischievous twinkle in her eye, was to take Amelia **wedding dress shopping**. This was no ordinary shopping trip; it was a ritual of sisterhood and unconditional acceptance. They swept through elegant Milanese boutiques, the air thick with the scent of fine lace and delicate silk. Sofia insisted on buying the entire wedding wardrobe for Amelia not just the dress, but shoes, accessories, and a whisper-light veil. This gesture went far beyond mere generosity; it was an unspoken vow of acceptance and love from one woman who cherished Luca to the other who was Luca's heart. Sofia moved with a quiet determination, meticulously ensuring every detail was perfect, a material manifestation of the deep, boundless love she held for Luca, a love she now poured into his future wife.

Amelia tried on a dozen dresses, each a masterpiece, but it was the **simple, flowing white silk gown** that stole her breath. It clung to her curves with understated elegance, moving like water, yet felt as comfortable and free as a second skin. It wasn't adorned with crystals or heavy lace; its beauty lay in its purity, its movement, and the way it made *her* feel unburdened, strong, and utterly radiant. Sofia, seeing Amelia's eyes light up, knew it was the one. It was perfect for the African sun, perfect for the woman who was finally embracing her wild heart.

Back at the farmhouse, with Amelia's emotions carefully managed and her wardrobe secure, Luca finalized the intricate logistics that underpinned their drastic decision to move to Africa. He had secured the **blessing of Amelia's father**, a man who, seeing Luca's unwavering love and decisive action, had entrusted him with his daughter's happiness. Luca painstakingly ensured every detail was covered: tickets were booked, passports stamped, visas acquired, and he even secured the plane tickets for Amelia's in-laws to meet them in South Africa, ensuring Amelia would have her entire American foundation present for this monumental, final step into her new life.

The days were a flurry of final goodbyes. Neighbors brought baskets of fresh fruit and bottles of local wine. Friends came with promises of visits. There were tearful hugs, long embraces, and the bittersweet flavor of endings that were, in truth, magnificent new beginnings. Livia and Leo, with their usual boundless energy, darted between suitcases, their giggles a constant reminder of the vibrant future awaiting them.

Finally, the morning arrived. The air, crisp and cool, held a thrill of anticipation. The bags, heavy with a new life, were loaded into the car. As they drove away from the farmhouse, leaving behind the beloved Tuscan hills, there was no sadness, only a quiet, profound certainty. Their hearts beat in unison, a compass set for the African sun, for the train, for the Falls, and for the destiny that had waited so patiently for them. They were ready.

Claiming the African Earth

The family flew south, leaving behind the cool marble elegance and sentinel cypress trees of Tuscany, exchanging them for the **glowing, ancient heart of the African continent**. It was a journey not just across miles, but across worlds, a deliberate crossing of a threshold into a future both challenging and utterly destined.

Upon landing in Zimbabwe, the transition was **immediate and profound**, a sensory immersion. The airplane's conditioned air, sterile and recycled, gave way to a sudden, encompassing wave of **thick, tropical heat**, a benevolent embrace that wrapped around them. It was heavy, laden with the earthy, mineral scent of **red dust** that promised adventure, mingling with the bright, intoxicating perfume of **frangipani and other tropical foliage**, a fragrance of life, raw and untamed. This wasn't just a smell; it was the very breath of Africa, filling Amelia's lungs with a sense of belonging she hadn't realized she craved.

Luca had arranged to view several houses, practical and promising, but as they drove into the **Borrowdale area of Harare**, Amelia was utterly captivated. This affluent suburb was a lush, serene tapestry woven from nature's most generous threads. Flowering gardens, ablaze with hibiscus and bougainvillea, spilled over high walls. Massive **Jacaranda trees**, not yet in their purple bloom, stood as ancient sentinels, offering wide, embracing shade. The streets were quiet, winding, leading to spacious, secluded homes behind high stone walls, each promising privacy and peace. The sunlight, filtered through the thick, verdant canopy, descended in luminous, shifting patterns, creating a sense of **seclusion and calm**, a sanctuary carved from the bustling city.

The house Luca had favored was a sprawling, light-filled structure that seemed to expand to greet the African sun. Wide, inviting verandas stretched across its facade, perfect for long, lazy evenings, and the cool, terracotta floors promised respite from the day's heat. As Amelia stepped out of the car, she didn't need to see the interior, didn't need a tour. She simply felt the house **breathe** around her, its old walls whispering tales of generations. It felt secure, solid, rooted utterly unlike the temporary, anxious spaces they had occupied, the transit points of their love story. This was a place to stay.

She looked at Luca, her eyes filling not with tears of sadness, but with a **radiant certainty** that erased months of doubt, a certainty that spoke of anchors dropped and journeys completed. "Babe," she said, her voice soft but resolute, claiming her ground. "This is our house."

Luca smiled, a deep, slow smile of profound relief. He understood the immense, emotional weight of her words, the true meaning of her claim. "Wherever you are, *Bella*, is where my home is," he responded, his voice thick with love, confirming their shared destiny. "You, me, and our kids follow." He knew that the home was less about the walls and more about the simple, undeniable fact that Amelia had finally, absolutely, claimed this patch of earth, this future, as her own.

He quickly, efficiently settled the family. The children were enrolled in a nearby international school, their days quickly finding a reassuring, familiar rhythm, their laughter once again echoing freely. Luca completed his paperwork with the clinic, officially ready to begin his three-year program the following month, eager to immerse himself in his new purpose. Amelia, already energized by the vibrant environment, wasted no time. She visited the local university, exploring options for either teaching part-time or engaging in meaningful volunteer work a **seamless transition** that showed their commitment was absolute, their roots already reaching deep into the rich African earth. Their life, once a turbulent journey, had finally found its profound, beautiful landing.

The Final Transit to Pretoria: A Full Circle Home

Within a week, with their new home in Harare already breathing with life and their children settled into their new school rhythms, everything was set. The invitations were out, the final details were meticulously arranged by Sofia, and the air thrummed with the anticipation of a long-awaited destiny. The family flew the last leg of their journey, a mere skip across the southern African sky, to **Pretoria, South Africa**.

Stepping off the plane onto the sun-baked tarmac, Amelia felt an immediate, powerful pull of memory, a spectral echo from a lifetime ago. This was the very city of their first, fateful encounter, the crucible where their impossible love story had first sparked. But this arrival was profoundly, unequivocally different. There was no longer the electric hum of anxiety, no lingering tremor of uncertainty. Instead, there was a deep, unifying feeling of **wholeness**, a serene confidence that settled into her bones like the warmth of the African sun. This was not a meeting; it was a homecoming.

Livia and Leo, their innocent faces alight with the unburdened curiosity of children on an adventure, were a vivid, tangible testament to the journey. Dressed in comfortable travel clothes, Livia, clutching her father's hand with fierce devotion, chattered ceaselessly about the wonder of the plane ride, her voice a delightful mashup of Italian and English. Leo, a sturdy, adventurous two-year-old, rode securely on Luca's broad shoulders, his tiny hands gripping his father's hair, a king surveying his new kingdom. They were the visible, tangible fruit of the long, impossible transit, the living, breathing proof that every mile, every tear, every doubt had been worth it.

They were no longer two strangers meeting at a train station, veiled in the mystery of what could be. They were a family of four, exquisitely complete, returning to the very starting line of their narrative, not to relive it, but to redefine its purpose. They were here to greet the arriving wedding guests Amelia's parents, Luca's extended family, and a handful of their closest friends all converging from across the globe, drawn by the magnet of their love. And then, together, they would finally board the iconic **Rovos Rail**, the luxurious train that had once carried them into the thrilling, terrifying unknown, ready now to carry them into forever, on a journey that would culminate in the most spectacular affirmation of their unbreakable bond. The circle was not just closing; it was expanding, embracing their past, celebrating their present, and promising a boundless future under the vast, ancient sky of Africa.

Inside the train, the world outside, with its endless demands and hurried pace, melted away. Time slowed to the perfect, deliberate tempo of romance. The **mahogany-paneled walls and gleaming brass fixtures** of their private suite shimmered under soft, ambient light, reflecting the quiet joy in their eyes. The rhythmic **click-clack of the wheels against the tracks** became a meditative, hypnotic soundtrack to their reunion, a lullaby of fate unfolding. Every creak and sway of the carriage was a reminder of their first journey, now reborn with the promise of forever.

Dinner was a **sensory feast** in the lavish dining car, an experience orchestrated for the senses. The rich, earthy taste of perfectly prepared **South African game** perhaps succulent springbok or tender kudu danced on their palates, each bite an exotic adventure. It was paired exquisitely with the smooth, **velvety texture of fine Cape wine**, a deep ruby liquid that shimmered in their crystal glasses, warming them from the inside out. The air was a delicate, intoxicating blend of fine linen, gourmet cooking, and the distant, **wild smoke of the evening Savannah**, carried on the breeze through the open windows. Every sound was filtered the light, joyous laughter of family and friends, the soft clinking of silver against porcelain, the gentle, hushed rush of the train carving its path through the moonlit landscape transforming the entire journey into a **moving sanctuary**, a cocoon of love and anticipation.

Later, with Leo and Livia sound asleep, tucked safely into their grandparents' cozy cabin next door, Luca decided it was time to recreate the moment that started it all. His heart thrummed with a nervous excitement, a delightful echo of his younger, more reckless self. He slipped out of their cabin, closing the door softly, and after a moment, knocked gently on their door, a mischievous glint in his eyes.

Amelia opened it, her gaze soft, expectant, her heart already racing. Luca stood there, bathed in the soft glow of the corridor, his eyes dancing with a familiar, magnetic fire. "Did you forget the..."

Before he could even finish the silly, half-forgotten line from that first night, Amelia, her love and anticipation overwhelming her, pulled him in. Her mouth found his in a **torrent of pent-up desire and profound relief**, a kiss that spoke of all the miles, all the tears, all the doubt, and every single triumph they had endured. It was a confirmation, an affirmation, a living testament to their unbreakable bond. They made love, slowly, tenderly, exquisitely, in the very vehicle of their first encounter, under the vast, unseen sky full of ancient African stars. Every touch was an emotion, every breath a connection, every whispered word a promise that bound their souls together forever, sealing their destiny within the gentle sway of the train.

Afterward, lying close in the gentle darkness of their cabin, the rhythmic **lullaby of the train** rocking them, Amelia's fingers traced the strong line of Luca's jaw. "Baby," she whispered, her voice soft with contentment, "you know, without that **Lonely Note** you left, we might never have connected again."

Luca sat up, his eyes sparkling, adopting a playful, dramatic pose, pretending he was **Shakespeare heading to Verona**to pen a sonnet. He reached for a piece of "hotel" stationary from the bedside table and, with mock solemnity, scribbled a note, then cleared his throat. He read it aloud, his voice low and solemn, yet brimming with tenderness:

"Darling Perfect Stranger,

Now I know your name and each cherished corner of your body. I have seen you cry, weep, smile, and laugh. You have stolen my heart, permanently. Thank you for giving me the best gifts a man could ask for: Livia, my lightning star, and Leo, my Lion King. The first day I met you, your eyes locked my heart and took the password with you. The transit is over, my love. I am finally home.

Amelia slowly walked to him, her heart overflowing, and wrapped her arms around his waist from behind, resting her head on his shoulder. She kissed his bare skin with a tenderness that held a lifetime of promises, of shared joys and overcome sorrows. Luca looked at her, his romantic vulnerability utterly exposed in his eyes, a depth of love so profound it was almost heartbreaking.

Amelia laughed, a soft, rich sound that echoed the rhythm of the train. "Boy, don't look at me like that," she teased, pressing another kiss to his shoulder. "Or do you want another baby?"

Luca lifted her into his arms, a full, joyous laugh erupting from his chest. "Girl," he declared, his eyes shining, "I have no say in that. I will never want to see you suffer like you did again, not for a moment. But if you want it, my love, I will be the happiest man. If you don't, I am perfectly okay with my two precious *bambinos*."

They held each other tight, allowing the **lullaby of the train** to gently rock them to sleep, united on the moving metal ribbon that was carrying them, not just through the African landscape, but inexorably toward their glorious destiny.

The Cathedral of Thunder

For three unforgettable nights, the luxury train carried them steadily north, the rhythmic pulse of the wheels counting down the final, destined miles of their transit, a slow, deliberate march towards their future. The landscape outside blurred into a symphony of changing light and shadow endless savannah, distant hills, and finally, the deepening green of approaching rainforest.

They finally disembarked near the mighty Zambezi River, the air already thick with a promise of something monumental. The wedding party followed the riverbank, a vibrant procession of love and joy, until they reached the precipice of **Mosi-oa-Tunya** *The Smoke that Thunders* **Victoria Falls**. It was not merely a vista; it was a revelation, a primal force of nature that commanded reverence. The air was a living thing, thick with the **sweet, damp musk of the rainforest**, the mineral scent of spray, and the primal, all-encompassing roar of the Zambezi. The very ground seemed to vibrate with the raw power of the **massive curtain of water**, which plummeted 350 feet in a blinding, chaotic white. The mist rose hundreds of feet into the sky, earning its local title, "the rain that never ends," cloaking the entire gorge in an ethereal, sacred veil.

It was the same terrifyingly beautiful place where Luca had scattered his father's ashes, the very soil that had witnessed his most profound release from grief and the unforeseen genesis of his love for Amelia. This was not a conventional church; it was a **cathedral of nature, built of water and sky**, a testament to enduring life and unending spirit.

Luca paused for a private, silent moment, closing his eyes against the invigorating spray, allowing the thunder of the Falls to wash over him. His heart swelled, connecting the past and the present, linking the beloved memory of his father to the vibrant reality of his new family. He whispered into the roar, a low, fervent sound swallowed by the thunder, yet resonating with absolute clarity in his soul:

"*Papà*, I know you are somewhere here in this mist. I came here for you. I came here to be complete. You witnessed my tears; now, witness my joy. Since the moment I met her, my life changed. A strong woman with a strong soul, she made me whole. Be here with us now, as my blessing."

He opened his eyes, and the world was Amelia, radiant and breathtaking, waiting to become his wife under the roar of the Falls.

The Bridal Mist: Vows in the Cathedral of Thunder

Amelia, radiant beyond words, stood before him, the very embodiment of grace and strength. Her **simple, flowing white silk dress** was unadorned, a deliberate choice that allowed the pure, unyielding strength and profound beauty she had fought so hard to reclaim to shine through. It moved with the gentlest breeze, a testament to her newfound freedom. The delicate fabric of her veil, caught instantly by the perpetual, shimmering spray of the Falls, made it look as though it was weeping brilliant, silver tears , tears not of sorrow, but of unparalleled joy and celestial mist, blessing their union.

Luca, impossibly handsome in a sharp Italian suit, his hair slightly damp from the spray, looked at her. His eyes, usually deep pools of dark intensity, now reflected the blinding, brilliant white of the crashing water, an incandescent fire that mirrored his soul. No longer did they hold the cold reflection of a past love or a distant doubt; they blazed with the pure, unadulterated passion of his future, his forever.

Livia, now a graceful four-year-old, her tiny legs moving with a newfound poise, was their flower girl. Dressed in the vibrant, fiery colors of a tropical sunset, a miniature reflection of the land around them, she scattered petals hibiscus pinks and marigold yellows with an earnest, focused dignity, her small hands scattering their joyful future. Her mixed-up languages, a delightful mashup of Italian and English, were the perfect, enchanting sound of their beautifully blended world, a symphony of their unique family. **Leo, the Lion**, now a sturdy two-year-old, was carried securely in the powerful embrace of his proud father, his tiny hands gripping Luca's collar amidst the beautiful, thundering chaos. He was utterly safe, nestled against the heart that beat for him, oblivious and serene amidst the monumental power of nature.

They stood before their assembled family and closest friends, a small, intimate circle bound by love and journey. The colossal, primal thunder of the Falls was their majestic witness, its roar a profound anthem to their love, ready to receive the vows written not on fragile paper, but etched indelibly upon their very souls.

Luca looked at Amelia, his gaze unwavering, his love pouring from his eyes. His voice, raw with emotion yet fighting the mighty roar with absolute, piercing clarity, reached her, touching her deepest core.

"My Perfect Stranger, my love in transit," he began, his voice deepening with every word. "I stand here, on the very soil where I let go of my past, where I scattered the last remnants of my grief, and I take you as my future. You, *mia bella*, gave me two impossible, perfect gifts Livia, my lightning star, and Leonardo, my Lion King. And more than that, you gave me my heart back, healed, stronger, and whole. Every goodbye that ripped us apart, every transatlantic flight that felt like an eternity, every argument that tested our limits, every moment of fear we shared I vow to never forget them. Because they were the fires that forged us; they proved that our love is stronger than distance, stronger than doubt, stronger than any shadow of my own fear. I vow to choose you, to hear you, to see you, and to never again allow a shadow of a kiss, or any ghost from the past, to divide us. I am no longer in transit. My final, forever destination, my only home, is you."

Amelia's own tears began to fall freely, mixing with the gentle, cool mist on her face, indistinguishable from the blessings of the Falls. Her voice, though quieter, held the deep, unwavering strength of a woman who had fought for her life, for her family, and for this extraordinary love.

"My Luca, you are the powerful stream of water that heals me, the sun that melts my fears. I vow to trust the doctor in you, the fierce protector; to trust the husband in you, my anchor and my soulmate; and to trust the father in you, the devoted heart of our children. You saved my life when I was suffering, pulling me from the deepest shadow, and you gave me the courage to accept this grand, terrifying, beautiful adventure. I accept this sacred African soil as our home, because your purpose, your heart's true calling, is here. And I vow that our children, and their children, will always know the story of how their parents were so irrevocably in love, they were willing to cross an ocean like it was merely crossing the street. You are my husband, my anchor, my only truth. Yes, Luca. For always."

The exchange of rings was almost a blur, a silver flash against the roaring white of the Falls, ephemeral yet eternal. When the officiant, his voice lifted above the thunder, declared them husband and wife, Luca didn't hesitate for a single second. He pulled Amelia into a kiss that was a torrent of relief, of incandescent joy, and of ultimate finality. It was a convergence of two souls, a moment of perfect, deafening intimacy against the backdrop of the most powerful natural sound on earth, a kiss that sealed their love forever.

The small crowd family, friends, a few curious onlookers cheered, the sound faint against the mighty roar of the water, yet the emotion was overwhelming, reverberating through the very ground. The Spadoni family was officially, irrevocably, gloriously united, forever bound by the majestic power of Africa and the boundless love that had conquered all transit.

Last Stop: An African Ever After

The thundering roar of Victoria Falls had provided the soundtrack to their vows, a force of nature as powerful and unyielding as the love they had fought to reclaim. But as the sun dipped below the horizon, painting the Zambezi in shades of molten gold, the celebration shifted from the primal majesty of the water to the refined, rhythmic elegance of the **Rovos Rail**.

The train station was no longer a place of departures, but a destination of joy. The vintage, wood-paneled carriages of the "Pride of Africa" vibrated with a new energy a "happy cacophony" that bridged two worlds.

From the observation car, a "delightful blend" of music spilled out into the warm African night. The soulful, operatic strains of Italian melodies intertwined seamlessly with the vibrant, earthy pulse of African drums.

Families who had once been strangers now moved in a shared rhythm. The "rhythmic beat of dancing" echoed through the halls, a celebratory pulse that continued long after the stars thick and brilliant like spilled diamonds had filled the sky. Every toast raised was a victory lap for a love that had survived the deepest frost.

Hours passed like a beautiful dream, the "I do" acting as the final, sacred stitch in the tapestry of their lives. Now, sitting in the quiet luxury of their suite as the train hummed southward, Luca and Amelia held the first developed photographs of their wedding.

The images acted as a "flashback," pulling them back into the vivid, sensory explosion of the day:

The Walk to the Waterfall: They looked at the shot of them walking toward the spray of the falls, the mist dampening their clothes, looking like two explorers discovering a new continent of the soul.

The most precious photo was of **Livia** and **Leo**. Livia, the perfect flower girl, scattering petals with a focused, Italian intensity; and Leo, the sturdy little ring holder, his hand tucked into his sister's as they guided their mother toward the man who had fought the world to keep them together.

As they looked at the pictures, Luca pulled Amelia closer, his chin resting on her shoulder.

"It wasn't just a wedding," he whispered, his voice thick with the memory of the ceremony. "It was a family affair."

Indeed, the ceremony at the thundering heart of the falls had been more than a legal union; it was a "connection of souls." They were no longer the broken people who had shivered in a D.C. bedroom or a silent Tuscan villa. They were a "family aware" fully conscious of the price of their happiness, the depth of their healing, and the boundless horizon that now lay before them. The winter rose had finally found its sun, and in the wild heart of Africa, it had bloomed into something eternal

A day later, with heartfelt goodbyes, the wedding party boarded the Rovos Rail for the return journey, their voices echoing promises of future visits. As the majestic train began to pull away, carrying their cherished guests back south, it left behind Mr. and Mrs. Spadoni, blissfully alone, standing on the sun-baked platform. The rhythmic **click-clack of the wheels fading into the distance** was no longer the drumbeat of separation; it was the quiet, comforting rhythm of permanence, a gentle cadence of their settled, entwined destinies.

Their plan was beautifully simple, a serene counterpoint to the dramatic transit that had defined their past: seven days of African safari honeymoon. A slow, contemplative immersion into the wild, untamed beauty of the continent that had witnessed their most profound vows. They would lose themselves in the vast, golden plains, under skies that stretched forever, tracing the paths of ancient elephants and feeling the pulse of a land as old as time itself. They would watch sunsets that bled across the horizon in hues of fire and amethyst, listen to the calls of the wild under skies thick with impossible stars, and simply *be* together, finally, irrevocably. It was a journey designed not to rush, but to deepen, to savor every breath of their new beginning.

They stood on the platform, arm in arm, their shoulders touching, Amelia's hand nestled in Luca's. The last shimmer of the departing train vanished around a bend, leaving them in the vast, echoing silence of the African landscape. Above them, the sky was an endless canvas of soft, ethereal blue, promising infinite possibilities. A gentle breeze rustled the nearby acacia trees, carrying the faint, sweet scent of distant blossoms and rich earth.

Luca turned to Amelia, his eyes filled with a love so profound it seemed to hold the weight of their entire journey, every challenge, every triumph. Amelia looked back, her heart overflowing, her face radiant with a peace she had never known so completely. The memory of the lonely note, the transcontinental flights, the shattered trust, and the desperate fight for connection it all receded into the past, becoming mere whispers in the wind.

Their love, once defined by movement, by oceans and airports, by the constant, yearning pull of "in transit," had finally found its **last stop**. It wasn't a physical place, but the sacred, unyielding space in each other's hearts, a sanctuary built of shared dreams, unbreakable vows, and an enduring, magnificent African love story.

The Honeymoon

The finale of their journey didn't begin with a roar, but with the rhythmic hum of a small bush plane gliding over the emerald veins of the **Okavango Delta**. Botswana welcomed them with an ancient, sprawling beauty a place where the desert sands of the Kalahari kissed the life-giving waters of the delta, mirroring the way their two turbulent lives had finally merged into one deep, steady current.

As they arrived at their luxury safari camp, the air was thick with the scent of wild sage and sun-warmed earth. They were greeted not by the stiff formality of a hotel, but by the soulful voices of the staff, whose welcome song harmonized with the wind in the acacia trees. Amelia and Luca, hands entwined, swayed to the beat, their feet moving instinctively in the dust of a land that already felt like home.

Livia and Leo were wide-eyed, their small faces lit with pure joy as they were handed glasses of frosted, fresh-squeezed **baobab juice**. The tangy, velvet sweetness was the "taste of Africa," and as they gulped it down with messy, satisfied grins, Luca laughed a sound so free of the city lights that it seemed to startle the nearby birds into flight.

As the sun began its slow, majestic descent, painting the vast savannah in strokes of violet, amber, and blood-orange, Luca and Amelia stood on the wooden deck of their tent. The light caught the unshed tears in their eyes, turning them into shimmering gold.

Luca turned to her, his voice a low, steady anchor. "Bella... I thought we would never make it this far," he whispered, his thumb tracing the line of her jaw. "For the rest of my life, I will continue to say sorry. I will spend every sunrise and every sunset loving you more than I did the day before."

Amelia couldn't find the words her heart was too full, the air too sweet. She simply smiled through her tears, a silent "I forgive you" that settled between them forever. Luca scooped her into his arms, carrying her inside the canvas sanctuary. He checked on the children, seeing them tucked into their beds in the adjoining section of the tent, before returning to Amelia. In the fading light of the African sky, he made love to her not as a stranger on a train, and not as a boyfriend seeking heat, but as a **husband** honoring a sacred covenant.

As she lay in his arms, Amelia let her mind drift back to that first night on the luxury of Rovos train. That night was a dark, anonymous escape a desperate spark in the shadows. Now, the "train" they had just left was filled with the echoes of their children's laughter and the weight of their parents' blessings. They had gone from strangers seeking a moment of heat to a husband and wife building a permanent, roaring fire.

In the middle of the night, the "sharp cry" of **Leo** broke the silence. Luca jumped up with the instincts of a protector, unzipping the partition to find his son startled by the unfamiliar sounds of the bush. He picked the boy up, whispering soft Italian comforts, and stepped out onto the deck.

Amelia followed, and they stood together under a sky so thick with stars it looked like a ceiling of diamonds. It was the first time Leo had truly seen the cosmos. His tiny finger pointed upward, his voice a whisper of awe as he started to "count" the stars *uno, due, tre...* his young mind expanding to fit the infinite beauty of his new world.

The Big Five and the New Dawn

The next morning at 6:00 AM, the horizon was a "bruised violet" as they climbed into the open-air jeep. **Livia and Leo**sat on Luca's lap, their eyes mirroring the burnt orange of the rising sun.

The safari was a "new discovery." It wasn't just about the thrill of the hunt for the Big Five; it was about the whispers of *"Look, Papa!"* as a herd of elephants emerged from the dust like grey giants. Seeing the world through their children's eyes turned the honeymoon into a family legacy. In the heat of the day, they camped under a sprawling tree, eating together in the dirt and the sun, a family of four that had survived the frost to find the light.

The week in Botswana ended not with sadness, but with a sense of arrival. As they boarded the flight to **Harare**, they left the "tourist" labels behind. They were no longer visitors; they were the **permanent resident of Harare, Zimbabwe**.

The air in Harare was thick with the scent of sun-warmed earth and blooming jacaranda, a stark, beautiful contrast of the Tuscan sky they had left behind. As the driver navigated the bustling streets, the city unfolded before them like a vibrant tapestry of their new beginning.

Livia pressed her face against the glass, her dark eyes wide and hungry, "memorizing her new home" with the intensity of a child who knew she was starting a grand adventure. Beside her, Leo was the picture of toddler peace, "going with the flow" as he slumbered, his head lolling rhythmically with the movement of the car.

In the front seat, Luca was already immersed in the logistics of their new life. He spoke rapidly with the driver about the routes to the hospital, the local markets, and the daily commute. But even as he discussed currency and transportation, his hand reached back, his fingers grazing Amelia's knee a silent, constant tether.

"Bella," he said, turning slightly to look at her with eyes that were no longer guarded, but bright with shared purpose. "Do you still want the driver to take you to the school this afternoon? To handle the fees and check the garden? Or would you rather wait until we've settled the bags?"

Amelia reached over to adjust Leo's head, making sure he was "nice and snug" in his seat booster. She looked out at the passing trees, a sense of competence and belonging washing over her.

"No, let's go today," she said firmly. "Livia and Leo need to meet their teachers. And the garden when I spoke to James, he said he'd already bought the flowers I asked for. After the school, I have so much to do... so much is still packed away in those crates."

They cruised through the winding streets until the car finally slowed, pulling up to a house draped in golden light. Luca didn't just rush to the door. He stepped out and stood for a moment, taking a "deep, shaky breath" of the warm African afternoon. He looked at his family the woman who had walked through fire to find him again, and the children who were the living pulse of their hearts.

He turned the key in the lock. As the door swung open, the house didn't feel like a collection of rooms; "it was waiting" for them.

Livia and Leo didn't hesitate. They burst inside, their small footsteps "claiming the space" with the echoes of laughter, turning a house into a home in a matter of seconds.

The air in the house foyer was thick with the scent of floor wax and the wild, sweet musk of the jasmine vines clinging to the porch outside. The afternoon sun didn't just light the room; it poured through the high windows in solid, honey-colored shafts, illuminating the dancing dust motes that swirled like tiny gold leaf around them.

In the distance, the hollow *thud-thud-thud* of Livia and Leo's footsteps echoed through the unfurnished hallways, followed by a burst of high-pitched giggles as they discovered their new rooms. The sound was the heartbeat of the house, a vibrant proof of life that made the walls feel less like stone and more like a sanctuary.

The front door, time had slowed to a crawl. Luca and Amelia stayed back for one heartbeat longer, their silhouettes framed against the bright African horizon. Their shadows stretched long across the polished wood floors, reaching toward the future.

Hand in hand, their fingers were interlaced so tightly it was impossible to tell where his strength ended and her grace began.

With a soft, deliberate *click*, the heavy oak door settled into its frame.

The sound was a finality. It was the sound of the "backwards steps" being erased. It was the sound of the transatlantic ghosts the airport goodbyes, the silent phones, and the frozen Tuscan nights being locked outside in the dust.

They stood in the center of their new hallway, surrounded by the cardboard boxes of their life, but they didn't see the mess. They were bathed in the glow of an infinite African summer that seemed to radiate from the very floorboards. Their love was no longer a message sent over a dark, lonely sea or a flickering face on a pixelated screen. It was no longer a dream "in transit," shivering and fighting to survive the cold.

Luca turned to her, his movements slow and reverent. He pulled her into his arms, his large hands splayed across her back as if anchoring her to this earth. He rested his forehead against hers, closing his eyes as he breathed her in the scent of the safari, the salt of her tears, and the unmistakable aroma of *home*.

In that shared breath, they both knew the truth. Their love had survived the storm, crossed the oceans, and navigated the untamed wilderness. It had been bruised by the frost and tested by the silence, only to emerge stronger, tempered by the fire of their journey.

As he tilted her chin up and pressed his lips to hers a kiss that tasted of forgiveness and a thousand tomorrows the world outside ceased to exist.

Their love hadn't just survived. It had finally arrived home.

Loved the Journey? Keep Exploring!

Loved the Journey? Keep Exploring!

Don't let the adventure stop at the final page. Scan the QR code below to go directly to my official website, where you can discover more of my spellbinding romance novels, step into the kitchen with my unique cookbooks, and explore my vibrant children's book series.

Scan to connect directly with Honeymoon Aljabri

Scan me

www.ingramcontent.com/pod-product-compliance
Lightning Source LLC
LaVergne TN
LVHW091258150826
845673LV00006B/1467

* 9 7 9 8 9 9 3 4 4 8 8 7 9 *